M

'Elsje Christiaens'
Drawing by Rembrandt Harmenszoon van Rijn, 1664
Metropolitan Museum of Art, New York

Alexander TARBET

cm

Cover Photo: clickclickbang.org
Cover Design: Douglas Cheape

ISBN-10: 1495996409
ISBN-13: 978-1495996405

For Dad

Mokum *(informal) (synonym)*
(orig: Yiddish), **Amsterdam**.

En met een air van gewicht voeren zij met spijt,
weer hun Mokumse meid weer terug naar het licht.

Perhaps gravity pulls them with an air of regret,
to an Amsterdam maid returned to the light.

'De Stad Amsterdam' by Jacques Brel.

I

Driving.

First to Groenlo, join the N18 north through Eibergen and Haaksbergen, then switch on to the A35 just south of Enschede.

Driving.

North toward Almelo, Hardenberg, Coevorden, Emmen. Emmen was halfway. If she slept he would drive on. Awake, she would insist they stopped.

Coffee, a sandwich.

Driving.

North through Veendam and still further north, Appingdam and eventually, through the still night, he would make out the unmistakable burning amber of Delfzijl.

Illuminating the corpulent clouds of steam endlessly spewing from the gaping mouths of the refinery's twin cooling towers, three tall gas flares paint the sky an iridescent fiery orange. Untidily heaped, a sprawling blanket of uncountable white lights lie below. Tiny pinholes thrown into dramatic relief against the nothingness of the cold grey River Eems. The ever-widening maw of the mighty river inexorably emptying into a darker and infinitely more forbidding grey: the North Sea.

'From here,' she had said on her first sighting of the industrial estuary town. 'It looks like little Hell.'

Her sister's family lived here, but he would not see them. He still shuddered at the recollection of his only visit since her death. Her brother following him out, tripping on to the pathetic postage-stamp sized lawn at the front of the house, blubbering and sputtering.
'My heart is broken for you, if there is anything...'
Becoming aware of the hand on his back he'd fought the urge to pull away.
'No, no - I'll be alright, really. I just have to go now. I'll be in touch…sorry.'
Some vestige of her memory had restrained him. The touch, a jolt of electricity, had caught him by surprise. Another shock came as he recognised the deep anger the simple contact had sparked within him. He had wanted to shout, to scream: What do *you* know? How could *you* do anything? How could anyone *do* anything?'
Moments later, he'd noticed an elderly woman staring open-mouthed at him from the other side of the street. He had been striding back to his car and, my God, had he been ranting? He recalled putting a hand to his mouth. To check, to catch the words. Feeling flecks of saliva on his cheek, he'd continued walking, but after a few metres he turned to look back over his shoulder. Wanting, no, *needing* to apologise. But she had gone.
The memory of that visit. The memory of that anger. He knew he had to push it back. To pack it away. Breathing slowly and deeply he began to concentrate.
Driving.
He had discovered something that day. Something comforting; calming; soothing. In the half-light of winter, in the hypnotic vibrating squeal of the windscreen wipers, and in the unrelenting drum of the rain, he had in fact discovered something quite extraordinary. Something miraculous. Breathing. He had to be calm to make it work.
Slowly it would happen. It was a sense at first. A feeling.

She was there. Beside him in the passenger seat. Sleeping, dozing, or perhaps, eyes closed, quietly listening to the radio. Concentrate on driving, just look out onto the road.

They were going to her sister's. Two or three times a month they would visit. Take the children something, not much, some sweets, or occasionally a cheap toy from a petrol station. The toys would always be broken by the time they came to leave and he would want to complain. She, of course, would laugh. They loved getting them. That to her was the important thing.

Stop.

Stop thinking. Concentrate on driving.

She was here. Here with him in the darkness. In the space between. He could smell her, her hair, her perfume.

Her.

Eventually a queue of traffic would appear, a dangerous manoeuvre ahead, some idiot speeding...something, something would cause him to look over, to look into the void where she had been.

Greater than emptiness.

Each time, on each journey, he felt a part of his very being splinter into a thousand tiny, fractured, glittering pain-filled shards. The very particles of his soul silently tumbling out into darkness.

Tears would make it impossible to see. The temptation to close his eyes tightly, to jam his foot on the accelerator. To let go, to cry out.

Breathing.

Calm down. He still had the drive home. He had to concentrate. He could still get her back for a few moments if he could just concentrate.

Breathing.

Driving.

Friday

14th December

1

hanging out

Bleary-eyed, Remco Elmers hunched in the weathered leather of the ancient Citroën's passenger seat and peered out on the greyest of grey afternoons. When he finally raised the energy to speak, it was all nasal flat-toned Amsterdammer vowels and grinding consonants. The gruff sound a living advertisement for roll-your-own cigarettes and cheap booze.

'Mokum, stag party, road trip, you name it. Party capital of Europe, right?'

It was Remco's car, but after observing his companion's hangover, Munro had considered it a matter of public safety to take the wheel.

'Go on,' he urged softly, mindful of the older man's delicate condition.

Remco obliged with a tired smile.

'Two, three in the morning and you're drunk, or stoned…or both. It is around this time that a lot of men become separated from their friends. Some by accident, and some deliberately, so they can sneak back up to *de Walletjes.*'

Walletjes, when literally translated, means 'Little-holes-in-the-wall' and was old Amsterdammer slang for the Red Light District. Sounded a little harsh to Munro the first time he'd heard it.

Harsh, but fair.

In these less enlightened and more prudish times, the area was now more commonly referred to as simply *de Wallen.*

Remco bravely soldiered on, his washed-out paper-bag face suddenly crumpling as he ineptly tried to rub the sleep out of one bloodshot eye.

'Okay, so now you need to piss. What do you do? You piss in the water. But you're not so steady and splash - in you go. If you're lucky, you climb out and make your way back to your room, cold and stinking with whichever disease the canal has seen fit to give you. If you're unlucky though,' he heaved a sigh, 'If you're unlucky you bang your head, you are too drunk to swim, or maybe you just breathe in at the wrong moment. Either way you slice it, it's all over.'

A raised eyebrow and careless shrug conveyed the timeless commonality and unremarkable regularity of the event.

'Why Ouderkerk?' Munro deliberately kept his enquiry brief. The freezing fog and constantly misting windscreen were making for poor visibility. That, combined with his own hangover, an ominously slick-looking road surface, and the fact he had no idea where he was heading, made him wonder if hitching a ride with the Diving Unit might have been the smarter option.

Casually oblivious to the dangers around him, Remco answered with uncharacteristic patience.

'The canals are full of mud, silt…and worse, so they hold on to whatever falls in. Naturally, because of all that shit the city has to dredge them. The dredgers scoop everything up, and, as right now they're shoring up this part of the river, it all gets dumped down here in beautiful Ouderkerk-aan-de-Amstel. With all the shaking around…'

Remco shook his head slowly before taking a sip from his machine-bought plastic coffee. Wincing as he turned his face toward his superior, he surreptitiously checked Munro's reaction as he spoke.

'It's not a pretty sight I can tell you. Bloated, knocked about, it can put you off your dinner.'

Munro allowed himself a half-smile, Remco needn't have bothered. Hard-earned experience had taught him many years ago to regard human remains as nothing more than evidence to be inspected, examined, and with a little bit of luck, harvested for information. He had seen the corpses of those he had known in life, and had observed the irrefutably fundamental change. It wasn't the lack of muscular activity evinced in the facial features, or the unnatural stillness of an inanimate body. He could only describe the change as shrinkage. A lessening. Not the feeling that something was missing, more the absolute knowledge that everything was. A religious man would regard this as the departure of the soul, but Munro was not a religious man.

This was the first time the pair had travelled out to Ouderkerk. A few weeks ago, two bodies had surfaced under a highway bridge a couple of kilometres downriver. Now, completing the hat trick, this last corpse had turned up only a stones-throw from the small drawbridge at the top of the town itself.

Only cursory post-mortem examinations were undertaken in these circumstances. Tragedies reduced to paperwork. Filing at this end, sweaty palms and a nervous tightness in the chest of the unfortunate official chosen to deliver the news at the other. Munro knew that occasionally these notifications were delivered in Amsterdam, but he also knew that typically the deceased was a tourist, and more often than not, British.

To find one body was nothing unusual, even two could be described as unfortunate. But three? Professional curiosity had forced him to make the trip south.

A cold breeze formed tiny ripples on the inky surface of the river as the four-man team busied themselves bagging the swollen and misshapen mass with a practised and silent efficiency. The procedure was carried out in the shallows, the all too experienced divers aware that a combination of gravity, gripping fingers and saturated flesh created a heady brew best avoided by even the strongest of stomachs. In spite of this precaution, when the wind briefly changed direction Munro envied them the nose-clips they had all kept in place.

Balancing awkwardly on the slippery grass bank, Remco somehow managed to roll himself a smoke. His delicate mission accomplished, he nudged Munro with his elbow and grumbled, 'You know, even the Coroner doesn't come all the way down here for the floaters.' Then, placing the cigarette between his lips and leaning on Munro's arm for support, he playfully waved his little finger at the nearest diver.

Pulling off the rubber helmet of his wetsuit, the greying, and for the moment, wildly wire-haired Chief of the Amstelland Police Diving Unit looked up, an easy smile creasing his face as he shook his head.

'Hard to tell. Fish have been at him,' he said.

As the two detectives climbed clumsily back up the greasy incline to the roadway, Munro lifted his own pinkie, copying the gesture.

'What's this?' he asked.

'Usually if they were pissing,' chortled Remco, his unshaven face splitting into a grin for the first time that day. 'Their dick'll still be hanging out.'

It seemed wherever they found themselves, Remco always knew of a good little café. This time though, Munro thought he would struggle.

Situated only eight kilometres to the south of Amsterdam, the small village of Ouderkerk-aan-de-Amstel was where the money came to live, and even through the rain Munro could see why. The expensive suburb perched neatly on the banks of the great Amstel River looked picturesque enough. In a Dutch sort of way. In the way the immaculate mansions were placed precisely the same distance apart, in the way each mansion was fronted by its own set of elaborately wrought ironwork gates, and most obviously, in the way each house sported a flagpole topped with the red white and blue tricolour of The Netherlands.

A simple trench, leaving tall ironwork gates irregularly dotting the slowly winding road edging both sides of the river, performed the role a wall would play in any other part of the world here. To the foreign eye the absence gave the ornate structures a strange and somehow absurd appearance. Obviously, fording one or two metres of stagnant water is much harder than climbing over a wall, and so in the pragmatically frugal style that epitomises so much of the Dutch psyche, the gates stood alone. Towering over the real deterrent, a stinking ditch.

Munro figured it must work. He knew quite a few casual housebreakers back home who would baulk at the thought of getting their designer tracksuits and fancy trainers filthy on their way in, and more importantly out, of a job.

The centre of the village itself maintained an air of deliberately understated exclusivity. Expensive restaurants, delicatessens and fashion boutiques politely jostling each other for the patronage of the locals. Commuters mostly, travelling each day into the city or making the short journey to the nearby 'super-modern' Amstel Business Park. The chances of turning up a decent bar here, especially one that would find favour with Remco, seemed remote.

Remote, but not impossible.

Remco appeared to sniff the air to get his bearings. 'It's on the other side of this bridge, fifty metres or so.'

Munro watched him walk away, and not for the first time marvelled at Brigadier Rechercheur Remco Elmers' complete undutchness. It wasn't just his physical appearance, or even his spectacularly scruffy exterior. It was something more. Something Remco.

The Dutch do 'unkempt' of course, but in general it is a carefully studied affair. The libertarian leftist politics of the Sixties and Seventies having left their mark on the city-dwelling Dutch, not in the laws particularly as historically they were always the most tolerant of Europeans, but more it seemed to Munro, in their clothes. In the studiously casual outward appearance of the urban middle classes. A revolution more corduroy than velvet.

Remco, on the other hand, was a one-off. Somewhat overweight, he stood erect at five foot four inches tall. A habitual wearer of a single breasted and badly fitted, brown suit, he owned just two ties. One red: a flowery and irredeemably stained silk-look affair, and one black: habitually flecked and scuffed with cigarette ash. Munro could never work out if a younger, fitter Remco purchased the ties, or if he was just lousy at tying knots. Either way, when worn they were always far too short; allowing friends and colleagues the pleasure of speculation over the shearing strength of polyester and plastic as immense pressure was applied to each of his, all too visibly strained, shirt buttons.

Munro took all this in once more. The antipathy, not only of the archetypal Dutchman, but the absolute opposite of what the powers-that-be regarded as the ideal Dutch policemen. Munro had taken to him the first minute they'd met.

By God, the wee man's done it again, he reflected happily, already halfway through his second beer. He liked the way they served it here. Holding only around a third of a pint, the fluted, paper thin glasses, called *fluitjes,* are conical tumblers that allow the beer to maintain its cold and lively texture to the last drop. The only disadvantage to this *'fluitje'* arrangement occurred in the more modern bars in town. There, the unsuspecting and increasingly thirsty drinker would often find himself confronted by what could only be described as 'bored-student-service'.

Thankfully, Piet Van Raak's bar in the heart of Ouderkerk had no such problem. Anachronistically sandwiched between two exceptionally fashionable restaurants and fronted by the Amstel River, it was a surprisingly decent example of an old-style *bruine bar,* complete with saw-dust, an original pocket-less billiard table and Piet himself, efficiently serving up the drinks.

Munro, mentally chalking another one up for his infinitely resourceful companion, lifted his beer in salute. 'Cheers. You know, you're a terrible loss to the alcoholic tourist business.'

'*Proost,*' Remco replied amicably, emptying his own glass in one smooth movement before signalling Piet for two more. The beers arrived just as one of the local uniforms popped his head around the door. Checking there was no one else in the bar, he called over to Remco.

'Easy one, it's another Brit. Passport and wallet were in his back pocket. I ran his name through the ALVP and he's registered there too.'

A remarkable number of people disappear in

Amsterdam each month. Closet gays, drug addicts, alcoholics, teenage runaways; the list of types Amsterdam could absorb was endless. The ALVP: *De Amsterdamse Lijst van Vermiste Personen,* provided the official roll call.

In his Police career, Munro had dealt with more than a few missing cases. Family men disappearing without a trace; and children. Children were the hardest. Families always asking the same questions, always desperate for news, and always demanding a more senior officer be placed in charge. In his own experience, when news was received from someone other than the missing individual it was almost invariably bad, and if a more senior officer became involved; it usually meant murder.

As a retiring Inspector had once said to the young Detective Constable Munro, more years ago than he cared to remember. 'If you always think the worst son, you'll usually be right.' It was one of the best pieces of advice he felt he had ever been given.

2

nearly a full roll

An ugly strip of land unambiguously marks the boundary between the Seventeenth Century Jordaan district to the west of the old city and the Nineteenth Century red-brick structures surrounding its southern edges. Bulldozed and redeveloped in the Sixties, the largest building in this hideous concrete redevelopment sits at the southern end of the Elandsgracht. It is the *Hoofdbureau van Politie:* Amsterdam Police Headquarters.

The Amsterdam traffic had been its usual appalling self, so it was almost seven by the time they made it back into the office. Remco, one eye on his first beer of the evening session, briskly headed off to file his report, and of similar mind, Munro also stepped up the pace as he made his way up the stairs to his tiny, grey, feature-free and windowless office. It was nearly six in the UK and he wanted to have his own report filed before the end of the working day.

According to the information culled from his sodden passport, John Patrick Gerrard was born in Manchester on the 25th of January, 1973. The black nylon wallet found in his jacket held a driving licence, one credit card, two hundred and ten pounds and three hundred euros. The euros were in new twenties, as if straight from a cash machine. At first sight, the contents made aggravated robbery look an unlikely cause of death. The licence was relatively recently obtained, considering the man's age, and also gave an address in Manchester.

Starting a new file, and bringing his details up-to-date, Munro reported Gerrard's latest address as drying out and chilling his heels in a stainless-steel drawer at the Onze-Lieve-Vrouwe Hospital Mortuary just off the Weesperstraat. The city morgue, situated somewhat ironically less than one hundred metres from the lower reaches of the same River Amstel.

As Interpol, Europol and Joint Police Operations Coordinator with responsibility for Amsterdam; Detective Chief Inspector Iain Munro had three calls to make. The National Criminal Intelligence Unit based in New Scotland Yard received the first. There, the name of the deceased and his date of birth would be entered onto the database. Munro made a young WPC promise to run Gerrard through the system before going off-duty. He also asked her to give any results to Chief Superintendent Michael Doherty with the specific instruction she tell him Iain Munro had said, 'He would know what to do with them'. Munro and Doherty went back a long way and as well as making sure the job was done speedily by involving the now slightly nervous officer's head of department, he also knew Mickey would get the gag.

He made the next call to Vice Consul Jack Downes on his out-of-hours mobile number. He had already couriered Gerrard's passport to the British Consulate building in the Oude Zuid as it would be their responsibility to contact the person named as emergency contact.

'I'm looking at it now,' Jack's English public school accent always raised a smile from Munro. He knew for a fact the man was born and bred in Hamilton, a tough town just twenty miles south of Glasgow. Munro looked down at his watch in surprise.

'Are you still in the office?'

'The joys of being on-call in Amsterdam I'm afraid,' griped the clearly disgruntled diplomat. 'Right now, I have four very unpleasant, and for the moment, passport-less Welshmen clogging up reception.'

He made the appellation sound like an STD.

'Steady now Jackie boy,' admonished Munro. 'We'll have none of that racial stereotyping. Didn't you get the memo?'

'I've put it with the others,' Downes sighed, before adding with a snort. 'We've nearly a full roll.'

There was a moment of silence. Munro pictured the Vice Consul deciphering the smudged handwriting on the inside back-cover of the waterlogged passport. The subdued tone of the reply was confirmation enough.

'I'll call now,' said Downes quietly.

'Thanks Jack.' He meant it.

Finally, Munro made his third and final call to the office of his direct superior. Based in Brussels, Sir James McFarlane was the most senior British Police Officer attached to Interpol and had recently been appointed Commissioner for Joint Police Operations within the European Union. This time his luck ran out. He left a message on Sir James' voicemail detailing the basics and left it at that.

As part of his duties, the report to Interpol would come directly from Remco, and, if he knew Remco, it would have been sent by now and the substantial, yet diminutive Detective Sergeant - it didn't quite sound as grand as Brigadier Rechercheur, Munro always thought - would be on his way to their favourite drinking hole, the Café de Doelen, where they had arranged to meet for another beer, or perhaps two.

It was only a fifteen minute walk from the headquarters on the Elandsgracht to the café, but today, as with every working day, Munro would have to make a slight detour.

3

language lessons

Bregje Van Til taught English from an office on the third floor of a very old building on the Nieuwezijds Voorburgwal. At five foot seven she was by no means tall by Dutch standards, but she was slim and fair with bright blue eyes. A recent change in hairstyle accentuated her slightly 'elfin look' as the hairdresser had put it, but she wasn't convinced, harbouring a niggling doubt that at thirty-five years old the cut may have been a little too young for her.

Most of her clients were corporate types relocated to Amsterdam from the UK or the US and required by their respective employers to learn Dutch. Unfortunately there was a hitch. Almost everyone in Amsterdam speaks English. Not as well as they think they do, in Bregje's opinion, but there it was. New clients would appear full of enthusiasm, eager to learn a new language and ready to be immersed in a new culture. Then, after a month or two the enthusiasm would wane. They would learn the basics, and Mokum would simply swallow them up.

She found herself pondering this problem more often these days and as a direct consequence had started taking Spanish lessons in her spare time. Quite a few Amsterdammers made the move to Spain each year and she had thought it would help her business if she could offer to teach them before they left, or even go to Spain herself one day and teach not only the Dutch, but maybe the English too. At the moment though, Bregje knew this was a pipe dream. She had only just started to learn, and she had responsibilities: the office, the apartment, and most annoyingly, a whopping great tax bill she had been avoiding for a bit too long.

Suddenly, giving her a small start she found her reverie interrupted as yet another responsibility made its presence felt. The warm, heavy, slightly damp sensation on the leg of her jeans meant only one thing: Whisky was awake. She looked under the table to find the dog's head resting on her leg, his large brown eyes peering upwards from the gloom. Glancing up at the clock on the wall, she reached for a cookie from the tin kept for clients before pouting at the dog's expectant face.

'He'll be here soon, don't worry,' she whispered.

Holding the small round ginger biscuit in front of the white retriever's muzzle, she wondered why she spoke to Whisky in English. *The dog didn't understand*, she thought. *Cookies, that's what this dog understands.*

Leaving a long trail of saliva on her jeans, Whisky rewarded her generosity in the usual way.

'Please don't mention it,' she complained under her breath as she made her way through to the small kitchen area to wash her hands and wipe down the affected area. Upon returning, she then became aware the dog had taken up a position by the door and was standing rigidly with ears fully cocked, and eyes focussed intently on the passageway into the hall. Bregje frowned as she opened the door.

'I don't mind telling you, that freaks me out a little,' she tutted.

Released from the room, Whisky bolted along the landing before coming to a complete stop at the top of the three flights of stairs leading down street-level. Then gingerly, he began to make his way down. The old Amsterdam stairwell wound down in the usual implausibly steep and impossibly narrow way, and on his first visit Whisky had spilled down the last few steps onto the first floor, as always learning his lesson the hard way.

Bregje was still watching him get to the second when the doorbell rang. Pressing the button to open the front door, she called down on the intercom.

'He's on his way.'

'Thanks Bregje, see you tomorrow,' replied Munro.

Another of my spectacular teaching successes, she reflected ironically. She didn't mind looking after the dog. In fact, she quite enjoyed the lunchtime strolls through the Jordaan; in spite of the slight feelings of guilt.

It had been Munro's idea. Jack Downes at the British Consulate had originally recommended her to him, and for the first few months it had gone well. Then the usual happened. She could tell it would. Munro wasn't particularly gifted when it came to languages and was beginning to struggle. Around six months ago, he arrived at her office at the normal time, only on this occasion he asked to speak with her before they began. She could tell he was losing interest and was prepared for the customary excuses, but much to her surprise he had offered to continue the lessons - or at least to continue paying for them. Instead of actually attending, he wondered if Bregje wouldn't mind using the appointed two hours to pop around to his apartment and take the dog for a walk. After a few weeks it became more convenient for Munro to drop the dog off at her office first thing in the morning, and pick him up again after work. Bregje had the feeling this was Munro's plan all along, but she was pragmatic enough to realise it was a pretty good arrangement for both parties. The dog was company between clients, and as the gaps between clients seemed to be getting longer, the regular income was also coming in very handy.

There was something else too; she could still recall Munro confiding in her one semi-drunken evening in the Doelen, that Whisky had been the only part of his failed marriage to survive. It had sounded terribly sad to her at the time, but as she reminded herself once more, she *had* been drinking.

By the time Munro had barged open the solidly built, but ill-fitted front door and entered the ground-floor hallway, Whisky was on the last flight of stairs. After carefully negotiating the last few steps, he then bounded enthusiastically around his master's legs, no mean feat as there was barely enough room for one person in the tiny lobby. Munro opened the door and the dog shot out, scrabbling his way down the last eight steps to street level.

Virtually all of the older buildings in the centre of Amsterdam have steps leading up to the main entrance. At first Munro had assumed this was due to the obvious risk of flooding, but the truth, as with everything in Amsterdam, is slightly more complicated.

The reason for the steps, and also the rationale behind most of the large rectangular windows for that matter, was tax; and not, as you would assume, tax avoidance either. Each step from the street leading up to a doorway, and each pane of glass, were originally taxed individually. These were the grand houses, built by the wealthy merchants of Amsterdam, recipients of uncountable fortunes amassed during the 17th and into the 18th Centuries in a period most commonly referred to in The Netherlands as *De Gouden Eeuw*: The Golden Age.

The Dutch being the Dutch however, could never find garish displays of wealth acceptable. This was, after all, one of the first Protestant controlled cities in the world. Lutherans and Calvinists held sway at different times and in different parts of the city throughout this period. Not for them the gaudy displays of gold favoured by the Catholic Church. Instead, the rich simply installed larger windows and built more steps in order to demonstrate their prosperity. The problem resolved the Amsterdam way. The arrangement allowing the merchants a level of ostentation, whilst at the same time demonstrating their public spirited largesse in bolstering the city's coffers.

If anything these large rectangular windows offered an even greater insight into the Amsterdam character. Yes they were taxed, and so acted as a display of wealth, but they were never shuttered or curtained. This was the Calvinist influence. It was a statement. *Look at us. We hard-working Christians have nothing to hide.* Except of course, the real living went on in an inner-room hidden from the street, often with a log fire and a stone, slate, or in rare cases marble hearth. Houses within houses, reasons within reasons, and arrangements within arrangements. Welcome to Amsterdam.

Coming from Glasgow, Munro had felt almost instantly at home here. Scotland herself had taken the full dose of Calvinism and everything that goes with it, including the 'Holy Willie's Prayer' aspect; the Burns' poem a firm favourite of the firmly agnostic Munro.

The fastest route home forced them across the Kalverstraat, or 'Holland's High Street', as the guidebooks like to call it. As always, Munro was greatly relieved when eventually the pair had forded the seemingly endless river of shoppers.

It was Friday the Fourteenth of December, and although the traditional Dutch Christmas had already gone by, the late-night shopping for the more universally celebrated version was still in full swing. Double Christmas, the thought brought a smile to Munro's lips. No one had ever accused the Dutch of missing a commercial opportunity.

Once clear of the throng, the next thoroughfare in need of negotiation was the Rokin. One of the main routes through the centre of the city, the Rokin bristled with an unholy mixture of bicycles, trams, buses, taxis, cars and pedestrians. Naturally in Amsterdam, the bicycles had the right of way. In this case they even had a cycle-path entirely devoted to them, which - as any self-respecting Amsterdam cyclist will tell you - they wouldn't be seen dead on. Quite how they weren't seen dead under the trams, buses, taxis and cars was a source of constant amazement to Munro, as once more he observed the implausibly incident-free waltz of Amsterdammers dodging and weaving their way home.

Eventually making it to the other side and still heading roughly eastwards, he unleashed the dog. Very few cars ventured into this area. Any motor vehicle foolish enough to attempt navigating the narrow one-way lanes bordering the canals and criss-crossing the very heart of the city could only travel at the speed of the slowest bicycle, or even more frustratingly, at the pace of the slowest flock of ambling tourists on one of the countless guided walking tours.

The pair parted company and began to thread their way into, and through the Grimburgwal. The tiny lane, running almost two-thirds the length of the Langebrug was, as usual, crammed. Gift shops, antique jewellers, art galleries, coffee shops, and an excellent *bruine bar* Munro and Remco occasionally frequented at lunchtime called The Gasthuys. All looked to be doing a brisk trade.

The narrow passageway itself only runs for fifty or sixty metres, so it wasn't long before, first Whisky, then Munro, emerged on to the bridge at the southern tip of one of Amsterdam's oldest canals. To Munro's left, the glimmering waters of the Oudezijds Voorburgwal curved gently towards the harbour at the northern edge of the city.

As usual, two or three junkies were selling stolen bikes on the Langebrug. Once in a while the police would make an arrest, the very definition of a thankless task. As it was, the bicycles only sold for twenty euros each, thirty at most, just enough for the next fix.

Each time he passed this way, Munro felt the bridge was a stark reminder of the human need for organisation. A primal instinct, which, even when confronted by the inevitable vicious selfishness of addiction, ably retained the capacity to survive against all odds and in all circumstances.

To a man, and occasionally woman, the junkies looked like shit. Grubby clothes, greasy hair and the unmistakably pale, greying skin of the afflicted drawn tightly over filthy, hollowed out faces. It was a fact of life in Amsterdam. Every so often your bike was stolen, so you went to the junkies for another. There are some junkies who scour the city looking for easy bikes to steal. They sell these bikes on for a few Euros to the junkies here on the bridge. Unsurprisingly, much of the inventory is damaged in the act of theft; so there is the junkie whose job it is to return the merchandise to saleable condition. He would appear like a ghost from the ether when required, fully equipped with an adjustable spanner and a bicycle pump.

The junkies actually selling the bikes to the public ride around on the Langebrug, softly whispering to anyone passing. '*Fiets-te-koop*,' or sometimes, displaying the same bi-lingual skills as the rest of the city. 'You want to buy a bike?'

Finally, there is the drug dealer himself. Obviously selling to feed his own habit, he often looks to be in an even worse condition than his clients. And so it goes on. Just another Amsterdam arrangement in a city built, not on military strength or political idealism, but on commerce and commerce alone. In this case, trade reduced to what must be close to its lowest level. Bicycles and crack cocaine.

Moving on, Munro then passed the southern tip of the Achterburgwal: the Voorburgwal's little sister, where, glancing left as he passed, he could just make out the twinkling cherry-neon marking the southern edge of the Red Light District. Unfettered by such human distractions, and knowing this particular route off by heart, Whisky had taken off in the opposite direction, his luxuriant white tail sashaying exuberantly as he disappeared into the Amsterdam University grounds.

After cutting through the University, Munro emerged from a low, dark passageway onto the airy open space of the grandly broad Kloveniersburgwal, and as he crossed the Doelen Bridge, he spotted Remco in the window of the café.

Whisky, already sitting patiently in the doorway to the bar, was causing much hilarity in a middle-aged English couple trying to gain entry.

'He knows where he's going,' laughed the woman.

Munro smiled back. Clicking his fingers at the dog he walked past the entrance until he was level with Remco in the window. Wanting to change out of his work clothes, he mimed pulling on a jacket and pointed toward his apartment. Remco in turn held up his beer and tilted his head quizzically.

Munro nodded for him to get one in.

Language lessons, he thought fleetingly of Bregje as he headed along the Staalstraat and turned left into the Verversstraat where his tiny top floor flat was located, *who needs them.*

II

She had saved him.
She was dead.
Was this her reward?
Was *he* still saved?
Where is the justice in this?
He couldn't sleep. He would drift off, but then wake with a guilty start.
How could he sleep?
He was disgusting. Unworthy.
She had saved him.
He had not saved her.
He *could not* save her.
They met at school. 'Childhood sweethearts' others would joke. This made them both uncomfortable. She would never joke about those times. She had known the pain memories of his childhood caused him, and had instinctively known when those memories were becoming too much. He would become morose, depressed. At those times she had also known how to soothe him. Holding him as one holds a baby. Stroking his hair gently as he wept. It could go on for hours. All the while she would be comforting him, assuring him.
'I'm here now. I'm here now…'
The one who should have been there though, the woman who had given him life? She had abandoned him. Betrayed him.

From as far back as he could remember his father had brought strangers to the house. They hurt him. They said nice things to him, some even brought gifts.
But always, they hurt him.
By the age of ten he had become quite proficient at hurting other things. It felt good not to be the lowest. To have the power his father and the strangers had.
By twelve he was in trouble.
A neighbour's dog had gone missing and eventually the body had been found in his father's shed. The policeman called to the scene, so appalled by the state of the creature, had punched his father full in the face before being restrained by a colleague. When it was established the responsibility lay not with the father, but with the boy, the not inconsiderable might of the Netherlands Social Services were brought to bear on the problem.
Psychiatrists, child psychiatrists, councillors, psychiatric specialists, one-to-one counselling, group therapy...this was the Netherlands of the sixties. New ideas on treatment emerged almost weekly. The only positive result from it all as far as he could tell was that when he was allowed home there were no more strangers. Even his father would no longer go near him.
More pain.
By his own admission now, an admission she had drawn from him in her careful, delicate way. He was pretty messed-up.
He recalled the day they met.
He had become a vicious bully, extracting money from helpless, smaller children, at once shocked and terrified by his sudden and unprovoked acts of violence. All attempts by the school to have him ousted were rebuffed by the social services. They claimed the best way for him to become a normal member of society was for him to attend his normal school whilst they

attempted to get to the bottom of his anti-social behaviour.
'And let all the other kids go to Hell in a basket!' he had overheard the Headmaster say on one of the many days he was sent to wait outside his office.
It was her third day at her new school. She walked straight up to him and handed over the money her mother had given her to buy sweets on the way home.
'What's that for?'
'That is so you don't need to hurt the little ones today.'
This was too unexpected for him to know how to react. She was so pretty. Whatever had happened to him in the past. Whatever he had become now. He was still a thirteen-year-old boy. He felt his face flush.
'Okay,' he mumbled
'Okay, I'll see you here at the same time tomorrow.'
She had saved him.
He had not saved her.

4

outrageous proportions

Munro caught a glimpse of himself in the mirror as he was changing and noticed he needed a haircut. He always needed a haircut. It was in his genes. His parents were both from the Isle of Lewis, the outermost of the Outer Hebrides, and his family had two things in common: the icy blue eyes of the Norsemen, who in ancient times and for generations were interwoven in the Island's history, and something unique to the Munro family: their hair, or more particularly, the unfeasibly fast rate it seemed to grow. He smiled as he recalled the long summers of his youth spent on the island. His parents had moved to Glasgow before he was born, but every July he and his brothers would be dispatched on the long tortuous journey to the family croft. At that time of year there was peat to be cut and carried, as well as many other dull, and, to city-boys like themselves, impossibly laborious chores to be completed. It struck him as odd that whenever his life became stressful, and on occasion downright dangerous, he would long for those days. The uncomplicated simplicity of honest work. He also didn't miss the irony of that sentiment, especially when observed by a policeman.

He remembered his uncle best of all. Munro always pictured the old guy sitting atop his ancient tractor, his thick white hair wild in the blustering wind. Whenever there was a *celeidh* or gathering at the house, it was always Uncle Murdo who slipped the boys a bottle or two. He was the archetypal loveable rogue and his young nephews had adored him. Wondering what had made him think of those days, he realised slowly that at forty years old he was beginning to recognise a few of the old rascal's features in his own reflection.

'Could be worse I guess,' he said to no one in particular, chuckling quietly at the memory.

Taking his utterance as a hint, the dog headed for the door, and Munro, now out of his work suit and into his jeans, black jumper and long black coat, started yet another uncertain descent down the five flights of the narrow and precipitous stairwell leading from his apartment to the communal front door.

Once into the lane and having gone only eight or nine metres, Whisky froze. Ears on alert, he waited for his master to catch up. This was where Gekke Henk lived. Munro felt this was overstating the case. Alright, Henk did have a tiny window box sized patch of earth just outside his front door. A patch he tended faithfully and carefully at all times of the day, and perhaps more unusually, night. And sure, whenever the old guy spotted a dog or cat passing down the lane he would leap out of his front door, wildly wave a silver umbrella and shout abuse at the top of his voice. But in a town as full of eccentrics as Amsterdam, calling Henk crazy did seem a little unfair. Happily on this occasion, it appeared Henk was either out or indisposed. A fact that didn't stop Whisky from cautiously sloping along the opposite wall.

Watching this daily pantomime, Munro began to feel guilty. The walk from Bregje's had only taken a few minutes and the dog was clearly still full of energy. Deciding to take a slightly longer route to the Doelen, he turned left on the Staalstraat instead of right, taking him by the Chocolatier and the corner diner, where, on winter weekends, he would have an entirely unhealthy yet delicious breakfast of bitter hot chocolate and appeltaartje while working on his Dutch by attempting to decipher the Sunday newspapers. At this corner he turned right onto the Zwanenburgwal. The route would take him around in a semi-circle, the southern edge touching the ever-present Amstel River before returning him to the Staalstraat. Here he would cross the Groeneburgwal and repeat the process. Another semi-circle later and he would find himself back on the Kloveniersburgwal, and as if by magic, back at the front door of the Café de Doelen.

He realised he had made the right choice when only half-way down the Zwanenburgwal the dog came to an abrupt halt, assumed the position, and deposited what to Munro appeared to be a dog-egg of outrageous proportions.

'You been saving that up for me?' he groaned.

Like every good dog owner, he always carried a few plastic bags. Top of the range and designed for the job they were too. However, Munro couldn't with hand on heart say he always used them. They were just handy to have when an irate passerby confronted him, or when Whisky chose a particularly public spot to perform. If he was lucky the misdemeanour would go unnoticed and Munro would sidle off, quietly secreting the dog's leash in his pocket. This was not to be one of those occasions. With all the intelligence and wisdom borne from centuries of breeding, Whisky had chosen to leave this particular effort directly under a large window. Inside, knocking furiously on the glass pane in an ultimately futile effort to move the dog on, a rotund, red-faced man of around sixty years of age spotted Munro with the incriminating leash still in his hand. Holding up the strip of leather in supplication, Munro reached into his pocket for one of the plastic bags, all the while muttering a steady stream of obscenities at the entirely unconcerned dog. Job done in every possible sense, the two continued. Munro holding the little green plastic bag with the bright yellow ties carefully pinched between thumb and forefinger.

As usual, he heard the rasping sound of the scooter engine straining at full tilt long before it came into view. Bicycles ruled the roost, he understood that. But the guys on the scooters rode with all the arrogance of the cyclists, at three times the speed and, unfortunately, without any of the skill. He had witnessed three or four minor accidents involving scooters, on one occasion a brommer; a curious hybrid of bicycle and scooter; the antagonists always speeding away before their victims knew what had, literally, hit them.

Echoing around the tall buildings and narrow canals, the sound grew. Although he could tell from the pitch it was travelling at speed, there was, as usual, no clue from which direction it might appear. Suddenly, causing him to skip onto the pavement, the rider brushed past.

'Arsehole!' he shouted, in as much shock as anger.

A pimply youth, helmet perched precariously on the back of his head, turned briefly and raised his middle finger. Turning back just in time, he was then forced to swerve wildly to avoid Whisky, who, in his previously referred to wisdom, had decided to view proceedings standing stock-still, half-on and half-off the pavement. The rider's curses faded into the icy breeze as he disappeared around the corner.

The same breeze had turned up a notch as they reached the Amstel for the second time. The dog, decided once more upon their destination, had put in a short burst of speed and was already sitting patiently in the vestibule of the Doelen for the second time that evening. As he approached the Café, Munro observed a scooter parked on the side of the road. Glancing around, he then spotted the owner standing impatiently at an apartment-block entrance. When eventually the door buzzed open, grasping a plain white carrier bag filled to capacity with take-out cartons in one hand and pushing the heavy entrance door open with the other, the same pimply youth entered.

'Hope it's on the top floor,' Munro murmured quietly as he dropped his own small plastic bag into the helmet hanging loosely on the scooter's handlebars.

Then, crossing the Staalstraat and passing over the threshold with an audible sigh of relief, he entered the welcoming warmth of the bar.

5

gezellig

The Café de Doelen, or HQ as he and Remco had christened it, is a *bruine bar* looking out over the Doelen Bridge, and it is truly a classic of the genre. One large room lined on two sides by the original brickwork, she is dominated by a beautifully tarnished, dark wooden counter. The heavily worn and enigmatically scarred wood standing testament to the many generations of dedicated drinkers and passing travellers seduced by the heavy smoky atmosphere and liver-quivering shots of Genever: the original form of gin first recommended as a juniper and spice-flavoured medicinal diuretic by a Dr. Franciscus de la Boe in the early 1600s and, 'quivering livers ever since,' as Remco never tired of joking.

One thing in the Doelen had always fascinated Munro: the step at the foot of the entrance. Smooth grey stone worn into a dull 'v' by the feet of the many thousands of imbibers who, over the years, had crossed the threshold. It made him want a drink every time he thought of it; and as he had just thought of it; he wanted a drink now.

The smoke had gone with the European wide ban, but to Munro's mind, it had been replaced by another pest. The use of cell-phones used to be politely discouraged in the more traditional bars of Amsterdam. A constraint long since relaxed, there remained a singular exception. When the place was relatively quiet, and when the landlady was holding court, in the Café de Doelen it was still a hanging offence. Consequently, as the familiar ring-tone sounded out across the room and was met with a collective groan from the regulars, it was with some relief, after checking his own phone, Munro watched Remco duck out of the door.

'*Lul!*' scowled Betty. A formidable woman of a certain age, the owner of the bar didn't seem to go anywhere without her two small dogs. A soft touch for animals in need of rescue, the Doelen also boasted an enormous ginger cat; a tough tom with what could only be described as psychopathic tendencies.

This was Betty's café, but these days she much preferred spending her time on the customer side of the bar, leaving the hard work to her daughter Daphne and the ready supply of student-workers from the University opposite.

Observing Remco sheltering from the cold rain under the mildly tattered green awning outside, Munro felt unexpectedly good. The Dutch have a word for it: *gezellig* - meaning warm, cosy, comfortable; a feeling of general, all round well-being. People and animals could also be described as *gezellig*, and as far as Munro knew, there was no comparable word in the English language. One word however, which has many comparisons in the English language is *lul*. Pronounced 'lool', it translates as prick, dick…etc.

'Correction: *lullen*,' pluralized Bette, this time raising a ripple of laughter around the bar as Munro's own phone began to ring. The door swung open as he reached it, and he ended up dancing a jig with Remco as they tried to pass each other in the doorway.

'Another beer?'

'Rude not to,' he replied before stepping outside.

Feeling a new razor-like sharpness in the chill wind, he pulled his coat closed.

'Munro speaking.'

'Sorry to drag you out the knocking shop so early Chief Inspector. Still fifty guilders for a Hilda is it?'

Munro recognised the voice.

'For your information Chief Superintendent it's all in euros now, and you dragged me out of the pub. This a social call Mickey or are you thinking of organising another fact-finding mission to the lowest places in the Low Countries?'

'Neither mate. Thing is, I've just had a chat with a young lady whose knickers have gotten themselves all in a twist over your new friend.'

'Gerrard?'

'John Patrick, to be precise. Turns out his name and date of birth popped up, but his records didn't: 'Clearance Required'. Not for the likes of her to look at. So she legs it up to my office, all aquiver at the thought of an Interpol request and a classified file. Then she tells me that you said...'

'Yeah, yeah, I know.'

'Well you were wrong.'

'What?'

'I don't know what to do with it, because I can't get at it. The file is actually tagged 'Special Clearance Required', not even for the eyes of a Chief Superintendent apparently.'

In spite of the cold, Munro could feel the skin tighten at the back of his neck.

'Best guess?' he asked.

'Could be a grass for the Serious Crime Squad, active or in witness protection. Or it could be your old lot -'

Just then the phone chirped in Munro's ear,

informing him of another call trying to get through.

'Sorry Mickey, what was that?'

'Your old crew, Special Branch. We're up to our bollocks in all sorts of Anti-Terrorist Units at the minute, not to mention Spooks. The name sounds a bit Irish I suppose?' Pondered Chief Superintendent Michael Francis Doherty with no discernable trace of irony.

'Sorry Mick, I've got another call. Listen, is there any chance you could-'

'Ask around? Sure. I won't be telling anyone who wants to know though, eh?'

'Probably wise, cheers.'

He pressed the hang-up button, but the other caller had already gone. He quickly keyed-in his voicemail number.

'Sir James McFarlane,' announced the caller ID.

I am honoured, thought Munro. In eighteen months on this job he'd met his boss only once, and although he'd been in touch with Sir James' secretary a few times, the man himself had never directly contacted him.

'Chief Inspector two things: first, take no further action on the Gerrard situation. That's a direct order I'm afraid. Don't worry, it's nothing serious. Also, I wonder if you could join me in Wassenaar at lunchtime on Monday. I'm giving a press conference there around eleven so we should have a chance to chat afterwards. Contact Nadine for the details. Thank you, ah...goodbye.' The farewell sounded awkward. An Edinburgh gent from the old school unsure of the etiquette required in something as modern as a voicemail system.

Still, considered Munro. *Situation*, it was an unusual word to use. *Case* maybe or even *Death* would have been more appropriate. And a meeting with the boss? He was still wearing a frown as he re-entered the café.

'Bad news?' asked Remco.

'*Ik heb geen idee*,' he replied. It was one of the first phrases Munro had learned, and in this instance it was very apt - he had no idea.

'Well drink-up. We've got somewhere to go.'

'Let me guess, John Patrick Gerrard?'

Remco's features opened in surprise.

'You want to fill me in?' he asked.

'You first,' replied Munro.

The little man shrugged amicably.

'Well, it appears on the night of *Meneer* Gerrard's disappearance,' he began, accentuating the more formal form of the title with a sarcastic nod. 'He found himself having a physical altercation with Ali Absullah, known to both locals and the police alike as Kwaaie Ali: bouncer, bagman and general gofer employed by the Sexy Castle Peepshow.'

'*Kwaaie?*' enquired Munro. He vaguely remembered the word, but couldn't quite get the connection.

'It means angry,' supplied Remco.

'So who reported this altercation involving,' Munro couldn't help smiling at the translation. 'Angry Ali?'

Remco snorted into his beer, then wiped his mouth with the sleeve of his jacket before replying.

'A couple of uniforms were passing. Didn't appear too serious. Gerrard said he was with a stag party and started apologising as soon as they arrived. He was pretty out of it according to them. They took his details and let his friends take him away.'

'What about Kwaaie Ali?'

'Just doing his job. Another drunk playing-up on the premises. He simply escorted him out.'

'Any obvious injuries to Gerrard?'

'Bloody nose, cut lip. Not worth calling anyone they reckoned.'

Munro knew how they felt. No-one wanted to spend

half a shift with a drunk in a hospital waiting room and the other half filling in incident forms. Especially not when there was little or no prospect of charges ever being brought.

'I'm surprised they bothered to write it up at all,' he mused.

'Ah, we're nothing if not efficient in the Amsterdam Police Force,' barked Remco. Then, as if to emphasise the point, he stood to attention, drained his glass, and with a thin white moustache of froth still twinkling on his top lip, headed for the door.

III

She never offered money the next day, and he didn't ask. Somehow, he instinctively knew he could no longer take advantage of the younger, weaker children.

That was the deal. She would become the only good thing in his life. Although he hadn't understood this at the time, he knew instinctively he'd been offered a lifeline.

A last chance.

As his overall behaviour improved, he began to attend his classes regularly, dividing his time between school and her house, only returning home late at night to sleep.

By this time, he and his father had long since ceased all communication. Her family, by complete contrast, accepted him with open arms.

Amsterdam had embraced the hippie movement and none more so than her parents. He remembered once confiding in her that he was having recurring nightmares and the next day her mother gave him an Indian Dream-catcher: a jumble of string, twigs and feathers. She told him to hang it above his bed for protection. He carried it home that evening, but something made him hide it in his bicycle satchel before going into the house.

It wasn't embarrassment.

It was more a question of separation.

Of cross contamination.

Two weeks after his fifteenth birthday he returned home to find the house empty. His father had simply packed a case and left. He felt nothing. No relief. No sense of abandonment.

Nothing.

When he told her the following morning, she was more upset than he was, taking him straight home to her parents and explaining the situation. He was both startled and more than a little embarrassed when both her mother and her father had burst into tears and hugged him. Eventually, when they had calmed down, her mother had stated simply.

'That's it settled, you will stay with us.'

Naturally, it wasn't quite settled.

The Social Services were still taking an interest in one of the few young men they assumed they had been able to help. Understandably, they wanted the fifteen year old placed in an environment of their choosing and it was quickly made clear they weren't at all enamoured with the 'alternative lifestyle' offered by her parents, and so began proceedings to have him placed in their care.

This placed a new kind of pressure on him. Once again, he became withdrawn and, as a consequence, even more dependent upon her. Now he refused to attend school. Something his adoptive family could hardly object to, as they continually argued vehemently against the restraints of a conventional education. It was becoming clear that something would have to give.

6

a lucrative business

Remco held the lapels of his coat together as he bowed his head into the thick, wet sleet.

'Now it's your turn,' he said, having to speak up against another soaking gust of wind.

'Sorry?'

Munro had joined him outside after settling up the bill and asking Martijn, the young mathematics student on bar-duty that night, to look after Whisky for a while.

'I believe in English to use the phrase 'you first' means, 'me second', if you know what I mean.'

'No need for sarcasm,' deflected Munro brightly, though he had already made the decision to keep Remco fully informed. They started to walk and Munro, falling into step, began relaying the contents of his call from Mickey Doherty in London. When he went on to tell Remco of the message he had received from McFarlane, his Sergeant stopped and turned to face him.

'I didn't need to know about that last part. You don't want to get into trouble, and I'm not sure I want to be party to anything that involves the disobeying of a direct order. I have a certain reputation to maintain.'

'Fuck off Remco.' Munro replied flatly, deliberately ignoring his friend's raucous laugh as they resumed their journey.

Turning it over in his mind, he realised it wasn't just that he had grown to trust Remco. When accepting this post he had made a promise to himself. No more secrets. No more lies. His ultimate departure from his last posting had involved half-truths, secret deals and unaccountable reports - basically all the usual Special Branch stuff. The position he had found himself in had not only ended his marriage, but had almost ended his life. As a direct result, he had determined each and every situation in this new job would be played with as 'straight-a-bat' as humanly possible. So far, so good.

Situated on the western edge of the Walletjes, the Sexy Castle Peepshow was doing a roaring trade. Watching the loud, high-spirited stag parties mingle happily with sightseeing couples, Munro spotted a number of middle-aged men peppered through the mix. They furnished the scene with a darker presence. Sloping self-consciously through the throng, it was their attendance that added the final ingredient. A faintly distasteful, but entirely necessary blue note to an otherwise harmless dirty joke.

Revealed through the open double-doors leading into the 'club', a large circular chamber almost filled the centre of the downstairs area. Inside, completely enclosed by an outer ring of stalls, naked girls and couples would perform. For two euros, the punters were allowed to view proceedings for a few minutes before the glass panel would opaque, only becoming transparent again when a further two coins were inserted. To the right, there stood a bank of four larger stalls. These were reserved for private shows. Individual girls performing to order behind full-length curved glass panels equipped with the same, but more expensively operated, system.

The whole place was scuffed and grubby. The matt-black paint, dull red lighting, and ubiquitous man-with-a-mop all coalescing to give the skin-joint a suitably seedy feel. Remco made his way to the cash-booth just inside the entrance. Practically shouting to be heard above a bass-line Munro could feel coming up through the soles of his shoes, he nodded a cold greeting.

'Kwaaie Ali on tonight?'

The bored looking youth behind the desk looked up once, then did a double-take as Remco held up his Police Identity Card. Attempting unsuccessfully to recover his composure, the extravagantly pierced cashier tried a casual shrug. Remco noticed his hand waver towards the telephone.

'Go ahead,' he smiled. 'Tell Joop, Remco Elmers wants a word.'

Remco had explained on the short walk north that this particular establishment was currently managed by a prominent 'local businessman' named Joop Huisman, his tone leaving Munro in no doubt as to Remco's opinion regarding both the man, and his occupation. His Sergeant had also taken the opportunity to fill him in on Kwaaie Ali. The bouncer had a reputation amongst the local police for being both physically robust, and frustratingly elusive.

'He's upstairs,' stated the cashier abruptly after a short conversation on the telephone. His face had flushed slightly, giving Munro the distinct impression that news of Remco's arrival had not been received with unconfined joy.

'Joop or Ali?' he quizzed quickly.

'What?'

Munro raised his voice. 'You said he's upstairs. Who is? Joop or Ali?'

The non-metallic parts of the young man's face had now turned scarlet.

'Erm, Meneer Huisman?' he replied unsteadily.

There were only two routes upstairs. An escalator to the left, and a wooden staircase on the right. Remco headed for the escalator.

'Lazy wee bastard,' grumbled Munro as he made his own way up the stairs to the second floor. At the top, he could just make out his Sergeant's unmistakably rotund figure at the opposite end of the room - silhouetted as it was, by a huge red neon sign proclaiming: *Over 200 films, Open from 11am-2am, 7 days a week!* Peering further into the gloom, Munro then became aware that what he had at first assumed to be walls, were in fact, doors. Altogether he estimated there must be fifty or sixty stalls lining the large open space.

'Shit,' puffed Remco.

'Worth a try,' Munro shook his head. He knew the only chance they had of getting their man had been if Kwaaie Ali had panicked and headed for street level.

'He's a clever boy,' he grudgingly conceded, assuming their target had simply walked into a booth, locked the door, dropped a couple of euros into the slot and settled in. Having learned from experience that unless you had a very good reason indeed, no-one wanted to go knocking on those doors. Especially not if they had an idea of what was occurring inside.

A band of illumination appeared to expand vertically on the rear wall. As Munro's eyes adjusted, the thin shaft of light revealed itself to be a door opening slowly into the darkness. Dramatically outlined against the light for a few short moments, the tall and slightly crooked figure of Joop Huisman filled the passageway.

'Brigadier Elmers, how nice of you to call. It is, as always, a pleasure to welcome a representative of our wonderful law enforcement agency. Now, how can I assist you?' Huisman, his greasy mouse-brown hair curling lankly against his sunken and deeply pitted cheeks, used the very polite and formal *u* instead of the more usual *je* to refer to the diminutive detective.

'You can cut out that shit for a start you fucking pimp,' offered Remco predictably as the three men met at the open door. 'This is my colleague. He's come all the way from the UK to ask you a few questions, so you'd better be on your toes you slimy fucker.'

'Please, please…in my office. It would be better in here.' A little flustered now, the UK reference seemed to have fazed Huisman. Munro deliberately remained expressionless as he felt his interest sharpen.

'Coffee gentlemen?' The offer was made with an extravagant hand gesture toward a gleaming stainless-steel coffee machine sitting on a table in the corner of the office.

'Meneer Huisman who owns this establishment?' Munro asked the question in English. He knew the offer of coffee was a simple ruse, giving Huisman time to think. But think about what? An everyday scuffle in the foyer?

More hand waving. 'This ah...club, is owned by a small consortium of local businessmen with whom, I am proud to say, I sit as a director on the board. The company is, as I'm sure your colleague here will confirm, entirely above suspicion of any illegal activity and is audited regularly. We pay tax just like any other business, and we expect to be treated in the same manner…'

Munro looked around. In stark contrast to the décor in the rest of the building, this was very much a modern working office. Two flat-screen state-of-the-art computers sat on opposing desks, and several filing cabinets lined the wall to the left. Dominating the office, a large smoked glass panel was attached to the far end. He guessed it was the technical stuff running the DVD signals into the stalls.

'Very good sir,' he began again. 'But who owns it? Who has the major share? Who makes the decisions?'

Munro had, of course, read the background reports on the Red Light District in his very first week in Amsterdam. Everyone knew the identity of Huisman's boss. The press were constantly running stories on him and the Organised Crime Unit did their level best to keep him under constant surveillance. That said, he'd picked up on Remco's animosity toward Huisman, and he had to admit he was quite enjoying the discomfort the question was causing.

'The company details are open to scrutiny by the relevant authorities and I don't think-'

Munro cut him off.

'I understand Joop, don't you worry,' he placed his arm around Huisman's shoulder. 'We'll tell Derk you suggested we contact him. After all, better the mechanic than the oily rag.'

Among numerous other interests, Derk Merel controlled almost all of the Red Light District. An organisation of many parts, his slice of the pie also included the local Hells Angels, which he used to collect a percentage from any transactions that took place within the area. Pimps, drug dealers and so on, everyone paid to have the area 'policed' by Merel's men. On one level it worked. Pick-pockets and potential muggers would discourage paying customers from visiting the area, and so were strictly contained. The truth was, you would rather have a visit from the real law enforcement authorities than from one of Merel's hoods any day. As for who ran Derk Merel? Intelligence suggested the Russian Mafia of involvement. But as ever, the trail stopped cold at the border.

Munro moved towards the door.

'Wait. Hold on, just a moment,' stammered Huisman. 'I thought this was about Ali?'

Munro cheekily mimicked the friendly, but formal tone adopted earlier by the now slightly distraught Huisman. 'Oh yes, ask *Meneer* Absullah if he wouldn't mind popping into the station on Monday afternoon. We're based at the headquarters on the Elandsgracht. Tell him to ask for Rechercheur Brigadier Elmers here. We just have one or two routine questions for him. Good evening sir.' Then, just for fun, he added. 'I can't begin to tell you what a pleasure it's been.'

'What the fuck was that all about?' enquired Remco with a bemused frown as they reached the large entrance downstairs.

'Not sure really. These girls here,' Munro gestured towards the row of prostitutes in the windows directly opposite the club's doorway. 'They regulars?'

'*Ja*, great spot this. See a bit of what turns you on inside and 'Abracadabra' - there it is, fully available outside.' Remco chewed on this for a second. 'I'll ask. This was a few months ago though.'

'Go ahead. I'll meet you in the café round the corner.'

Only seven or eight metres from the peepshow entrance, the Kijkuit coffee bar faced on to the Oudekerksplein. The Oudekerk itself, a cavernous and ancient church, all but filled the square.

The majority of the doorways facing onto the plein were given over to black prostitutes shipped in from various poverty-stricken regions of Africa, and as Munro ordered a coffee and took a seat near the window, he wondered exactly what the 14th Century builders would make of the triple-x-rated circus surrounding their, originally unpretentious, architectural masterpiece. Adding a melancholic note, the dimly lit square echoed with the rattle of coin on glass as the inmates desperately attempted to attract the attention of potential customers. Munro, for obvious reasons, always found this particular part of *de Wallen* profoundly depressing. Undoubtedly some of the monies collected in order to renovate and remodel the now magnificent church building had come from the slave trade; a lucrative business for the Dutch in the Seventeenth, Eighteenth and even into the Nineteenth Centuries. *And here we are now*, thought Munro. *Progress? Not really*.

He finished his small and appropriately bitter coffee, only ordering another two as Remco entered.

'Got lucky, two of them were working that night. I told them to meet us in here for a chat. To be honest, we might have more luck talking to them in a proper interview room, but the Bureau on the Warmoesstraat is being gutted. Going to go all high-tech apparently.' Remco did not appear enthused by the prospect.

'The girls remember anything?'

'Seem to. They know Ali pretty well. He jumps in if there's any bother with the punters. Gets a backhander for his trouble from the girl's pimp if he's needed.' Remco warmed his hands on the tiny coffee cup. 'Thing is, fights are quite rare here, so they reckon they remember our boy. Obviously I had to tell them I'd post a couple of uniforms in the lane if they didn't want to join us. Terrible for business that.' He grinned a Remco grin, and Munro fleetingly considered registering it as a trademark.

'I'd imagine so,' he replied appreciatively. 'Listen, make sure the girls sit at the window here when they come in. Stands to reason their handlers will be checking on them. We might get a word.'

Although realising how unlikely it was they would get any worthwhile information from a pimp, you never knew. It was always better to ask. You may not get an answer, but as had already happened this evening, you sometimes got something from the reaction to the question.

Remco nodded as he tapped his fingers absently on the table. 'What about Huisman?'

'I know,' Munro's brow furrowed. 'You know him better than I do, but it looked to me like he was shitting himself about something.'

'Definitely. He's usually a cool bastard. Do you think it's got anything to do with Gerrard?'

Munro could only shrug.

'Don't tell me,' Remco sighed. '*Geen idee.*'

The girls arrived a few minutes later. Obviously keen to get it over with and back to earning on one of the busiest nights of the week, they quickly dropped into the seats opposite the two detectives. Remco, dispensing with introductions, spoke in English to the tallest of the pair.

'Tell him what you told me.' he said bluntly.

'Ali is a good man you know,' she began in an accent Munro identified as Eastern European. Possibly Czech. 'Everyone says he is angry all the time, but he has always been kind to me. Tomorrow he has a party for his brother, a doctor I think...yes, his brother has just become a doctor and Ali is very proud.' She wagged a finger at Munro. 'He is a good man,' she reiterated.

'The fight,' interrupted Remco. 'Tell us about the fight.'

'It was no fight.' Her face twisted into a scowl. 'The man was yelling at Ali, shouting he would kill him. His friend was trying to stop it, trying to pull him away, but the man got free and tried to hit him . Ali punched him once. And that was that.'

Munro turned to the other girl. 'That what you saw?

'I was…busy. I only saw the man sitting on the ground with blood on his mouth. My customer nearly shit himself, he ran away when he saw the police.' The memory made her smile, and Munro realised she was beautiful. In fact, they were both blonde, and both stunning. He knew he shouldn't have been surprised, they did work in two of the most lucrative windows in the District. Spots only ever occupied by the most attractive merchandise.

It was an old story. A great many of these girls were lured each year from the poorest parts of Eastern Europe with promises of modelling contracts or au-pair work. Tragically upon arrival, they would find their dreams shattered and their passports confiscated. Quickly and efficiently brutalised, they would then be put to work.

Munro took a deep breath. Looking directly into his coffee, he gathered his thoughts before going on.

'You said his friend. There was only one?'

'Yes, but he spoke to the police as well.'

'Did either of your…your boyfriends see this too?' There was no point antagonising them, they would know what he meant.

'No, he was…he is different now.'

He understood. Pimps would often steal girls from each other. It was literally a cut-throat market, and high earners like these would be a prize worth fighting for.

'Well anyway, thanks for your time.' he said quietly.

As Munro stood, reaching out to shake hands with each girl, he noticed the shorter of the two stifle a giggle as the other held his hand a little longer.

Looking him directly in the eye, she purred. 'You know, I have much more time if you want to pay?'

'Never any reason to be lonely in Amsterdam,' joked Remco gently as the girls left.

Munro noticed the almost despondent expression on his friend's face. A claustrophobic room, a beautiful girl almost half your age and a handful of Euros for sex. Munro was no moral crusader. In fact he felt strongly The Netherlands' method of dealing with the world's oldest profession was by far and away the safest and most honest system. But he agreed with the Sergeant he knew had served his time as a beat-cop in the Walletjes. He couldn't think of any place on Earth that could conceivably make him feel more alone either.

On the way back to the Doelen, he asked Remco to make two calls on his cell. The first to the ALVP to ask if Gerrard had been reported missing in Amsterdam or from the UK, and the second to the Amsterdam Police Records Department to find out if they had a current address for Kwaaie Ali. As Remco sheltered in a side street to make his calls, Munro spotted a scooter parked up on the pavement. Secured by three spring-clips, a red metal box sat on the pillion.

His phone balanced precariously between head and shoulder, Remco scribbled furiously into his notebook. Finally, he grunted once into the mouthpiece, nodded his thanks and caught the handset as it fell.

'Right,' he turned to Munro. 'Let's get to the bar, it's fucking freezing out here.'

As they approached the café, Munro could hear the scooter engine sputtering into life. Speeding down the one-way street the wrong way, it zipped passed them. Then, as the rider banked to turn right to cross the Doelen Bridge, a wide red box flew out to the side and crashed noisily against one of the cast-iron stanchions. Munro watched with some amusement as the contents, three white pizza boxes were caught by the wind and spun, Frisbee-like, into the canal.

'This scooter thing of yours is going to get you into trouble one day,' scowled Remco as he trudged on, his head pitched forward against the freezing rain.

The Doelen was packed. Each night at this time, theatre-goers from the three venues within very short walking distance from the café would want to finish their evening discussing the play, opera, or comedy show they had just attended over a coffee or hot chocolate. This made it the least favourite part of the evening for the staff. Making six or seven coffees per round near the end of a long shift was pretty much exactly what you didn't want to be doing, and as it was Friday, the place was even busier than usual.

Munro and Remco squeezed in and managed to catch Martijn's eye as he bustled around behind the counter. This was quality bar-work. With numerous orders on the go, Martijn was obviously more than capable of counting the costs up in his head, and somewhat incredibly, in all of the time Munro had frequented the Doelen he had never seen a single bill queried.

'I'll bring them over.' Martijn gestured towards a nook at the very back of the café where two chairs were still free.

'Thanks,' mouthed Munro as he and Remco jostled their way through the crowd. Once there, they realised why it was, in a thronging café, the two seats had remained vacant. Obviously looking too *gezellig* to disturb, Whisky lay curled around the legs of both chairs in a deep sleep. Barely acknowledging Munro's arrival, the dog opened one eye slowly and lifted his head a little to look up. Then, his tail thumping a couple of times against the floor, he had a gentle stretch followed by a tiny wriggle before falling back into a more comfortable sleeping position.

'I missed you too,' sighed Munro.

They sat down carefully, their feet at slightly odd angles in order to avoid treading on the dog.

'What did you get?'

Remco pulled his notebook out of his coat pocket and looked at it for a moment before replying. 'What do you want first: the good, the bad, or the ugly?'

'Good?'

'We've got a current address for Ali Absullah.'

'Bad?'

'It's in Kolenkit.'

Munro grimaced. The police regularly denied allegations in the press claiming certain parts of the council-owned estate were no-go areas for them.

'Great. Go on then, give me the ugly.'

'More odd than ugly really. Gerrard was reported missing by his girlfriend two full days after he was supposed to return to the UK.'

'Not by other members of the supposed stag party?'

'Not even by his friend. I've asked them to check on the flight details to see if his tickets were bought at the same time as anyone else's. Maybe as a group booking.'

'Curiouser and curiouser said Alice,' mused Munro. Remco reached up to take the two beers from Martijn.

'Who's Alice?' he asked.

'Nobody,' Munro smiled at the barman. 'How's things?'

'They'll be gone soon, thank fuck,' Martijn turned to glower at the theatre crowd chattering noisily behind him. The dog, clearly disgruntled by the commotion caused by the delivery of the drinks, pulled himself to his feet and took three slow steps to the nearest wall. Once there, he slumped to the floor again with a huge sigh.

Remco shook his head and frowned. 'What the fuck's up with him?'

'It was Betty. She went upstairs and gave him a plate of her vegetarian stew,' Martijn laughed and pointed at Munro. 'I would sleep with the window open tonight if I were you.'

'That's great, just great.' moaned Munro quietly, under Remco's gut-busting laugh.

IV

In a last ditch effort to resolve the situation, the authorities appointed a panel. They were sensible enough to realise the removal of the troublesome fifteen year-old from his, admittedly unorthodox, yet unquestionably loving adoptive family, would not help matters. Upon his sixteenth birthday they would have no jurisdiction over him and he would return, in all probability, more resentful of authority than ever.

A compromise was reached.

He would attend a meeting twice a month with an appointed committee, which, in turn, would check on his school attendance and general well-being. The panel of three consisted of a social worker, a child psychiatrist, and a youth worker from the church: in this case a newly ordained Predikant. The inclusion of the Predikant was unusual, but this particular cleric represented a group within the Church specialising in helping young people in difficult circumstances find training and work.

It didn't take him long to work out the social worker and the psychiatrist talked the same shit as all the others and he instinctively regarded them as enemies - yet another part of the establishment conspiring to take him away from her.

But the Predikant.

He seemed different.

Apart.

On the first and only meeting - whilst the other two prattled on about the importance of education - the minister was silent. Examining him. Watching him more closely than the others. Until, in reply to one of the many questions he had become bored of deflecting, he had lost his temper - telling them all to 'fuck-off and mind their own business'.

It was at that point, he recalled it now as if it were yesterday, the Predikant had risen to his feet.

'Where is your mother?'

Startled a little by the question, coming as it did out of nowhere from a tall thin man dressed entirely in black. A man whom at this moment had fixed him with a steady, ice-cold glare.

'Why do you think *we* are here?'

Fear gripped his heart. 'I don't know, I didn't ask-'

'We are here because you sinned,' roared the Predikant. 'You tortured an innocent animal. You turn on your fellow pupils. You cause pain and anguish to all around you, and you will not escape unpunished. Your mother has withdrawn her love, do not risk losing the Lord's. The Almighty sees your weaknesses and you shall pay a terrible price.'

The remaining members of the panel froze. He could still see their faces twisted in shock as they stared in horror at the clergyman.

He though, he felt the tears of relief well up from deep in his soul, his pain burning in his eyes.

The psychiatrist was the first to recover and grabbed at the Predikant's shoulder.

'What the hell do you think you're doing?'

The tall man replied calmly. 'What I have to.'

For years he had been told it wasn't his fault. Everything that happened. Everything he had done. And yet he could feel the guilt squeezing through every part of him.

His father. The strangers. His mother's betrayal.

Everything *was* his fault.

He felt a great weight had been lifted. He could be punished. At last there was a chance his torture would end. He sobbed and, leaping forward, he clutched at the Predikant's coat.

'Yes,' he cried out. 'Yes. Please, let me be punished.'

Astonished by this reaction from the formerly reticent and recalcitrant young man, the psychiatrist abruptly fell back into her seat.

Thinking back on that day, he realised his sins had been so horrendous and so irredeemable. It had taken not one, but two emissaries from the Almighty to save him.

Saturday

15th December

7

glad you brought the flowers

'Holy shit!' Munro squinted at the dog.

Whisky, his head resting on the mattress and his nose only a few inches from his owner's, had been waiting patiently and silently for him to wake. Another wave of dog-breath, with just a hint of cabbage and God knew what else, wafted his way.

'What the fuck was in that stew? he groaned. Turning his head, he rubbed his face roughly in an effort to force himself awake. Then he noticed something.

It was very quiet.

Mornings in Amsterdam were often quiet. Especially at the weekends, when it appeared the whole town had a hangover until eleven or twelve. But this was different. It was silent. And much, much brighter than usual. In winter he never usually closed the curtains, there was no need as the sun didn't fully come up until long after he had risen to walk the dog. But this morning? He checked his alarm clock again.

The snow had fallen steadily through the night and lay thickly on the sloping roof opposite his bedroom window. As Munro peered out, the reflected light bypassed his eyes and pierced his dehydrated brain.

Aspirin-time. He vaguely remembered something about Martijn and Remco arguing over which late-night café would be better for a last drink as the young barman closed up the Doelen. Eventually, he and Remco had decided to go for something to eat in one of the all-night Thai cafes in the Nieuwmarkt whilst Martijn, declining the offer of food, had gone off to join his friends at some club or other. Friday night was just beginning for the young student and Munro wondered if, even in his youth, he'd possessed half as much energy.

Carefully stepping over the dog, he made for the bathroom. There were only three rooms in the small apartment, and all could be accessed from the tiny hallway. Tiny, because the original landing had literally been cut in half by his front door. An arrangement, as the genius responsible must have discovered too late, meant it was impossible to open the door inwards. This in turn forced anyone opening the door from the outside to retreat back down a couple of steps to allow it to open fully. Munro had been assured this kind of comically absurd alteration was not all that unusual, most of the old apartments had been renovated in the fifties and sixties by the residents in a frenzy of enthusiastic, and mostly misguided, attempts at DIY.

His bedroom was directly opposite the front door. The bathroom on the left. The kitchen to the right. An ambitious estate agent would describe the kitchen as 'compact'. Or possibly a 'galley kitchen' with 'everything close at hand'. In other words, an area not much wider than a corridor with a cooker at the end. A sink and work surface ran along the length of the confined space, leaving barely enough room for the tiny table and two folding wooden chairs, which made up the only other furniture in the room. The compact size of the flat didn't really bother Munro. He never spent much of his time there, and he had also gained the distinct impression the dog felt very secure in the warm enclosed environment. *Gezellig* even.

Showered, shaved, dressed, and feeling a little more human, Munro immediately felt a chill as he opened the door leading onto the landing. Stuffing his hands into his coat pockets he began to make his way down the perilously steep staircase. Another heroic descent later, including a successful negotiation of the three bicycles leaning against the wall on the ground floor, and the pair emerged from the main door and on to the street.

As Whisky slinked past Gekke Henk's front door, Munro observed the tiny half-meter rectangle of earth Henk called his garden had been cleared of snow.

'Busy boy.' he noted aloud.

One thing he did recall from last night, was the arrangement he had made with Remco to meet at eleven in his usual weekend breakfast haunt. This left him around an hour to wander around the city.

The mornings were his favourite time of day here. So very little had changed in the centre of Amsterdam that with the streets almost deserted, he felt he could choose any of the last four centuries for his walk. And as an added bonus, this morning's addition of unevenly heaped snow handsomely served to heighten the illusion.

Almost exactly an hour later, after a leisurely circumnavigation of the Herengracht, he returned once more to the end of his lane and the breakfast café feeling in good spirits, and more than ready for a coffee and a slice of his favourite cinnamon-coated appeltaartje.

Munro nudged the glassy-eyed Remco as he sat down. Balancing his coffee on a saucer with one hand, he pushed the dog under the table with the other.

'What the fuck did we finish on last night?' he asked.

'Thai whiskey, compliments of the management,' sighed Remco in reply.

'Bastards,' he cursed, laughing gently. 'Are you ready to go to a party then?'

'I am if you are,' A grin, 'better have some breakfast first though. We might need the energy.'

On the drive west, through and out of the other side of the city, Remco stopped his car at a corner flower kiosk and purchased a small bouquet of flowers. In answer to Munro's puzzled expression he tossed the flowers on to the back seat next to Whisky, before stating simply, 'It is a party.'

The Dutch obsession with flowers never ceased to amaze Munro. Bouquets here weren't exclusively given for weddings or birthdays. It was good manners to bring a bunch whenever visiting anyone at home and, as a consequence, they were available to purchase relatively inexpensively almost everywhere.

The Kolenkit estate is located in the western section of the area known as Bos-en-Lommer, and in common with many other architectural experiments undertaken in Europe in the sixties, the concrete low-rise housing development had won many awards.

At around the same time Amsterdam had gone horizontal, his home-town had gone vertical. Munro remembered vaguely reading something about Glasgow City Council in that particular era adding an extra two floors to its own concrete tower blocks in order to make them the tallest in Europe. In the end, the angle of the developments hadn't mattered as in each case the results had proven disappointingly analogous.

As they stepped carefully around the discarded syringes and consciously tried to avoid inhaling too deeply the fetid, urine tainted air pervading the darkest corners of the communal hallway, Munro hoped there was a special place in Hell reserved for over-ambitious, well-connected architects and trough-snorting city planners. Ideally, he reflected, somewhere like this.

The address Remco had obtained for Kwaaie Ali placed him on the fifth floor. After climbing to the third, the two men began to notice a marked difference in the conditions in the stairwell. There were no more syringes, a distinct smell of bleach, and even a couple of colourful flower pots perched proudly on the steps of the fourth floor entrance. The two men exchanged a fleeting look of surprise before turning the last corner onto the fifth landing. Abruptly, they found themselves face to face with two very large, dark-skinned men. Both were dressed identically: puffy black *North-Face* jerkins and matching black tee-shirts and jeans. Turning aside, Munro could see Remco was sweating profusely and more than a little out of breath. With a gesture that managed to be both inquisitive and aggressive, one of the men curtly tilted his head. Remco pulled a handkerchief from his pocket and dabbed his forehead.

'We're from the hospital,' he began, holding up the flowers. 'Colleagues, for the party?'

The larger of the two stared intently at him for a few seconds. Then standing aside, he gestured for them to pass through.

'Okay,' he grunted, pointing the way along the concrete landing. 'It's along there, number five-eight-two.'

'Thank you.' smiled Remco politely as they squeezed through between them.

Munro waited until they were out of earshot.

'Security?'

'Of a sort. A lot of these neighbourhoods have set up their own little police forces. Unfortunately, the line between protecting your own interests and criminal activity is a pretty fine one. Add religion into the mix and it makes arresting anyone for even the pettiest of crimes in these places a fucking nightmare.'

At the Absullahs' apartment, Munro pressed the doorbell. Seeing Remco raising the bouquet in anticipation as several locks were turned on the large and obviously heavily-fortified door, he allowed himself an appreciative half-smile.

'Yes?' A short, handsomely smooth-skinned youth craned his head warily into view. Munro decided to play the odds.

'What's up Doc?' Grabbing the startled young man's hand, he slid his way gently, but forcefully through the door. Once inside, he began to shake the hand vigorously.

'I don't think I...'

'You don't.' Munro released his grip. 'Is your brother in?' Making out low voices mingled with what sounded like some kind of Arabic music, he headed on through the hallway to what they imagined to be the living room.

'I'm so glad you brought the flowers. Otherwise we'd have stuck out like a sore thumb.' Munro murmured under his breath.

Momentarily stunned by the scene before them. The two detectives stood side by side, just inside the door of the lounge. The low ceiling somehow accentuating the feeling of depth, two, or possibly three apartments had been combined to create one huge room. A room so out of scale to what they had expected, and so full of people - all of whom were dressed in traditional white Moroccan costume - it had taken them completely by surprise.

With a strange kind of slow Mexican wave, heads began to turn in their direction. Conversations were cut short, and those nearest the two interlopers began nervously backing away. A quiet began to fill the room, the elderly man providing the music on a small electric organ slowing to an untidy stop. The tinny drumbeat continuing to tap in the background for a short time, before bizarrely speeding up as he fumbled for the right button. Then there was silence.

Remco looked up at Munro quizzically. 'Sore thumb?'

A booming voice sounded out from the back of the room. 'What the fuck are you doing here?'

Munro couldn't help but locate the source. A full head taller than the other party-goers, Kwaaie Ali began moving towards them. The men in the room, all dressed in long white cotton robes, white baggy trousers and matching knitted caps, made an impressive sight as they parted to allow him through.

'Oh shit!' hissed Remco.

'Well put.'

'No I mean, shoes!'

'Fuck!' Munro looked around quickly. No-one in the room was wearing shoes - no-one except Remco and himself of course.

Munro tried to smile. 'On the plus side, it might distract them from the fact we're gatecrashers.' Raising his hands in an attempt at a conciliatory gesture toward the advancing Ali, he noticed Remco handing the flowers to the young man who had let them in. He obviously wanted his own hands free for whatever came next.

'Listen,' Munro began. 'It's just a couple of questions,' he held his arms open, trying to appear relaxed.

'Yeah, the same fucking questions you ducked out of last night,' barked Remco.

'Helpful.'

Munro glared at him.

'Very helpful, thanks.'

'What?' Remco returned his gaze defiantly as Munro felt a hand grasp the lapel of his coat, effortlessly lifting him onto his toes.

'No Ali, there's no need.' It was the young man. Still holding the flowers in one hand, he had placed the other on the big man's arm.

'Really, I mean it,' he insisted quietly.

The previously iron grip, slowly eased.

'Thank you,' he said carefully, before turning to the two detectives. Glancing at both in turn, Ali Absullah's little brother smiled, revealing a set of perfect white teeth.

'Perhaps it would be better if we spoke outside. Yes?' Moving his hand gently onto the big man's shoulder, he began to usher the three men back out on to the landing.

'Now gentlemen, how can we help you?'

'*You* can't.' Remco aggressively jabbed his finger at the youth's chest. Ali inched threateningly forward onto the balls of his feet.

'I think what my colleague means to say is that our business here is with Meneer Absullah,' Munro gestured politely towards Ali. 'We wouldn't wish to interrupt your celebrations any more than we have already. I'm sorry, I don't have your name?'

He'd already deduced that this was the newly qualified doctor. But it was obvious the extensive refurbishments that had taken place in the Absullah's apartment weren't paid for by occasionally helping prostitutes and mopping out coin booths. Nor for that matter, he thought, could they have been undertaken on the wages of a newly qualified junior medic.

'My name is Youssef.'

Now it was the young man's turn to reach out and shake Munro's hand. He did so slowly and deliberately. By reversing the roles played out earlier, Munro could sense it was of some importance to Youssef Absullah that he regained control of the situation.

'Well the thing is Meneer...'

Munro paused smiling.

'Sorry, I guess its Doctor Absullah now. Congratulations, by the way.'

'Thank you.' The large brown eyes remained fixed on his own as he gently bowed his head.

'My colleague here has a few questions to ask your brother, just routine really. So why don't we go back inside and leave them to it for a few moments?'

Munro took the young man's arm, gently steering him back towards the door. Glancing back over his shoulder, he observed a look of surprise flit across Remco's face as he turned to the scowling, and quite clearly at the moment, appropriately named Kwaaie Ali.

'This is some place you've got here,' began Munro as they passed through the open door and back into the warmth of the hallway. 'Must have taken a quite a bit of effort to do all this.'

Smiling, Absullah turned to face him. 'And money Inspector, and money. I can see how your mind works. It is Inspector isn't it?'

'Chief Inspector actually, but we won't stand on ceremony.'

'Well *Chief* Inspector, please allow me to explain what we do here. Or rather, what we are.'

There was a moment's hesitation, a frown. 'Look at these,' he began again, holding up the bouquet. 'This is why we are here. The Dutch don't want to do the back-breaking manual labour involved in the harvest of their own national product, so my parents and many thousands of others from Morocco and Algeria were brought here to do it for them. It was cheap labour and it made economic sense. Naturally, I don't deny the poverty they left behind. There was no real choice for them.'

Youssef Absullah led Munro through a side door in the hallway and into the kitchen. Then, picking up a large earthenware vase from the table, he began filling it with tap water.

'We are a community here and we want there to be a choice, at least for the children of these immigrants. How many of us do you think are doctors? And how many do you think were left to grow up on these estates? An afterthought. An unfortunate by-product of a discredited and redundant economic policy. We also want another choice. A choice for our families in our villages at home.' A shrug and another smile. 'You think we want a lot maybe?'

Munro took a seat at the table and watched as the bouquet was carefully unwrapped and the flowers placed, one by one, into the vase. 'Maybe,' Munro replied, flattening his palms on the table. 'But as you have just made clear, you don't regard Holland as home. You refer to the Dutch as a foreigner would. And yet here you are. I don't see your community moving en-masse back to North Africa anytime soon.' He was fishing for a reaction. Most of what he had heard had felt just a little too rehearsed.

'Please understand, I am grateful,' Absullah spoke slowly. 'My father was a Professor of Chemistry in Morocco. In Holland he was a manual labourer. Sometimes he would work sixteen hours a day in the harvesting time. Why did he do that? For me, and for my mother. For this I am grateful. Ali has worked for years in that disgusting place in order to help pay for my studies. For this I am grateful. Finally, and I'm sure this will surprise you, to *Nederland*. For the opportunity to learn. To be able to help my people. For this above all, I am *truly* grateful.' Putting the flowers aside he sat down opposite Munro. 'This community is a non-religious registered charity. Together, we have built a clinic near Oudja, in the village of my father's birth. All are welcomed there for treatment and many travel days to reach us. The money we raise goes on supplying our clinic with Western medicines. Not the out-of-date stock the drug companies give away to salve their consciences, but the drugs used here in Europe. We use the young men to collect recyclables, sell raffle tickets, and even rattle buckets on the Kalverstraat. I assure you, and you are more than welcome to check, everything is properly licensed, and all funds are audited and accounted for.'

'Sounds familiar,' grumbled Munro. Then, ignoring Youssef Absullah's puzzled expression, he asked. 'Does this charity have a name?'

As he pulled his notebook from his coat pocket, he noticed a broad grin spread across the young man's face.

'I'm sorry, it's just...you are from Interpol. I was expecting something a little more-'

'Technologically advanced?' offered Munro with a smile.

'Yes, I suppose so. Anyway, the name of our charity is the *Noord-AfrikaanLiefkliniek*. I have the registration number here too if you require it?'

'No that'll be fine, thanks. There is just one more thing, and I hate to repeat myself, but it must have taken quite an effort to do all this.' Munro gestured once more toward the hallway and the rest of the apartment. The slightly built man's shoulders shook as he began to laugh.

'I'm sorry. Ali's always telling me to shut up, but once I get going it's hard for me to stop. There is no secret. All of these men work. Some are employed by the charity, but most work in shops or fast-food places. Even my meagre wages go into the pot. What can be achieved by the many, as you can see Chief Inspector, easily outstrips what can be achieved by the individual.'

Smooth, deliberated Munro, *bit too smooth*.

Leaning forward and putting his elbows on the table, he clasped his hands together and stared intently at the young man.

'Does the name John Patrick Gerrard mean anything to you?'

'Gerrard?' A fleeting glance at the flowers by the sink, or perhaps toward the window, out onto the landing where his brother was being questioned by Remco. 'No, I'm afraid not.'

Munro let the silence take hold before asking again.

'Nothing?'

'No.'

'Well, thank you very much for your time. Congratulations again.' Munro stood to shake hands and allowed himself to be shown out.

Remco was leaning against the wall outside. Attempting in vain to light his cigarette against the wind, he noted Munro's thoughtful frown.

'HQ?' he suggested hopefully.

V

He remembered her parents' shock when they were first told. They had no time for organised religion, but by their own rules they had to respect her right at seventeen years of age to choose the direction of her life. Together they had left Amsterdam behind. Her parents simply couldn't understand it. No-one but he could ever truly understand her beauty.

Her grace.

Her sacrifice.

In the act of saving him, she herself had been saved. A few years later, when her parents were informed of his choice of career - his calling, they pleaded with her to return home. Angrily she ended all contact. From that point on, the only link she would have with her family was through her sister in Delfzijl.

Now they were in a new place. Different. Clean.

They were happy here, but as always with him, there were many more sacrifices to be made. Due to his own upbringing he could not countenance the thought of having children. Without complaint, without even the slightest dissent, she had agreed. He knew now, her silence in the car on the way home from visiting her nephews and niece in Delfzijl. The eagerness with which she volunteered to teach in the Church Sunday School. He knew what he had taken from her.

A life of sacrifice - but not a lifetime.
He could not save her. He had stolen her life, traded it for his.
Where was God's love for her now?
Where was His forgiveness?

8

outer shitkanistan

'Jesus-fucking-Christ!' blasphemed Remco loudly.

'You're not kidding,' agreed Munro.

Betty's stew was now having a truly unwelcome effect on the dog. Leaving his own door open, he backed away from the noxious fumes emanating from the interior of the car. There were a few seconds silence before both men burst into laughter. The left-over tension from the encounter in the tower-block suddenly relieved.

'I think we should give that a few minutes,' Remco suggested. Regaining his composure, he looked on in surprise when for some mysterious reason, the phrase set Munro off laughing again.

Back in town, Remco carefully parked his car in one of the reserved spaces in front of the Nieuwmarkt Bureau van Politie. The police station, a late-seventies red brick building, squatted awkwardly in the south-west corner of one of the oldest and most beautiful market squares in the city. On the other side of the Nieuwmarktplein, across the flat expanse of cobbles and behind the cafes and mostly Thai restaurants, the red lights of *de Wallen* blushed darkly along gloomy alleyways. However, on Munro's left, and in almost perfect contrast, there stood one of the many reasons Munro had fallen in love with this place.

The widest and possibly oldest canal in the city, the reflection of the gaudy Christmas illuminations shimmered on the murky and now icily viscous surface of the Kloveniersburgwal. In the dim and distant past the impressively broad waterway had served as the main artery connecting a young and burgeoning Amsterdam to the River Amstel. These days, this grand old lady of Mokum serves a far lesser purpose. Constricted and confined by many bridges, the once mighty, rod-straight canal is reduced to little more than a tourist attraction. And now, perhaps even more ignominiously, she would provide a direct route south, guiding Munro, Remco and Whisky to the Café de Doelen.

'So basically, we've got nothing.' Remco placed the two beers on the table before lifting Muis, the ironically named ginger tomcat, from the seat across the table from Munro and placing him carefully on the window ledge. Only he could do this, the unevenly tempered cat instinctively recognising in Remco something of a kindred spirit. Munro knew from painful experience that anyone else attempting such a thing would almost certainly be risking serious injury.

Kwaaie Ali had basically confirmed the prostitutes' story, and whilst he had asked Remco to check up on Youssef's charity, Munro didn't feel there would be much to run with. But still…

'Doesn't feel right does it?' he mused. 'I get told to leave it alone. Joop Huisman. The stag party that wasn't. the girlfriend reporting Gerrard missing. It all kind of-'

'stinks.' As Remco completed his sentence, an icy blast fired into the bar. It had grown dark and Munro could tell the temperature outside had dropped from frosty to bitter.

'Told you we'd find him in here. Come on, you're freezing the place.' Marco de Veer all but dragged his partner through the open doorway. A hesitant Jack Downes entered. Turning slowly and deliberately, he closed the heavy door behind him.

'And the lovely Remco, we are honoured tonight,' boomed Marco with an ostentatious roll of his hand.

Both Munro and Remco stood, returning the hug and traditional three kiss greeting from the two men. Marco was a force of nature. Destined to be the centre of attention at any party - and to create a party if there wasn't one at hand.

'I'll get the drinks. Jack sit down.' He waved his finger at Munro. 'He's got something to tell you.'

'I'm sorry Iain, it's probably nothing.' Jack Downes seemed to spend his whole life slightly embarrassed by Marco's exuberance, right now he appeared more uncomfortable than usual. Remco, for once surprisingly sensitive and understanding the diplomat's need for privacy, left the table to help with the drinks.

Jack spoke slowly. 'Iain this has to remain confidential, I could lose my job.'

Munro smiled. 'Maybe should've thought of that before telling Marco.'

'He knows the score, in fact it was he insisted I speak with you.' The British Vice-Consul, always an exceptionally dapper little man, removed his scarf and carefully folded it on the table. Taking a deep breath, he began relating the day's events in his customary, cut-glass accent.

'John Patrick Gerrard.'

'There's a surprise, go on,' nudged Munro, with wry smile.

'Well it's not right. Today, on a Saturday no less, I get a call from the Foreign Office. I'm told his passport's a forgery and I'm to send it to them straight away for examination. I'll tell you if it's a forgery it's the best bloody forgery I've ever seen, and I've seen a few. It stated on the passport that it was issued *by* the Foreign Office. FCO as clear as day. I mean, why put that on it?'

Munro nodded. Anything out of the ordinary, anything that drew added attention to a forged passport didn't make much sense.

'That's not the half of it. Guess where I've been today?' Jack didn't wait for an answer. 'I'll tell you, at the bloody Onze-Lieve-Vrouwe hospital trying to avert an international incident.'

'That's where Gerrard's body is,' added Munro.

'Was,' Downes held up his hands in a gesture of disbelief. 'Until two Embassy staff from The Hague turned up with orders to transport him, with immediate effect, back to good old Blighty. The Coroner's not a happy girl. Threatened to kick up all sorts of fuss. Got me over there to try and sort it out, then she gets a phone call from her boss. Promptly tells me to forget it. Walks out, slams the door. Finally, I call the Embassy to find out what's going on. I mean Amsterdam is my patch after all, but I'm given the cold shoulder, told to leave it alone or I'll be handing out work visas in Outer Shitkanistan.'

Munro thought for a moment before replying. 'I was warned off it by Sir James last night.'

'Oh?'

'Afraid so. Look, you don't need to get involved in this, I'll happen by the Coroners' office on Monday. If she'll make a complaint I'll take it to McFarlane.'

'I'd appreciate that Iain, it just - it doesn't seem right, the whole thing kind of-'

'stinks?' Remco, with Marco in tow, had re-joined them.

Marco, squeezing Jack's shoulder gently, smiled and added in a breathy voice. 'See, much better to get that off your chest.' Then at much louder volume. 'It's Saturday. The night is young. Yet here I am in this dreary café. There's only one thing for it,' he jabbed his index finger upwards. 'Let's get drunk.'

By the time she arrived, Bregje immediately realised she had some catching up to do. Martijn and Jean-Baptiste had joined Munro, Remco, Jack and Marco. The two regular student barmen obviously having a few drinks before going on to a club later.

At the bar, Betty was holding court with 'the usual suspects' as Munro had christened them. These were veteran regulars: Koos, Thon, Leo and, of course, Kapitein Hans - so called as he travelled to and from the café each night in his small motorboat. Bregje gave each three kisses and was rewarded with a hug from Betty.

Formalities completed, she then called over to Munro's table. 'Hoy, hoy! This is a Dutch pub you know - in het Nederlands uh?' From the door she had overheard them laughing and joking in English. Bregje wouldn't have minded, but she knew Jack Downes was fluent in Dutch. Meaning Munro was the culprit. She also knew full-well what the reaction would be.

'Absoluut! Idiote Schot!' Betty pushed herself off her barstool and making her way to their table, arm raised and finger waving, she began chastising Munro for his lack of enthusiasm and obvious lack of appreciation for the beauty of the Dutch language. Daphne, Betty's daughter, who must have drawn the short-straw to be working on a Saturday night, handed Bregje a beer.

'Nice one,' she grinned.

Bregje followed Betty over to the table. Standing behind her favourite landlady, she beamed her best smile at Munro before saluting him with her glass.

'...and do you know what else?' Betty continued. 'You have one of the most intelligent and beautiful girls in Amsterdam walking your dog instead of teaching you what you should be learning. *Lui varken!'* Scowling and throwing her hands up in mock exasperation she returned to her stool, pausing only briefly en-route to acknowledge the impromptu round of applause from the old guard perched at the bar.

Instantly embarrassed, Bregje could feel her face begin to colour. Marco came to her rescue.

'Well, someone get this goddess a seat. Intelligent *and* beautiful. At last, I appear to have met my equal,' he gushed.

Jack Downes rolled his eyes. 'For God's-sake, don't encourage him.' Leaning over, he gave Bregje a peck on the cheek as she sat down.

'Lui varken?' quizzed Munro.

'Lazy pig,' chorused the table loudly, dissolving into fits of mocking laughter.

Sunday

16th December

9

drawn toward the light

Munro fumbled for the lamp-switch before eventually giving up and scrabbling for his mobile on the bedside cabinet. Holding the phone to his ear, he was momentarily mystified by the continued ringing. Suddenly, realising the chirping sound was actually coming from the telephone in the kitchen; he rolled out of bed and narrowly avoided tripping over the dog as he stumbled through the tiny apartment.

'Hello?'

'It's me.'

'Remco?'

'*Ja,* listen, we've got to get to *de Wallen.'*

His head was slow to clear. 'What time is it?'

'Just after six. My car's still up at the Nieuwmarkt so I'm getting a squad car to pick me up. I'll meet you there.' The line went dead.

Munro filled the small bathroom sink and immersed his head a few times in the cold water. Rubbing his face and hair dry vigorously with the warm towel kept hanging on the radiator, he observed Whisky pad across the room and snuggle back down into his warm basket. Once dressed and wrapped tightly in his heaviest black overcoat, he then experienced more than a pang of jealousy as he negotiated the narrow staircase, pushed open the communal front door into the Verversstraat, and felt his bones ache in protest at the scything wind and brutal cold.

To Munro, a murder scene in the early stages of an investigation had always appeared slightly surreal, but this was on a completely different scale. Illuminating a hive of activity, one huge arc light splashed an unnatural bright fluorescence on the main entrance of the Sexy Castle Peepshow. The myriad of surrounding tiny lanes buzzed with activity as, drawn toward the light and enclosed in sky-blue plastic overalls, forensic officers swarmed in and out of the building. Holding up his identification card to the nearest uniform, Munro was directed toward the Oudekerksplein where a Mobile Incident Unit had already been established.

The Hoofdcommissaris van Politie, Hendrik Uylenburg, reached out to shake his hand.

'Chief Inspecteur Munro, how are you?'

The still slightly groggy Munro, climbing the steps leading up to the prefabricated hut had been surprised by the sudden appearance in the doorway of Amsterdam's Chief of Police.

'Cold.' he replied austerely.

Uylenburg released a sharp grunt of laughter.

'Come in. I'll introduce you.'

Munro followed him into the small white rectangular room. Standing at the far end, two men looked up from a map unfolded untidily on the desk.

'I have placed Hoofdinspecteur Meyns here in charge of this investigation; he will be assisted by Inspecteur Baart and his team.'

Munro shook hands with both men as they were introduced. Both were in plain-clothes. Meyns looked as though he had been round the block a few times.

Overweight, close to retirement, and clearly not too happy about being dragged out of bed at some ungodly hour on a Sunday morning, he glowered at the Hoofdcommissaris with slightly glassy eyes. Baart was the opposite. Young for an Inspecteur and although casually dressed, it was all designer gear. He had even somehow managed a shave. Meyns turned his withering gaze on Munro.

'I believe you interviewed one of the victims,' he growled.

Shrugging, Munro opened his arms.

'I just got here. I don't even know who the victims are.'

The Hoofdcommissaris turned to Inspecteur Baart.

'Has forensics cleared the inside yet?'

'Yes sir,' Baart replied eagerly, 'they've marked the no-go areas and, if I may be excused, I have the manager of the establishment over at the Nieuwmarkt Bureau-'

'Bring him here.' Meyns interrupted with a growl.

'Well there's not really an interview room here, I thought I'd-'

'*Here.*'

The young Inspecteur immediately looked toward the most senior policeman in the room for support. Uylenburg blankly returned his gaze. In an instant, Baart had turned on his heel, scurried down the steps and could be heard barking into his radio, demanding Joop Huisman's immediate presence.

Uylenburg raised an eyebrow at the older detective. 'Take it easy Jaap, you were young once.'

'Not me,' sneered Meyns, before adding in a voice dripping with sarcasm. 'Oh, and Hendrik, when you've finished showing *Meneer* Munro here the sights, I'd like him back for a chat, if it's not too much trouble?'

Munro would never have believed it possible, but beneath the blindingly harsh white of several arc lights, the Peepshow now appeared somehow seedier than before. Activity was centred on the second of the four larger cubicles to the right of the downstairs area.

'Hi boss.' As Remco turned to face the two men, Munro was surprised to find he was actually addressing the Hoofdcommissaris. The two shook hands firmly.

'Remco. Still sleeping in hedges I see,' jibed Uylenburg with a wintry smile. He had a point. Even by his own unique standards, Munro's Sergeant was looking pretty rough. Entirely unfazed, Remco spoke directly to Munro.

'Passing patrol car noticed the side-door on to the Oudekerksplein was open at three-twenty this morning. Went in to investigate and found...' his gruff voice trailed off.

'What?'

'This you have to see for yourself.' Clapping his hands to get the attention of the forensics team, Remco walked Munro up to a line of yellow tape glued to the floor. 'Lights… turn off the lights.' Assuming he was with the Hoofdcommissaris, his instructions were immediately followed and the arc lights inside the club were, one by one, switched off.

The Peepshow's everyday dull-red illuminations battled ineffectively against the darkness as Munro's eyes slowly adjusted to the gloom. Through the door of the stall he could see a faint glow emanating from behind a tall, curved, grey-white panel. On the glass itself there were two small patches of beige. One, at around four feet from the floor, had a faint reddish tinge. The second patch, three feet lower and to the left, was pure flesh-tone. Remco fished around in his pocket before coming up with a two-euro coin. Then, holding the metal disc in the air like a magician, he tiptoed past the crouching forensics officer in the doorway and inserted it into a slot set into the left wall of the cubicle. There was the familiar sound of metal rattling into an almost empty collection box, followed by a loud clunk. For a half-second the window cleared. Blonde - pale - flesh. Then back to grey-white. Remco's sharp kick at the panel startled the forensics officer, causing him to emit a strangled curse. One more clunk and the window once again became transparent.

Sitting on a round metal stool attached to the rear of the booth, she leaned forward. One cheek and one knee pressed against the glass. In her twenties, early thirties at most. Blonde. Naked, except for stockings: one pulled up on the right thigh, the other slack around the left ankle. The makeup had been clumsily applied. Smudged lipstick. Heavy dark eye shadow and thick black lashes curved extravagantly over milky blue, sightless eyes. The tint of red smeared on the glass appeared to be rouge: heavily and roughly applied.

'Can she be moved yet?' The Hoofdcommissaris' voice was thicker now than before.

'Yes sir,' replied the forensic officer rising from the doorway. 'We're finished in here, but I think the Prof wants us to wait until they've cleared upstairs.'

'Upstairs?' Munro turned to Remco.

'You two go ahead,' Uylenburg laid a hand on Munro's shoulder. 'I've got half of this year's budget to sign away on this mess. Don't forget to go and see Meyns after.'

Munro knew the Hoofdcommissaris to be in his mid-fifties, but couldn't help noticing he now looked a little older. Running a hand through his thick white hair before replacing his cap, Uylenburg seemed to stoop a little as he made his way out of the club.

'Can't blame him for being pissed off,' puffed Remco as they made their way up the wooden staircase.

'When this shit hits the papers, all Hell's going to break loose.'

More arc lights; this time surrounding a stall to the immediate right of Joop Huisman's office. Three figures stood off to the side, whilst a fourth, kneeling on one leg, fired off multiple camera shots into the booth. Recognising the Pathologist, Munro reached out to shake hands.

'Esther?'

Glancing up before taking a step back, Professor Esther Van Joeren held up two surgical gloves streaked with blood.

'Formalities later I think,' she grinned. 'Didn't know this was one of yours?'

'I don't know that it is at the moment.'

'Help yourself.'

In her late thirties, her mop of blonde curls neatly tucked into a blue shower cap, the tall slender Doctor moved quickly toward the open door of the stall.

Unusually for someone in her line of work, Amsterdam's most senior Coroner and best respected Forensic Pathologist always seemed to Munro to be unnaturally jovial. This was a woman who enjoyed her work, and a morning like this had evidently put a spring in her step.

'Oh, if this *is* one of yours is there any chance I can keep him? You know, at least until I've finished examining him,' she quipped cheerfully.

'You talking about Gerrard?' Munro peered inside the tiny black cubicle 'Weird one that. Why don't you make a complaint?'

'I would, but the Hospital Director told me…'

Munro didn't hear the end of the sentence. Sitting, bent almost double, his head between his knees and hands taped crudely behind his back, he immediately recognised Kwaaie Ali's unmistakably huge frame. The stall was spattered with blood. Darkly congealing, the gory mess almost obscured the hard-core sex-scene playing silently on the screen set into the rear wall.

'Close-range shot to the base of the skull,' Van Joeren used a pen to point out a small blackened hole just above the hairline. 'The bullet travelled upwards through the brain at an angle of around forty-five degrees. The bone it took with it did the rest of the damage, with the whole lot eventually exploding out through the forehead and eye socket here.'

'The bullet?'

The Pathologist held up a clear plastic bag containing a small misshapen lump of metal. 'Dug it out of the wall above the screen.'

'Yes, the screen…'

'I know, I know. Its Michael here,' smiling indulgently, she pointed over to the photographer waiting impatiently for them to finish. 'We've got all the shots we need, but he wants to take some with the screen on. Thinks it might look arty.'

Back in the warmth of the incident unit, Munro related most of his previous day's activities to Meyns. Looking even more exhausted than before, the older officer sat up in his chair when Munro told him of the Kolenkit visit.

'Let me get this straight. You visit him at home and the next thing we know his brains are all over the Walletjes. Jesus the press are going to love that. Did many people see you there?'

Munro closed his eyes for a moment as a wave of white-capped heads rotated towards him in the Absullah brothers' oversized lounge. A gruff voice interrupted his reverie.

'No sir, we were very discrete.' Remco stood in the doorway holding two cups of steaming liquid. Carefully avoiding Munro's glare, he handed him a coffee.

'That's something I suppose.' Meyns rubbed his face roughly with his hands. 'Okay, here's the question. Do you think this Gerrard's death has anything at all to do with this?'

Munro thought carefully before replying. 'The honest answer is, I don't know.'

He felt for Meyns. The first twenty-four hours of any murder enquiry was crucial. Information gathered in this period almost always had a huge impact on a case. Munro guessed that was the reason he had ordered Huisman brought here. You had to try and keep everything together. Close at hand. After twenty-four hours forensic evidence would begin to deteriorate, witness accounts would begin to change, and solving the crime, hour upon hour, would become a more difficult and exponentially longer process.

'Fair enough,' Meyns conceded. 'Listen, it's Sunday morning, I'm short-staffed and you two are up to speed. I wonder if you could you do me a favour?'

Munro opened his arms. 'Name it.'

'Take the girl. The Coroner's is moving her now. When she gets the body back to the hospital she'll run a check for ID. I know it's not really your job, but it means I'll have two more men here for the investigation.'

'We could interview Huisman,' Remco volunteered. 'You know he was pretty twitchy when we spoke to him before.'

Meyns shook his head. 'No. If this is a gang thing it'll have to be Amsterdam officers who deal with it.'

Munro understood. Kwaaie Ali was executed, leaving the girl as either a witness or, in all probability, just the icing on the cake. An expendable commodity utilised to emphasise a point.

They watched the first body stretchered out through

the main door of the club and carried on to the Oudekerksplein. As the ambulance pulled away, having to turn sharply on to the narrow Warmoesstraat, a uniformed police officer pointed and pressed a small remote control unit at a row of three retractable steel bollards set into the cobbled stone. Glancing across, Munro noted a similar arrangement guarding the entrance to the square from the Oudezijds Voorburgwal on the other side.

VI

He had to stop.
The huge articulated lorry threatening to jack-knife on the slick road had slewed slowly to the left before the driver, skillfully steering the front wheels into the skid, managed to regain control.
The incident had broken his concentration.
She had been closer than ever.
It was as though he could reach across and touch her, holding her hand on the long stretches of carriageway between Delfzijl and home.
The long lay-by, designed for use by articulated trucks, was almost full. A caravan offering various forms of fast food and hot drinks stood alone on the grass verge. He assumed most of the potential customers in the parked vehicles would wait until the rain eased, understandably reluctant to leave the warmth and comfort of their cabs for a greasy burger and plastic cup of lukewarm coffee.
Turning off the windscreen wipers he felt his gaze lose focus as the raindrops obscured his view.
He was empty.
There was nothing left.
The trips were exhausting him. He couldn't go on continually torturing himself with her memory.
It had become an addiction. And there was something else. This time he had felt something other than gezellig

in her presence.
Something darker.
Something hidden.
He had to stop.
He would go home now and clear out her things. Her clothes could go to the church. One of the charities would be grateful.
She would have liked that.
Allowing his head to fall forward, he covered his face with his hands. Kneading his temples slowly, he released a great sigh and, feeling his breath still waver with emotion, allowed his eyes to close.
He could not remember how long he had remained like this before it happened. It was feint at first, becoming softly louder. Coming initially from his right, the voice seemed to centre on him.
'I'm here now, it's alright...I'm here now.'
Afraid to open his eyes lest the spell be broken, he began to shake. A warming, then joyful burning flood seemed to rush into him.
Everything became clear.
At last he knew what he had to do. It was all so obvious. She could be saved. She *would be* saved. He let out a whoop as he gunned the car out of the lay-by.
Plans swarmed in his mind. There was so much to do. He needed structure. A formula. It would come to him, he knew that now.
He forced himself to slow down as he neared the town. Discipline was required now.
He had to have *her* patience, *her* will.
Once home he could begin to plot his course.
Their course.
Once he got back to Winterswijk.

10

life in the old dog

Bregje sat on the edge of her bed. It was still dark outside and she waited to see if the doorbell would sound again. She was hoping the first ring had been kids on their way home from a night out. Listen to me: *kids*, she tutted inwardly, an old lady at thirty-five. The doorbell did ring again, only longer and more insistently.

'Fucking assholes,' she cursed as she pulled on her dressing gown and made her way to the intercom in the hall. Nights were usually quiet here in the Oud-Zuid. The area between the Vondelpark and the Hobbemakade was a pretty exclusive district, one of the reasons she could only just afford to rent the tiny one bedroom flat.

'Ja?' she practically barked into the intercom.

'Bregje?'

'Iain?'

'Sorry Bregje. I know it's early, but something's come up.'

She pressed the button to open the main door and heard the buzz echoing up the staircase.

'That'll make me popular with the neighbours,' she murmured to herself. Leaving the apartment door on the latch, she stomped slowly through to the kitchen. Much to her surprise, the clock on the wall informed her it was already eight-thirty. Munro called from the hall.

'Hello?'

'In here.'

Sheepishly, he stuck his head around the kitchen door as a bounding wall of joyous retriever flooded the tiny room.

'You do know this is Sunday?' Bregje tried to sound angry, but before she'd managed to finish the question she'd noticed something different in Munro's expression.

'I just need you to look after Whisky for me today,' he said quietly.

'No problem,' she shrugged. 'Do you want a coffee?' Covering her face with her hands she tried, with no obvious success, to stifle a yawn.

'I wouldn't mind.' he replied through one of his own.

Munro pulled out a chair as Bregje filled the kettle. In the mirror above the sink she could see him looking around in vain for somewhere to hang his coat. Finally, he folded it across his lap and sat down. She didn't really know why, but for some reason she felt herself smiling.

'Hey Whisky, *hoe-gaat-het?'* The familiar voice from the bedroom caused them both to look up. Bregje let the kettle drop on to the draining board with a metallic clang. Turning around slowly and feeling the heat rise in her face, she lowered her head and leaned back against the counter top. Martijn appeared in the doorway. His mop of dark curls in disarray, he was dressed only in a pair of slightly faded boxer shorts. Reaching up he began opening cupboard doors.

'Where are the cookies? This dog needs cookies.'

'Here.' Bregje handed him a metal jar from the table.

'Thanks,' he beamed at her. Then, nodding a greeting

to Munro, he went on enthusiastically. 'Hey, why don't I take a shower and we can take him to the Vondelpark before I have to open the café.'

'Okay,' she agreed, her gaze remaining fixed on the wooden floor. Youthfully oblivious to any embarrassment he may have caused, the student tempted Whisky out of the kitchen by means of a cookie waved in the air.

'Good night last night was it?' Munro rubbed his hands together before holding them out in front of him, palms toward her.

'What are you doing?' she frowned.

'I think I'd better go and leave you two lovebirds to it, but it's freezing out there. So before I do, I thought I'd just get a wee heat off your face.'

Tilting her head to the side, Bregje raised her middle finger.

'What is it you say?' she asked.

Her English almost perfect, she was now at the stage where she loved trying out new phrases. 'There may be life in the old dog yet?'

'My goodness,' Munro rose to his feet shaking his head. 'Don't run yourself down gorgeous,' he said with a snort, making his way to the door. 'That's why I'm here.'

11

exactly what I need

'Finally!' Professor Esther Van Joeren punched the air. 'You're here.' Somewhat alarmingly, she now appeared even more animated than usual.

'Something on the girl already?' Munro glanced at his watch. 'I didn't think you'd have even started on her yet.'

'I didn't need to.' A corkscrew of blond hair fell forward over her left eye and was quickly tidied away. 'Follow me.'

Barging the double doors aside with the palms of her hands, she marched through to the examination suite. Two tables stood in the centre of the large tiled room. Both were occupied, and both were draped in dark-green sheets. Only one was spotted with ominous looking darker stains.

'First things first, we know who she is.'

'Nice work.' Remco rummaged around in his jacket for his notebook.

'It's alright, Michael here has the file.' Van Joeren gestured toward the young man in the corner Munro recognized as the photographer from the murder scene. 'Now to the interesting part...'

Quickly pulling on a pair of surgical gloves, she then carefully removed the sheet from the table nearest the door. Arching her arm over the body, she pointed to the right side of the pale, naked girl's temple.

'We found this when we removed the make-up.' Standing aside to let them have a better view, she looked up at Munro. 'The cosmetics were applied after death by the way. Obvious really, apart from the bloody awful job someone has made of it, the compounds aren't absorbed the way they would be with living tissue.'

He could see a small indentation at the side of the skull. It was almost a half-centimetre deep with a faded, thin bluish-red circle at the centre.

'This the cause of death?' he asked.

'Nope, and neither is this.' Van Joeren pointed out a similar yet much larger and deeper indentation in the rib cage on the same side of the body, the circle this time almost seven centimetres across. 'There's one more on the right leg here. I can't tell until I open her up, but I would guess her skull is fractured and she's got at least two broken ribs to go with that broken femur.' She leant over the leg, squinting at the wound before going on. 'You'd have to be pretty strong and have the right tools to do the other two, but this one took a remarkable amount of force.'

'Torture?' offered Remco.

'Nope, and this is where it gets a little bit weird.'

Munro wondered briefly just what would qualify as a big bit weird to an Amsterdam Pathologist.

Van Joeren ploughed on. 'These injuries occurred after death. There's no real swelling or bruising from these blows. I think *this* is what killed her.'

At first Munro couldn't see what the professor was referring to, but after moving a little closer he could just make out a wafer thin vertical line, ten or twelve centimetres below the sternum.

'A thin blade, I'd say at least thirty centimetres long, inserted from below the ribcage and thrust directly into the heart.' Van Joeren enthusiastically mimed the act using Munro as the victim. 'Death may have taken less than twenty or thirty seconds. The initial blow would have put the heart into spasm and left her completely incapacitated. If I'm right, the lack of defence wounds on the hands and arms would support that, but as I say, I haven't really started on her yet.'

'Any signs of sexual assault?'

'I've found no genital bruising at all so far.' A fleeting look of sadness crossed the Professor's face. 'Which I would have to say is unusual working in that place.'

'Fingernails?'

'The whole body was scrubbed clean before the make-up was applied. You saw the stuff on her face, but also, concealer was used to mask the stab wound.'

Remco glanced up. 'Concealer?'

Van Joeren smiled. 'It's what keeps us girls looking so perfect.'

'Okay Prof, you know the next question.' Munro was already more than a little impressed. Receiving such a candid briefing before a full examination was a rare privilege.

'Time of death,' she delivered the words slowly. 'I took an internal temperature reading at the scene, but unfortunately it didn't really tell me anything. Obviously she wasn't killed on the premises or we'd have found where he cleaned her up, and if the body was outside for any time at all in this weather her core temperature would have plummeted. Once I get inside I can check out her internal organs. We'll get the blood back from the lab and I'll get a look at the stomach contents. Should have a better idea then…as for now?' Munro could see she was trying to help, unconsciously sucking on her bottom lip.

'This is just a guess you understand.' Another pause. 'I'm saying between two and four hours before she was discovered.'

'Good enough,' nodded Munro. 'I'll owe you a drink if you're right.'

The pathologist flashed him a grin. 'Too right you will. Now, if you will excuse me I have some work to do.'

'Just one last thing. Did you find anything new on Kwaaie Ali?'

'The big guy?' Esther Van Joeren glanced at the other table. 'No, pretty much what I told you at the scene.' Her genuine note of disappointment struck a chord with his own.

'This is exactly what I need,' Hoofdinspecteur Meyns had finally been persuaded to relocate to a hastily cleared incident room in the Nieuwmarkt Bureau. 'Another fucking headache.'

'Sorry. I thought you should know.' Munro stepped back, allowing two uniforms carrying a large notice board to pass between them. Photographs of the dead girl and a blood spattered Ali Absullah flashed in front of his eyes.

'You say you have an ID?'

'Dental records flagged up straight away.' Munro let the folder he was carrying fall open and glanced down at the contents. 'She was reported missing by her parents nine months ago.'

Pinching the bridge of his nose, Meyns slowly reeled back. Leaning against the wall he spoke quietly. 'Get a copy of that file to Inspecteur Baart. He's collating everything for the twelve o'clock briefing.' His skin looked pale and Munro could see dark patches of sweat soaking through his shirt.

'Did you get anything from Huisman?' he asked.

The old detective managed a smile. 'Not really. He's as slimy as they come. One thing though, when we showed him a photograph of the girl he just about had kittens.'

'Did he know her?'

'He said not, but you never know with him. He also turned up with his lawyer so we couldn't really have a go at him. Look I'm sorry, but I have to get on. Stick with the girl. It could be something, but I have to say this still looks like gang thing. Most likely some sick bastard mixing work with pleasure.'

Remco handed Munro a cheese and ham roll and a plastic cup of coffee as he climbed into the unmarked police car his Sergeant had acquired for the journey. It was at least an hour and a half's drive to the recently deceased Jitske Bolthof's home-town on a normal day, but now, with a blanket of snow drifting across the flat expanse of the eastern plains of the country it was likely to take a whole lot longer. Much too long to risk his precious Citroën.

'We need to call in somewhere before we get going.' Remco mumbled between mouthfuls. 'Someone's asking for us at the Westerdoksdijk.'

12

be careful what we wish for

'Aye, aye, Skipper. What's all this then?'

Reflecting the buzzing, bright fluorescent light-panels in the ceiling, the pure-white porcelain tiles lining the holding cell at the headquarters of the Amsterdam Water Police seemed to Munro an unnecessarily cruel touch. This was not a good place to have a hangover. Munro assumed by the look of him, that Kapitein Hans wouldn't take issue with that assessment. In truth, Hans didn't exactly look capable of taking issue with anything at the moment.

'I'm sorry guys, but you're the only cops I know. This is the third time. And if they confiscate my boat…' Hans ran his fingers over the closely cropped grey stubble on his scalp. Sitting on the only padded bench in the room, his shoeless toes only just reaching the floor, the already short man seemed to have shrunk in the featureless cell. Remco, still nursing a little of his own hangover, was not in sympathetic mood.

'Hans, we're not fucking traffic cops - or water cops for that matter,' he grumbled.

'Hold on,' Munro, feeling a little more generous, interrupted quietly. 'Listen, we're a little bit busy today. Why don't you just tell us what happened, and we'll see if there's anything we can do?'

'It was last night, after the Doelen closed. A couple of us went up to Koos' flat for another...well, to visit.' Koos, another regular, lived in the top floor apartment above the café. Remco's already limited patience was wearing thin.

'That makes it at least two in the morning. Just how fucking drunk were you?'

Munro shot him a warning glance. Guessing the rest of the story, he placed a hand gently on Hans' shoulder.

'Where'd they pick you up?' he asked quietly.

'That's the pisser! I was already home. I tied the boat up at the Zeedijk and was just climbing out when they got me.'

Munro felt the hairs rise on the back of his neck.

'Hans, which canal did you take home?'

'The Oudezijds of course. It's the quickest way.'

'What time did you leave Koos' apartment?'

'I don't really…I'm not sure.'

Hans had moved back against the wall, and Munro realised both he and Remco were leaning in towards him.

'Sorry,' he smiled, retreating. 'It's just that something happened near there in the early hours of this morning. Think carefully now, did you see anything unusual on your way home?'

'On Oudezijds you mean?'

Munro nodded.

'Not unusual really. It was so bloody cold the streets were deserted. There was a cop van parked on the Oudekerksplein, so I just cut the engine and drifted past.'

'Too late,' Remco cursed as he turned away.

'There was the other guy though,' Hans mused.

'What other guy?'

'Tall guy. Came out of the alley in front of the

peepshow. He was in a bit of a hurry - jumped into a sports car and shot off.'

'What kind of sports car?'

'Soft-top, definitely a Porsche. Silver I think.'

'Fuck me!' exclaimed Remco. 'You think he dived out the front as our guys came in the back?'

Munro's expression remained neutral. 'Get on to Meyns. Tell him what we've got, and that we're sending the Kapitein here right over.'

Hans looked confused. 'What's going on? Can you stop them confiscating my boat?'

'I'll speak to the Water Police; I don't think it'll be a problem.'

Grabbing Munro's hand, Hans began to shake it enthusiastically. 'That's great, fantastic...thanks.'

Munro turned his face to Remco. 'Tell the Hoofdinspecteur he better get the Skipper here some armed guards too.'

The handshake slowed.

Munro looked sympathetically at the small man as he spoke, 'Sorry Hans. I suppose we should all be careful what we wish for.'

The Commissaris van Water Politie practically leapt out of his seat as Munro entered.

'Here he is, the man himself. Come in. Please, sit down.' Beaming, he gestured toward the chair on thc opposite side of his desk. 'How about a coffee?'

Munro had met with Jan Pelser several times before, but never had the usually dour Chief of the Amsterdam Water Police been in such high spirits.

'Having a good day?' he asked.

'Good? Bloody brilliant, thanks to you. I tell you, if it wasn't for that business down in *de Wallen* we'd be on the front page tomorrow.'

Munro did his best to mask his surprise.

'Glad I could help,' he murmured.

'Just under three hundred kilos, can you believe it? We haven't even worked out how many pills.'

'Ecstasy,' Munro surmised immediately.

In recent years, and in every major city in Britain, ecstasy tabs had been selling for only three or four pounds a tab. With that kind of margin the only way to make a decent profit for the maker is to produce the pills in massive bulk, and as ever, the commercial and technical expertise of the Dutch had helped to make them the world leaders in the illegal trade.

'Where'd you pick it up?'

'In the Riebeekhaven. Just where you told us it would be. Listen,' Pelser crossed his arms and leant forward on the desk. 'I'm glad you're here, I really wanted to thank you. I know it was heading for the UK and your guys could have seized the stuff there. I also know you could have given it to the Douane.'

Could have? deliberated Munro silently. With three hundred kilos of ecstasy kicking about - it *should* have gone to Customs.

'You arrested the crew?' he enquired quietly.

Ja, but it's a container ship. It's like the United Nations on there. I'd imagine most of them had no idea what was on board, and until we get some interpreters sorted out...' the Commissaris shrugged.

'Which...' Munro hesitated for a moment, choosing his words carefully. 'Which channel did the tip-off come through?'

'Let me check,' Pelser leafed through a few sheets of paper on his desk before raising his eyebrows in surprise. 'I had assumed it was the Interpol, but it says here it was Joint Police Operations. You work for both though, right?'

'I do,' Munro replied thoughtfully. 'I do. Listen, I think we need a favour-'

'Ah, your drunken sailor? Don't worry, we'll lose the blood-test results, let him off with a warning. One good turn and all that.'

Eventually Munro gave in to Remco's huffing and puffing.

'Alright, on you go,' he conceded with a sigh.

For the last forty-five minutes they had been trapped in a traffic jam caused almost as much by the stubborn nature of the native population as by the weather. All morning the television and radio stations had advised motorists to undertake only the most essential journeys. Munro knew at the very moment this caution had been broadcast, each and every Dutch driver had determined his or her own trip to be of paramount importance. Wondering idly if the roads would have been quite so busy if the warnings had been issued on a working day, he gave permission for Remco to turn on the siren in the unmarked police car. Edging their way on to the hard shoulder they began at last to make progress.

'You know we're headed for the Bible-Belt?' The prospect of overtaking kilometres of mostly stationary traffic had instantly lightened Remco's mood. 'And us working on a Sunday too,' he tutted in mock disapproval.

'How far now?' Munro's back was beginning to ache.

'Another hour or so at this speed, it is the eastern outpost of the Gelderland Police Force you know. Another couple of kilometres and you'd find yourself in Germany. There you go, what did I tell you?' The top left corner of the large road sign was completely obscured by a patch of frozen snow clinging to the icy metal. Around halfway down Munro could just make out their destination. Remco seemed to have his timings right - it *was* only another forty-five kilometres to Winterswijk.

13

first place you looked

'And the winner of the ugliest Police Bureau in The Netherlands is?' announced Munro, climbing stiffly out of the car. The *Winterswijk Bureau van Politie:* two metre cubes of dull red brickwork thrown together in the style of discarded children's building blocks. The uniform on reception took Remco's police identity card and examined it slowly.

'We're here to see the boss,' nodded Remco with a grimace.

'Een ogenblikje alstublieft.'

Turning away, the middle-aged Desk-Sergeant slowly disappeared into the back office.

Ruefully Remco shook his head.

'Welcome to the countryside,' he grumbled.

It was a lot longer than the 'blink of an eye' before the uniform reappeared. Casually returning to his newspaper, the heavily weathered Desk-Sergeant absently pressed a button just below the counter and the double doors leading off to the right of the grey reception room squealed noisily open.

'Upstairs, second on the left,' he sighed without lifting his gaze.

'Dank-u-wel,' smiled Remco. The formality of his

Dutch steeped in irony.

Commissaris Johan Hesselink met them at the door of his office. Tall, balding, wafer thin with skin the texture of dry parchment, he lowered his head curtly with each hand-shake. His pale features visibly stiffening as he took in Remco's appearance, he spoke directly to Munro.

'I hope you will forgive me, but I've taken the liberty of making a few arrangements in order to make your time here as productive as possible.'

Munro felt his heart sink as the colourless man continued.

'I have despatched Jitske Bolthof's parents to Amsterdam in order to identify the body, and I've brought in the husband. He's waiting for you in the interview room.

There had been no mention of a husband in the missing person's report filed by her parents.

'I also have to inform you of a…' the Commissaris hesitated for a moment, '…of a rather delicate situation.'

Taking his seat with an almost pained expression, Hesselink reached for a manila folder on the top of a neat pile to his left. Placing it in front him he clasped his hands together, resting them carefully on the unopened file. Munro observed neither he nor Remco had been offered a chair.

'What do you know of Winterswijk Chief Inspector?' The note of condescension in the Commissaris' voice also did not go unnoticed.

'Not a lot,' replied Munro.

The grey face furrowed into a frown at the brusque reply.

'Well,' he began, a small wave of his hand brushing the apparent slight away. 'The church is very influential here. Architecturally of course, the church tower dominates the town, but there is also a deeper, more significant influence. A spiritual and social authority.' Warming to his subject, Hesselink gestured with his forefinger raised upward toward an antique framed map on the wall behind him. 'This is the area we must police, and I have a force of just twenty-eight. Twenty-eight, imagine that. One policeman per one thousand and fifty-three residents. In summer, with the campers and holidaymakers, you can double that figure.'

They all loved their numbers. Munro had met many 'Hesselinks' in his career, coming to the sad realisation long ago that there would always be room for uniformed accountants in the senior ranks of every police force.

The Commissaris droned on. 'Statistically we have the lowest crime rate of any sector in Gelderland, and this brings me back to my original point. The church is very active here and you must understand the impact that has on our work.'

Remco rolled his eyes.

Hesselink glared angrily at him. 'As this is a sensitive matter perhaps Chief Inspector Munro and I should discuss this alone?'

'I'm sorry,' sighed Munro. Enough was enough. Trying, and failing, to keep the anger from his voice he slowly placed a clenched fist on the table.

'Sir, as I'm sure you appreciate we are in the early hours of a murder enquiry. So maybe we could get to the point. I'm assuming you've got a problem with the Priest.'

It was almost impossible to detect, given the Commissaris' deathly pallor, but Munro could have sworn the man blanched.

'We don't have *Priests* in our church Chief Inspector. Our *Predikant,'* he pronounced the word slowly and carefully. 'Has been with us for many years, and is very much a pillar of our community.'

He'd half-hoped he'd been wrong.

'But?'

Clearly uncomfortable, Winterswijk's most senior police officer closed his eyes for a moment before speaking.

'Eight months ago, one of our patrol cars spotted a white Volkswagen van parked in a lay-by on one of our quieter roads. The road has a certain reputation. We don't condone that sort of thing you understand, and in normal circumstances my officer would simply have moved the vehicle on. In this case, however, he identified the van as one belonging to the church, and believing it may have been stolen, he decided to investigate further.'

His voice remained steady, the flat-tone reminding Munro of any number of policemen he had heard giving evidence in court.

'In the rear of the van he identified Predikant Kotmans. He was not alone and both he and his companion were in a state of undress. My officer, a parishioner himself, recognised the woman.' A pause as Hesselink's watery grey-blue eyes fixed once again on Munro. 'It was Jitske Bolthof.'

'Did the officer take any action?'

'Not officially. He left the scene without making his presence known.'

'Unofficially?'

'He reported it to me. As I have said we're a small force here. I told him to keep it quiet. It really wasn't any of our business.'

'Where is this Predikant now?'

'It's Sunday, he has two services today. The first from eleven until two, and another between four and seven. I've made an appointment for you to visit him before the evening service begins.'

Standing abruptly, Hesselink made his way to the

door, obviously discomfited, he opened it quickly and dismissed the pair with a brusque nod. 'Please keep me informed of any further developments.'

The flimsy grey carpet covering the floor of the airless and stiflingly warm interview room in the Winterswijk Police Bureau somewhat bizarrely continued up the walls before neatly disappearing behind a scruffy set of nicotine stained ceiling tiles. The material served a double purpose. Not only preventing any sound from escaping the room, it deadened any resonance within, adding an extra dimension to the already uncomfortably claustrophobic atmosphere. Set just above head height and running the length of the far wall, a band of cold yellow light glimmered through a rectangular, wire-toughened window. In the middle of the room, Willem Bolthof's thin frame curved untidily into a plastic chair. The frail, greasily unkempt man's hand trembled as his cigarette hovered above the silver foil ashtray on the wooden, graffiti-scarred table.

Munro began quietly. 'When did you last see your wife Willem?'

'She left me. We hadn't been getting on. Arguing...you know.' Raising the same shaky hand, Bolthof wiped his forehead with his thumb. The hair smeared stickily across his brow. 'It was…it was almost a year ago. She packed a few things and walked out.'

'Were you angry?' Remco, impatient as ever.

'Yes, well...kind of. It was over. We'd been unhappy for a long time. I think in the end it was almost a relief. I…' Bolthof glanced up at the two detectives as if for encouragement. 'I drink. It's a problem. I'm trying to get help. I was hoping if I could get better...'

'Did you know where she'd gone?'

'I thought she went to her parents place. But they called me a few weeks later, looking for her.'

'That's a long time ago. Weren't you worried about her?'

'No, yes, of course, but…' Bolthof stopped. Drawing in a long unsteady breath, he regained what was left of his composure before starting over. 'The call ended in an argument. I was drunk and...well, let's just say we never got on. It was one of the things we always argued about. Her parents are *church* people.'

The way he said it reminded Munro of Jack Downes' views on passport-less Welshmen.

'Were you aware,' Munro thought carefully before rephrasing the question. 'Did you know your wife was having an affair?'

Leaning back, Willem Bolthof tried on a smile. It didn't fit. 'Jitske? No, you've got that wrong.'

Remco rapped the table with his knuckles. 'I don't suppose you knew about her little sex-job on the side then either.'

Munro just had time to wince inwardly at the callous phrasing of his sergeant's question when, taking them both by surprise, Bolthof exploded out of his chair. Lunging across the table, his outstretched fingers grasped for Remco's neck. Munro reached up and smoothly gripped the thin man's left hand. Then, pushing his thumb hard into the palm, he twisted the hand around and upwards, effortlessly forcing Bolthof down on to the wooden surface.

'Easy now, easy,' he whispered, leaning over. 'Listen carefully…we're sorry, but we have to ask you these questions.'

Feeling the tension beneath him ease, Munro slowly released his hold. Red-faced and falling back into his seat, Bolthof began rubbing his wrist. A single tear rolled down his flushed cheek.

'She's dead isn't she?'

'I'm sorry Willem, her body was found this morning.'

From the other side of the table, the pathetically shabby man appeared to dissolve. Then, bent double as if in great pain, Willem Bolthof released a long, keening, high-pitched whine.

'He's got a temper.' Remco stated simply as they waited for the heating system to clear the windscreen.

Munro slowly looked across.

'Remco, we told him his wife was having an affair. Might have been involved in the sex business, and was now dead. I think we can allow for a little emotion.'

'I know, but well, you know the statistics.'

Over ninety percent of all murders stem from a domestic situation, and almost all are committed by the victim's partner or spouse. It was the first place you looked. In this case unfortunately, as they were both keenly aware, this didn't look like your average murder.

Munro glimpsed a flash of red brick as a large piece of ice slid down the glass. Putting the car into reverse, Remco struggled around to look out of the rear window.

'There is something bothering me though?' Thoughtfully Munro placed his hand on Remco's arm.

'Why do I feel as if I'm getting my arse felt?'

'What?'

'Look, we've pulled in the poor cuckolded husband for questioning. And now we're sent off for tea with the vicar?'

Remco returned the gear stick to neutral and switched off the engine. 'What the fuck are you talking about?'

This time, the Desk-Sergeant bolted upright as Remco slammed both his and Munro's identity cards on the counter.

'Brigadier? A word.'

Beneath his full head of greying curls, the uniformed

Sergeant's face was almost purple as he approached.

'Hello again,' Remco's smile was not one which warmed the soul. 'This is Detective Chief Inspector Munro from both Interpol *and* Joint Police Operations, and he needs you to do something for him.'

'Sir?'

'Put a call out to the nearest patrol car and get them to pick up Predikant Kotmans. Have him brought here for questioning.'

'But sir I…I'll have to clear that with the Commissaris.'

'No you don't,' barked Munro. 'I'm using my authority to issue this order, and unless you fancy a starring role in a report detailing the inefficient and obstructive culture prevalent in the outlying regions of the Gelderland Police Force, I suggest you get on with it.'

As the clearly distraught Sergeant began speaking into his radio, Munro turned to Remco. 'I don't suppose you know of a good little café near here?'

The little man grinned, '*Natuurlijk.*'

'Assuming he's at the church they should return with the Predikant in approximately thirty minutes. Is there anything else Sir?'

'Thank you, Brigadier…?' Munro reached out to shake hands.

'Verboven sir.'

'Brigadier Verboven, actually there is just one thing. When the Predikant arrives, can you contact us at the...um-'

'Café Oostboom,' supplied Remco.

The Oostboom wasn't quite the bruine bar he would have hoped for, but as it was only seventy or eighty metres from the police bureau, Munro figured it would have to do.

'They've cleaned it up,' groused Remco as they sat down at a highly polished table in the rear of the café. 'I hate it when they do that.'

Munro watched with some amusement the frown on Remco's face darken into a scowl as the waitress approached with two large, plastic encased menus.

'When were you last here?' he asked.

'Eighty-six I think, camping with friends.'

'Nothing stays the same Remco, even cafés change.'

'Out here maybe.'

Munro knew what he meant. Obviously the feeling would be stronger for the Amsterdammer, but he could sense it too. They were a long way from home.

The cheese and ham toasties arrived with their second beers just as a flushed looking Hesselink strode purposefully into the café. Bent at the waist with his palms flat on the table, he waited impatiently for the waitress to move away.

His voice soft yet hoarse with barely suppressed anger, he directed his enquiry at Munro.

'What do you think you are doing?'

Peering through the crook of Hesselink's arm, Munro noticed three elderly regulars watching the action intently from the opposite end of the room.

'Sure you should be in a Café in uniform sir? I thought that was against regulations.' Smiling, he turned to his Sergeant for guidance.

'Reportable offence actually,' mumbled Remco helpfully through a mouthful of toast.

Hesselink's eye twitched as a livid thick vein on his forehead became more prominent.

'I'll have you both disciplined, who do you think-'

'Listen to me,' interrupted Munro. He then took a slow sip of his beer, counting to three before placing the glass carefully back on the table. Looking up, he wondered if he could actually see a pulse. He spoke slowly and deliberately.

'This, Commissaris, is a double-murder enquiry. A double-murder that took place less than twenty-four hours ago. Now I know you don't get many of those out here, and I'm happy for you, really I am. But sir, you have to understand that by sending Jitske Bolthof's parents to Amsterdam, dragging in her husband *and* informing Predikant Kotmans of our arrival, you have jeopardised the integrity of our whole investigation.'

Hesselink straightened up, and, hesitantly, he began to speak. 'I told you it was to make your time here-'

'As productive as possible, I heard you the first time. Now I assume your presence here means Kotmans has arrived.'

'Predikant Kotmans? Yes, he-'

'Good. We're on our way.'

14

second chance

With the exception of his white starched collar, Predikant Jan Kotmans was clad entirely in black. Sitting, head bowed and hands clasped, he remained perfectly still as Munro and Remco entered the interview room. Remco pulled out the chair opposite whilst Munro, intrigued by the tranquillity of the clergyman's pose, opted to stand. Leaning back against the wall beneath the long window he positioned himself directly on Kotmans' left.

'Praying, Meneer?' Remco's opening line caused Kotmans to look up. Then casually, as if only just realising his whereabouts, the clergyman's long face creased into a slow smile.

'How may I assist you gentlemen?'

Tall, lithe and athletically built, Munro could see how Jitske Bolthof would have found the man attractive. His full head of sandy hair, cut short and streaked with grey, was styled in an almost boyish side-parting. The cut jarred against his heavily lined facial features, the overall effect making Kotmans almost impossible to age.

Remco returned the smile. 'Your Church Meneer, is it a part of the Dutch Reformed Church?'

'It is not.'

'The Hersteld Hervormde Kerk then.'

Tilting his head, Kotmans nodded stiffly.

'You disagree on a few things with the Dutch Reformed Church?' Remco's tone remained conversational.

'A few fundamental things, yes.'

'Let me see if I can remember.' Remco raised his hands from the desk and hooking the little finger of his right hand with the index finger of his left, he ostentatiously began to count.

'Female clergy, you're against those.'

Kotmans' face remained expressionless.

'No abortion under any circumstances. Same-sex marriages, you don't like the idea of that at all do you?'

At this, the Predikant's eyes narrowed. His attention still directed toward Remco, he replied carefully. 'We believe in the sanctity of marriage. A union before God between a man and a woman. We are of the opinion that this sacred bond would be undermined by the inclusion of, shall we say, others.

Jumped straight in, thought Munro, *didn't even touch the sides.*

'How about adultery?' he enquired offhandedly.

Kotmans twisted toward him. 'I'm sorry?'

'That's a start I suppose, atonement and all that.'

'No, I mean, I don't understand.'

'I think you do.'

Munro let silence fill the room.

The preacher slowly turned back to Remco. 'What is this all about?'

Munro slid down the wall until their faces were level.

He spoke quietly, observing the clergyman closely.

'Jitske Bolthof.'

'A tragedy of course.'

'In what way?'

'Murdered, and in *Amsterdam*.' Disgust filled Kotmans voice at the mere mention of the city. 'Dreadful, just dreadful.'

'You knew her?'

'Her parents are members of my congregation, naturally Jitske used to attend with them. That is, until her marriage to Willem made it difficult for her. Her husband is not a religious man.'

'Are you married Meneer?' Remco swung back on his chair.

'I am a widower. My wife died of cancer thirteen months ago.'

From his low angle, Munro noticed Kotmans' body tense as he spoke. A tiny display of emotion he felt sure would have been imperceptible from across the table.

'Please listen carefully,' Munro's back protested as he straightened up. 'This is background stuff. We have no desire to tarnish your good name or bring any kind of shame to Jitske's family.' He leaned forward, placing his hands on the table, bowing his head before going on. 'If, as I suspect, your relationship with the victim has nothing whatsoever to do with her murder, you have my word the matter will be dealt with in the most discrete manner possible. Now, that said. Let's try again.'

Munro walked around the table, settling into the seat next to Remco before repeating the name.

'Jitske Bolthof.'

Silence.

'It was...' Kotmans began slowly, his gaze faltering for the first time since they had entered the room. 'It was regrettable. My wife was ill for a very long time. Near the end Jitske used to visit almost every day. I think she rather pitied me. I'm not very good with emotions you see, and I was...I was in a bad way.' A faint smile curled the edges of his thin lips. 'Doubt gentleman, doubt is the enemy. After my wife's death,

Jitske and I became very close. She had her own problems of course, but she never doubted in the power of the Lord. In many ways she helped restore my faith.'

'When did you last see her?'

'Around nine months ago. Naturally my home in town belongs to the church, but I also have a small farmhouse around six kilometres south of here. When Jitske left her husband she stayed there for a while.'

'Did you stay with her?'

'I could get away on Friday nights, sometimes Saturdays. She hated all the sneaking around, but I had no choice. What could I do? I was recently widowed. Even if she was to get a divorce...' Kotmans shook his head slowly. 'I'm afraid my congregation wouldn't stand for it. Finally, I returned one day and found a note. She said she was going to stay with a friend, and that's the last I ever heard from her.'

'Did the note say who this friend was?'

'No.'

'Do you still have it?'

'I'm afraid not, I threw it out.'

'Of course you did,' huffed Remco.

Munro fixed his gaze on Kotmans. 'Where were you last night?'

'My goodness, you don't think I…'

'I don't think anything at the moment Sir, but I do have to ask.'

'Alright, let me see, well, on Saturday evenings I usually go to the farm to work on my sermon, and yesterday was no exception. I think I must have gone to bed around ten or ten-thirty.'

Remco leaned forward. 'You were alone?'

Kotmans glared back at him defiantly. 'I was alone, yes.'

As Remco escorted the Predikant out of the building Munro made his way back upstairs to Hesselink's office.

Knocking on the door gently, he waited for the Commissaris' permission to enter.

Hesselink glanced up briefly before returning to his paperwork. 'You have completed your enquiries?'

'You talked to Kotmans.'

'I beg your pardon?'

'Not only did he know why we were here, he would never have admitted to the affair with Jitske Bolthof if you hadn't discussed it with him beforehand.'

'That's enough Munro.' Hesselink applied his signature with a flourish before placing the pen carefully on the desk. 'I did discuss the matter with Predikant Kotmans. As the ranking officer in my own Police Bureau I would be bound to assume I had the right to do so. Furthermore, it appears the conversation I had with him produced results. He has confessed to an affair that ended several months ago, and, as I'm assuming Jitske Bolthof died a little more recently than that, it would appear you are now free to get on with the business of finding the person or persons responsible for her death. Please drive safely on your journey back to Amsterdam Chief Inspector. Goodbye.'

And fuck you too, thought Munro as he silently turned and left the office.

The light was beginning to fade as Munro tapped Remco's arm, gesturing him to pull the car over. Dwarfing the surrounding buildings, the magnificent Winterswijk Grote Kerk was appropriately, if unimaginatively, named. Shivering as he climbed out of the car, Munro sucked in the clean cold air and peered up at the church tower, marvelling at the architectural and masonry skills involved in the planning and creation of such an immense and strikingly beautiful structure.

Approaching the church from the rear, he strolled through a simple set of black ironwork gates and along a cleared stone path through the small graveyard. Thick wedges of snow obscured the inscriptions on the gravestones facing eastward. Most of the others leaned awkwardly, wiped clean by several generations of brutal winter weather. As he neared the church, there was a change in the texture of the grey granite. Originally more roughly hewn and sheltered from the wind, these stones were clearly from a much earlier period.

Buried in 1602, Johanna Catharina Beker lay beside her husband: Hermanus Derk Beker, and the couple's two sons: Jan Derk Beker, born 5th October 1590, and Jan Derk Beker: born 7th January 1592. Munro, confused for a moment, realised the sad truth. Both sons had perished in infancy. He could barely contemplate the family's pain. The worst kind. A hope reborn and renamed, then cruelly twisted into grief. The mother, Johanna, was only twenty-nine years old when she died. The same age as Jitske Bolthof. Two short lives, centuries apart. Both darkened by misery and heartbreak. Both robbed of a second chance.

Lost in contemplation, he slowly made his way round to the large cobbled square at the front of the church. The Grotekerkplein had been cleared, and in the far corner a small yellow snowplough had been neatly parked next to an uneven mound of snow. Recognising Predikant Kotmans' voice echoing inside, he approached the massive iron studded wooden doors of the church. Hesitating in the vestry, a reflected metallic flash of light caught his eye. Turning toward the source, Munro observed a row of three retractable steel bollards silently disappear into the ground at the other end of the square. A few moments later, a flat-bed truck entered, and two workmen began to load up the plough.

'Boss! We've got to get moving.' Remco stood at the corner of the church. Panting and waving his phone in the air, he pointed in the direction of the car.

Once back in the enveloping warmth of the passenger seat, Munro felt his face begin to tingle. Distracted by his own thoughts, he hadn't noticed just how cold it had become outside.

Remco's expression was grim.

'Do you want the bad news, the bad news, or the really bad news?' he asked.

'Go on then.' sighed

'The Prof. wants your blood for sending Jitske Bolthof's parents to identify the body without letting her know.'

'Not guilty.'

'I told her it was down to Commissaris *Lul-hoofd.'*

Hoofd translates as head.

Munro smiled. 'Don't be too hard on him. I'm sure he'll be fine once they get that poker out.'

Snorting, Remco retorted. 'Broomstick.'

'What?'

'In *het Nederlands* we say broomstick.'

It was Munro's turn to laugh. Turning to Remco, he observed his Sergeant's smile fade.

Remco paused before speaking. 'Meyns is in hospital. Had a heart attack a few hours ago.'

'Jesus,' Munro let the information sink in. 'How is he?'

'Not advised to start any long books.'

'Is this the really bad news?'

'Depends on your point of view. Inspecteur Baart's in charge of the case for now, and…are you sitting comfortably?'

'Fucking Hell Remco!'

'He's arrested Derk Merel.'

'You're joking.'

Remco pulled the car out from the kerb and executed an unwieldy u-turn.

'I wish,' he sighed.

'Merel may have ordered the murders I suppose?'

They had reached the outskirts of Arnhem before Remco had broken the silence.

Munro shook his head.

'And Baart's unpicked that connection in a couple of hours? Can't see it. It's not Merel's style. He's been very careful in the past to avoid-'

'shitting on his own doorstep?'

'Exactly.'

Baart was ambitious, anyone could see that. But the idea that the gangland boss, with his contacts and organisation, would take the risk of committing a double murder in the heart of Amsterdam appeared somewhat implausible.

Remco's mobile rang. 'It's for you,' he smirked mischievously as he handed the receiver to Munro.

'Munro? It's Esther.'

'Call me Iain. What can I do you for Professor?' he quipped, raising his voice against the noise of the car as Remco barrelled along the, now much quieter, highway.

'We need to talk. I can't get through to Baart.'

'I think he's probably quite busy at the moment, can I help?'

'Someone should. Can you come here? I'm still at the hospital.'

'I've got a better idea. Do I owe you that drink?'

'The Bolthof girl?' Munro heard paper rustling. 'Time of death between eleven-thirty and one, push me and I'd say a little later than midnight'

'Fair enough,' he smiled, before enquiring politely, 'Do you know a café called the Doelen?'

15

coincidence

Awkward, thought Bregje, as Whisky raced behind the bar to greet Martijn. Jean-Baptiste practically leaping from his stool on the customer side, flashed her a quick smile as he followed the dog around to the beer taps. Barely masking his concern, the young barman looked over at his friend as, disconsolately, Martijn shuffled into the tiny kitchen area.

Keeping his voice low, Jean-Baptiste leaned toward her as he poured the beer.

'What happened?' he whispered.

Bregje pulled an exaggeratedly anxious face. 'It was just some fun, but then in the park today he became so serious.'

'I'm sorry, I should have said something.' The fair haired student-lawyer dipped his head apologetically as he handed Bregje the fluitje. 'He's had a thing for you for a while, we all knew. I guess I just assumed you did too.'

'I told him I didn't want anything too, you know, too permanent at the moment, and he just - he was so upset.'

'Don't worry, he'll survive. Don't take this the wrong

way, but Martijn falls in love a lot.'

The combination of freezing weather and the early evening calm meant the café was unusually quiet. Apart from herself, Martijn and Jean-Baptiste, there were only three others in the bar. A scruffy collection of what Bregje assumed to be students. Carefully nursing their drinks, they sat huddled around the iron stove in the corner. It reminded her of her own student days. Weary, cold Sunday nights spent squeezing the last few drops out of the weekend.

Remco's raised voice could be heard long before the door flew open. '...one day, trouble, I'm telling you,' he ranted as they burst in, bringing with them a chill wind and a small flurry of snow.

Bregje quickly stepped around them and closed the door. 'It's snowing again? Jesus, when is it going to stop?'

Business had been bad since the cold snap set in. Her type of students didn't need much of an excuse to call off a lesson, and it was beginning to look like December was going to be a pretty lean month.

Munro strode up to the bar and handed Jean-Baptiste a fistful of plastic bags.

'Couldn't dispose of these for me could you?' he enquired politely.

Remco scowled in reply to the barman's puzzled expression. 'They were keeping the seats of those scooters on the bridge dry. What can I say, he's a lunatic.'

The group in the corner turned their faces toward the newcomers. One stood.

'What did you say?' he snapped.

Remco shot Munro an irate glare before shaking his head.

'You see what happens?'

All of the young men were standing now. Tight faces

and tighter fists. Taking the initiative and smiling broadly, the short, stout Sergeant sauntered over.

'I don't know why you're mad at me. I told him not to do it.' He gestured with a thumb over his shoulder. 'However, there is one thing,' reaching into his coat pocket, Remco pulled out his police identity card. 'I didn't check if the tax was up to date on them. Do you have the paperwork with you or do you want me to run the registrations through the system?'

He was still beaming as the trio scampered out of the cafe.

Taking a table near the back of the room, Bregje joined the two detectives. Although she felt relieved to be away from the bar, she gave Remco a puzzled look. She knew Munro preferred a barstool when the café was quiet, and this evening it was quieter than most.

'We've got company coming,' he explained, nodding at the empty chair.

'Anything I can help with?'

In the past, Bregje had assisted Munro with recordings of interviews he'd had Remco smuggle out of the office. Munro felt that although he could comprehend most of what had been said, he was missing out on much of the nuance. There was Remco obviously, but it would be fair to say understanding tone and subtle use of language were not his strongest points.

Bregje's real specialty was dialect. It was what had captured her imagination at university and she took great pleasure in pigeon-holing people. Not only on where they were brought up, but also when and where in the Netherlands they had moved in the past. Her strike rate was impressive enough to make it her regular fall-back party trick.

Munro frowned distantly. 'You know, I wish we had recorded it. We interviewed a guy today and I didn't get anything close to a read on him.'

'God-botherer out east,' supplied Remco. 'Preacher caught with his pants down.'

Hiding a smile in his glass, Munro took a few welcome swallows of beer before turning his attention to Bregje.

'Trouble in paradise?' he asked.

He may have had some difficulty picking up the language, but he had no problem picking up on the tension in the café. Bregje glanced over her shoulder and briefly caught Martijn's eye. He looked away quickly.

'Let's just say it didn't work out,' she smiled back at him frostily.

Munro tilted his head back. 'And days may come of milder, calmer beam, but there's nothing half so sweet in life, as love's young dream.'

Remco tutted, 'Where does he get this stuff?'

'That one's Thomas Moore I think,' sighed Bregje.

Surprised, Munro saluted her with his glass.

'She's a smart lassie that one.' he nodded.

Bregje felt her cheeks begin to redden.

'Who needs another beer?' she asked, standing quickly, then, remembering who was at the bar, she hesitated for a moment before resolutely setting off to order the drinks.

As Professor Esther Van Joeren bent to shake the snow from her hair, Remco leaned over to Munro. '*De Zwarte Weduwe* scrubs up pretty good uh?'

It was a nickname used by most of the policemen Van Joeren came into contact with - though not many were brave enough to call her The Black Widow to her face.

Wearing a short maroon leather jacket over a snug fitting black t-shirt and well-worn, skin-tight jeans, the arrival of Amsterdam's top pathologist was also attracting some attention from behind the bar.

Even Martijn seemed to have perked up.

'Franck Baart is a complete asshole!' Van Joeren all but threw her briefcase onto the table.

Munro stood to shake hands.

'Well, we're not on first-name terms, but you'll get no argument from me.' he smiled.

'Where's that drink you owe me?'

'Here,' returning from the bar, Bregje handed one of the fluitjes to the Professor. 'I'm Bregje, and if you ask me, they're *all* assholes.'

Van Joeren raised her glass. 'Call me Esther, and in the words of the Chief Inspector here, you'll get no argument from me.'

Munro waited until the two were seated.

'So, what seems to be the problem with our esteemed colleague?' he asked brightly.

Esther half-turned toward Bregje and waited. Munro nodded his approval. Shrugging, she reached into her briefcase and pulled out a sheaf of folders.

'I've been trying to get through to him all afternoon. I have got his fucking bodies for God's sake!'

'You've something new?'

'At first I wasn't sure…but now?' she dumped her case on the floor and looked down at the stack of buff-coloured files. 'Do you know what Policemen and Forensic Pathologists have in common?'

Eyebrows raised, Munro looked around the table. 'Surprise me.'

'We don't like coincidences.'

'Go on.'

'It was Michael, my photographer; he noticed something familiar about the marks on the Bolthof girl. He couldn't remember where, but he swore he'd come across something similar before. It didn't occur to him until he was downloading the images he had captured in the examination room, so naturally we assumed it was something he'd seen on-line.' Esther tapped the stack of folders with her forefinger deliberately. 'This is what we came up with by running the exact dimensions of the traumas through the database.'

'You'd have done that anyway I presume.'

'You would have thought so wouldn't you? But standard procedure is to run the fatal-wound data first. Then, only when the examination is completed, are the other injuries entered into the system.'

Munro was beginning to understand.

'These files contain post-mortem matches, and you guys are the first to put them together?'

'Exactly. As far as I can tell, in each of these cases the circular wounds occurred after death. In most, the bodies were either badly decomposed or had been so damaged as to make at least one of the three wounds undetectable.'

Bregje stared down at the heap of folders. 'How many people are here?'

Esther held up a hand at the interruption. Turning her head to Munro, she continued. 'There are two reasons we spotted the connection. One: Michael spends a lot of his time studying post-mortem pictures, which makes him useful, if a little weird. And two: this time whoever did this either wanted us to find the wounds, or didn't care if we did.'

For once, Remco's beer sat untouched.

'What about the concealer?' he asked.

'Purely cosmetic, if you'll forgive the pun.'

Grimacing, Munro set his own beer to one side and began to thumb through the folders on the table.

'Which brings us back to the lady's question,' he spoke softly, not sure he wanted to hear the answer.

'I'm sorry,' Esther deliberately turned to face Bregje. 'So far, we have four. Five, if you count Jitske Bolthof.'

The words sent a chill around the table.

'In that case,' Remco took a deep breath before slapping the table with the palm of his hand. 'We need a map.'

'We do?' Bregje looked up at Munro.

'We do,' he replied.

'There's one in the car.' Jumping out of his chair, Remco made for the door.

Munro, examining the contents of the top folder, spoke quietly to the Professor. 'Give me the basics.'

'Are you sure you want to do this here?'

'If you're right, we're going to need your pal Baart on board. Convince me, and I'll try to convince him. Although, if what I've heard of his performance today is anything to go by...' Munro shrugged.

Esther appeared to mull this over for a few moments before reaching into her briefcase for a notepad.

'Alright, here we go.' she sighed.

Flicking the first couple of pages over the top of the pad she paused again, scanning the page.

'All of the victims are women. As we have already discussed, all have injuries which correlate in one way or other to the circular marks found on the right side of Jitske Bolthof.' She frowned before going on. 'I'm afraid that's about all they have in common. Their ages vary from twenty-four to seventy-two. Ethnically: four of the five are Caucasian, one is black.'

'Give Bregje the list of locations.' Reaching out, Munro touched Bregje's arm. 'When Remco gets back with the map, see if you can pinpoint where the bodies turned up. Look for a pattern, anything.'

Bregje nodded, she knew she should be appalled. Horrified even. But in truth, she felt more than a little thrilled at the prospect of assisting in a murder inquiry. Maybe that was wrong. Shrugging mentally, she suppressed a smile. Then again - maybe not.

'Now Esther,' Munro pressed his elbows on the table

and leaned in towards the Pathologist. 'How about telling me the real reason this hasn't come to anyone else's attention?'

She met his gaze evenly for a few seconds before bowing her head in resignation. 'This is where I ran into difficulties. Officially, there's only one murder.'

'Jitske Bolthof.'

'I'm afraid so. Three of the others have been recorded as accidental deaths.'

'Let me guess, the last one threw a lucky seven.'

'Lucky seven?'

'Jumped straight to heaven. Suicide?'

Esther nodded, holding up the pad. 'The report says she threw herself into the Rhine at Arnhem.'

'A bridge too high,' murmured Munro.

'Sorry?'

'Doesn't matter. Do you have dates?'

Glancing down at the open notebook, she read aloud. '14th of July this year, then the 14th of August, 24th of October and the last, not counting Jitske Bolthof today, was the suicide on the 4th of this month.'

Bregje held up her hands. 'I'm going to hate myself for saying this, but you should give the dates to Martijn. If there is a pattern, he'll see it. Numbers are his thing. You should see him with a Sudoku book.'

Munro nodded again to Esther.

Looking a little ill at ease, she tore out a page of her notebook and handed it to Bregje.

'Some incident room,' she noted, making a show of looking around.

'Erm…not me,' Bregje placed the paper carefully on the table. Glowering impatiently at her, Munro snatched up the sheet and strode to the bar.

16

holy man

'Well, you're right about one thing,' groaned Munro.

Multi-coloured pins, harvested from the posters lining the steep staircase leading down to the toilets, had been pushed through the map and into the table's already scarred surface.

Esther, half-standing, squinted down.

'What?'

'I really don't like coincidences.'

Bregje chipped in. 'God-botherer out East?'

Although not exactly a pattern, she had no trouble putting two and two together. Doetinchem, Borculo and Aalten. All in the east. And all within twenty kilometres of Jitske Bolthof's home town. The only exception was Arnhem. Not so far east, but on the direct route to Amsterdam.

'Told you she was a smart one.' Munro's expression remained grim as he pulled the photographs from each of the files. Lining them up on his side of the table, he examined them closely. 'These all match?'

'Exact dimensions.' Esther Van Joeren looked slightly flushed.

I'm not the only one finding this exciting, thought

Bregje, sharing a smile with Remco.

'There's no chance some weirdo at the morgue's responsible?'

'Three of the victims did go to the same hospital for examination. But Jitske Bolthof-'

'With you?'

'The whole time.'

The pictures slipped out of focus. Rubbing his eyes, Munro felt a wave of fatigue wash over him.

'It's been a long day,' Remco yawned in sympathy.

Munro felt his knees creak as he pulled himself to his feet. Rolling his shoulders he stretched out his arms.

'You're no' wrang wee man,' he groaned in his broadest Scots as he gathered up the empty glasses.

It was time to get started. All he had now was a collection of disparate facts. What he needed was a plan.

A few of the regulars had pitched up. Munro exchanged greetings with Koos and Thon as he approached the bar.

'Goejeavond gentlemen, you heard anything from Kapitein Hans today?'

'Have I,' Koos rolled his eyes heavenward. 'I tell you, if that lucky bastard fell into the canal he would come up with a gold watch.'

'He got to keep his boat then?'

'Why don't you ask him yourself? He's on his way here, called me five minutes ago.'

Returning with the drinks, Munro passed on the conversation from the bar. If Hans had fingered Baart's favourite candidate he would surely be in the most protective of protective custodies by now. Esther met the news of his release with a sigh of relief.

'At least Baart should listen now,' she reasoned.

Munro's reply lacked conviction. 'He should.'

His own assumption, based on bitter experience, told him that changing the tack of an ambitious and focussed detective on this kind of high profile case wasn't going to be quite that simple.

'Got it!' Martijn stood at the end of the table with the sheet of notepaper triumphantly held aloft, trying manfully to avoid eye contact with Bregje.

Remco attempted an upper-class English accent.

'You have...in your hand...a piece of paper.' His impression was more Richard Chamberlain than Neville.

'Not always good news,' added Munro.

'The 12th of September, 5th of October, 10th of November, 23rd of November, 11th of December…' Martijn glanced down at his scribbled notes on the sheet, '...and then today, the 16th. Followed by the 19th and 21st of December.' He beamed down at the table.

Bregje looked up. 'And these are?'

'Dates of course - the dates you're missing.'

Munro met the Pathologist's horrified stare. 'Tell me Martijn,' in spite of an empty churning in the pit of his stomach, he maintained eye contact with Esther. 'How exactly did you come up with these dates?'

'Easy, they're not dates really, well kind of-'

'Get to the point,' growled Remco.

Martijn looked around the table nervously. 'Thirty-one, that was the key. It's a very special number. Anyone interested in mathematics knows that.'

Remco looked as if he was about to burst, *'For fuck's sake!'*

'Prime numbers, it's a sequence of prime numbers. On the list you gave me, you have the 4th of December and the 24th of October, forty-one days apart, *that's* the red herring,' he nodded appreciatively. 'Then the 14th of August, no good. But *then* you have the 14th of July and Hallelujah. Thirty-one days.'

'You've lost me,' Bregje shook her head.

All awkwardness forgotten in the moment, Martijn laughed out loud. 'Don't you see? You work your way back. The thirty-first day after the 14th of July falls on the 14th of August. The twenty-ninth day after that is the 12th of September-'

'Why twenty-nine?' Remco scratched the back of his head.

'Twenty-nine is the next lowest prime number. It goes like this: 31, 29, 23, 19, 17, 13, 11, 7, 5, 3, and of course, 2.'

'But we didn't give you the 12th of September,' Remco's voice rose in exasperation.

Munro silenced him with an angry look before turning to the barman 'The four other dates fit?'

'In the sequence? Of course. They all fit perfectly.'

'No chance it's a coincidence?'

'In Mathematics we don't have much time for coincidences.'

Munro rubbed his face slowly with both hands.

'Join the club,' he said quietly.

'My God,' Esther jumped to her feet and began pulling the folders together and stashing them untidily into her briefcase. 'I've got to get back to the hospital. I'll get on the database and start working on the new dates.'

'Holy shit!' Remco leaned back in his chair as the significance of the missing dates dawned on him. 'Holy-fucking-shit!'

Bregje's head was swimming. 'He's killing people on specific days?'

'It won't just be specific days.' Munro opened his hand toward Esther's seat.

The Professor lowered herself back into the wooden chair before speaking. 'This must have taken a phenomenal amount of planning. These victims weren't at the wrong place at the wrong time. They were selected. In some way connected - at least in his mind.'

'They're all women?' Remco raised his forefinger.

'Apart from Kwaaie Ali,' interjected Esther.

Undaunted Remco carried on. 'Four of the five we know about are from the Winterswijk area.'

It was Munro's turn to interrupt. 'He's not hiding them anymore. He wants us to make the connection. He's come all the way to Amsterdam to make us sit up and take notice. The question is, why now? He's been at this since July.'

'At least.' Esther exchanged another look with Munro. He could feel the adrenalin begin to kick in, pushing the tiredness to one side. Forcing himself to calm down he took a deep breath.

'There is one other thing.' One by one he looked at the faces around the table, making sure he had their full attention. 'In three days, our boy's about to do it again.'

Bregje was the first to break the silence. 'This is crazy. He must know you're on to him, you said so yourself. How could he get away with it?'

'Because he's nearly finished,' Remco lifted his glass. 'This bastard doesn't care if we know about it. He only has two more murders to commit. One on Wednesday and one on Friday. Then he wins the prize. A full fucking set!'

Munro contemplated his own beer for a few moments. 'We need to knock him off-course. Rattle him somehow. Or else…' Bregje was right. This *was* crazy. The Sunday night drink in the bar had taken a bizarre turn - spiralled out of control.

Too much information.

'What about your *Holy Man* from the East?' She suggested thoughtfully.

'Fair point,' agreed Remco. 'He's all we've got at the moment.'

Munro was unconvinced. 'Based on a nine month old affair?'

Remco shrugged, 'When barrels need scraping?'

'Alright,' he conceded. 'This thing's got roots in the East, I'll give you that. But the next murder's going to be here. This guy *wants* everyone to know what he's doing. And as we know from this morning, good old Mokum is the only venue worth playing.'

Esther nodded in agreement. 'So how do we slow him down?'

'We don't,' he had the beginnings of an idea. 'We wind him up.'

As with all good ideas, this one had an element of risk. He considered this for a moment before embarking on an explanation. *As it happens,* he reflected as he spoke, *quite a large element.*

Monday

17th December

17

a matter of severe gravity

'Did you get into the office this morning?'

'Did what I had to. Got out quick though.'

Munro chortled. 'Can't say I blame you.'

'Anyway, good luck - I think you're going to need it.' Remco's customary gruff tone carried a note of genuine concern.'

Ending the call, Munro tossed his phone onto the untidy pile of newspapers crumpled in the passenger seat. Screwing up his face he rubbed his nose, conceding his friend might well have a point.

Wassenaar and a meeting with the boss. The car was stationary, as he knew it would be. Which was why, after rising early to iron his shirt and pick out his smartest suit, he had dropped Whisky off at Bregje's office before heading south. No point both of them spending two hours cooped up on what should be a forty-five minute journey. Stay on this road and it would lead you through Den Haag and on to Rotterdam, Antwerp, and eventually take you all the way to Brussels…eventually.

Today, as with most days, the A4 was living up to its reputation as one of the largest parking lots in Europe.

Munro didn't mind as he was in no particular hurry

to get to this appointment. He had no doubt McFarlane would have read the newspapers this morning, and little doubt as to the reaction his superior would have had to the articles naming Munro as the leading expert on the enquiry.

The press had devoured the information. Protests at the lateness of the hour. Moans about early editions having already been printed and fears over one editor's standing orders not to be disturbed on a Sunday night, all instantly blown away by the chance of an inside line on the biggest story of the year.

Sexual predator responsible for double murder in de Wallen.

The journalists were contacts Remco had built up over his considerable years as an Amsterdam cop. Each had been promised an exclusive and, right at this moment, each would be weathering a shitstorm from their editor.

The story was in every daily. The *Dagblad* and *Het Parool* had chequered their front pages with thick black headlines. Even the *Telegraaf*, usually a more conservative tome, had splashed out, their normally staid layout awash with gory details.

Gory details hashed out around a pockmarked table in the Doelen late into the night before.

'Make it sexual,' Esther had insisted, scribbling dates into her notebook from the piece of paper Martijn had marked up.

'Was it?' Bregje was confused, no-one had mentioned sex until now.

'It always is. He may not have assaulted the victims sexually,' Esther held up her pen. 'But I'll bet he wanted to.'

'And stopped himself,' Munro filled in. 'He's probably very proud of himself for that.'

Bregje understood. 'He'll want to set the record straight.'

'He has to.' Munro tried not to sound too desperate. 'We make it dirty,' he handed Remco the notebook he'd been working on. His reward came in the form of an appreciative grin.

'Alright, alright, I'm coming,' Bregje shouted impotently at the ringing telephone. Her progress was hampered by Whisky as, directly in front of her, the large white retriever laboriously zigzagged his way up the steep staircase to her office. Unconsciously, she began searching the English lexicon in her brain for an adjective.

'Doggedly, I suppose,' she laughed out loud.

She'd let Whisky lead the way as the pair wandered around the Jordaan. The events of the night before had given her a disturbed night, and the sharp cold air felt good in her lungs. Cleansing.

'Hello?'

'Bregje, its Esther. I need you to do something for me.'

'Of course.' Surprised, Bregje unravelled the scarf from around her neck and sat down. Looking around for a pen and a scrap of paper she balanced the telephone on her shoulder before speaking.

'Go on?'

'I've sent you an e-mail with the names and dates of birth of all of the victims so far. I want you to do some online digging for me. Look for newspaper articles, personal websites - anything that connects them.'

Bregje remembered exchanging phone numbers and email addresses the night before, at Munro's insistence, but she had assumed from Esther's demeanour that the Professor was profoundly uncomfortable with any amateur involvement.

'I don't understand. Isn't this police work?' she asked.

'It should be. Unfortunately right now, Franck

Baart's chasing his ass around Police Headquarters trying to justify the arrest of Merel in light of, shall we say, certain revelatory newspaper reports. It's a mess down there. I'd ask Remco, but it looks like he's high-tailed it back to Winterswijk. Not sure if he's got anything to go on, or he's just getting out of range for a few hours.'

'It's just...I have a class here in half-an-hour,' as she spoke, Bregje knew how pathetic it sounded. 'Sorry, forget that. I'll get on to it.'

'Thank you Bregje,' the gratitude was sincere. 'I would try myself, but…well, it looks as if we've turned up one of Martijn's missing dates.'

'Another body?'

'Floating in the harbour two hours ago. From what I can tell so far, she's going to be favourite for the 11th December.'

Her students arrived together and on time. These particular pupils always did. They were a mixed group in almost every sense. Bregje could hear the two Frenchmen, two Englishmen and one Danish girl chattering noisily as they hung their coats in the hallway. Recruited straight from university, they were all employed by the same company. An American high-tech outfit with a European Headquarters located to the south of the city. No doubt tempted there by favourable rates and tax incentives.

No such breaks for me, reflected Bregje. Unhappily reminded of her own outstanding tax bill.

She had been busy since Esther's call, printing out separate pages for each student. This was going to be a different kind of lesson.

Only after Whisky had met each member of the group, and been rewarded with the requisite amount of fuss and adoration, did the clatter die down. When everyone was seated around the large rectangular table,

Bregje distributed the sheets.

'Today I need you to do me a favour,' she began. 'Do you all have your laptops with you?'

This was a redundant question. These were trainee technical engineers; never found more than three feet from their matt-black, slim-line and portable lives.

Esther waited as a ruffle of power cables spread across the wooden surface of the table. Computers were plugged in and switched on. The shortage of power points resolved by the utilisation of the extension normally used to power the refrigerator and kettle in the kitchen area.

Each sheet had a date of birth, a name and one additional piece of information: a date of death.

'I need you to go online and find out everything you can about these people. I'm looking for some kind of link between them.'

'Is this instead of our lesson?' Freda the Danish girl, and by far the most advanced student, looked concerned.

'These people are all Dutch. Anything you do find will be in het Dutch. So translate.'

Bregje could see the others smiling at this. Pleased to be doing something less boring than my lesson, she thought. Realising the knowledge didn't really bother her, she wondered again if perhaps it was time for a change.

'Wow,' exclaimed one of the English students. 'You could cook a chicken with this wireless signal.'

The announcement brought a chorus of appreciative murmurs from the others. Bregje decided not to explain. The office below was occupied by a small recruitment agency that, a few months ago, had installed a wireless network. Unfortunately for their communications supplier, they hadn't got around to activating the password encryption. There were two notable beneficiaries Bregje knew of. Herself, now with free and unlimited access to the Internet, and the owner of the cafe two doors along the Nieuwezijds; his bar takings almost doubled by a mysterious, yet wholly welcome, influx of Amsterdam University students.

'Oh dear,' it was Freda again.

For the last fifteen minutes the room had been silent. Only the clicking of keyboards and occasional ticking of mouse buttons disturbing the peace.

'How awful.' Her young face twisted down to one corner in disgust.

'What is it?' Bregje crouched behind the girl's shoulder and squinted at the screen.

'This woman, Maartje Weidman. She was seventy-two when she died. Fell down her stairs at home and lay there for twelve days before someone found her.'

Bregje remembered the photograph from the night before. The Professor explaining how the blackness splashed down the victim's right side had occurred as a result of blood pooling inside the body.

'A matter of severe gravity,' as Munro had quipped darkly.

He knew that. Bregje had felt a chill run up her spine. The killer knew that would happen. Esther had brightened up considerably as she described how, from the picture it appeared the sole of the woman's shoe had caught on the lip of the skirting board. That, along with the angle of the leg had meant most of the blood had settled just a fraction higher than was intended. Near the hip, leaving two-thirds of a uniformly round bruise exposed.

'My God!' Still scrolling down the page, the girl shook her head in horror. 'She, she…you read it.'

Standing abruptly, Freda offered her seat. Reading slowly, Bregje realised why this particular every-day tragedy had made the headlines.

Eight years before her death, workmen replacing tiles on Maartje Weidman's roof had found a hollow in the eaves. And from that cavity, in the space between the roof and the attic wall, one of the men had pulled a child's skull. The police were called and the end of the search had revealed three complete sets of bones from three new-born infants. Each had been crammed into the tiny nook some three decades before. Bregje, noticing she had instinctively brought her hand up to her mouth, pulled it down quickly as she scanned further down the article. Weidman was released without trial. She claimed each child had been still-born and, with only bones to work with, there had been no evidence to the contrary.

'How about that for irony?'

Bregje hadn't noticed the young man peering over her shoulder. He pointed to the last two lines of the piece and read aloud. 'Mevrouw Weidman spent fourteen years as a member of the Winterswijk Hersteld Hervormde Kerk's Save the Children committee.'

'Wait. What was that?' James, one of the English students, looked up from his laptop.

'This old biddy-'

'No, the other bit, the church.'

'The Hersteld Hervormde Kerk?' Bregje made her way around the table.

'Yup, there it is: Anna Leys. Released on probation on the recommendation of the Director of the Winterswijk Hersteld Hervormde Kerk's Youth Initiative Programme. No wonder she threw herself of a bridge,' he snickered unpleasantly.

'What did she do?' asked Bregje.

'Beat up an old man in his home apparently. Stole his money.'

'Nice girl,' she stated flatly as she placed a hand on the young engineering student's back to steady herself.

Trying to get a better view of his screen, she hid her amusement as his face reddened.

'What about anyone else?' Bregje looked at the others.

'Nothing about the church.' The young Frenchman looked disappointed.

She had that connection already; his sheet held Jitske Bolthof's name.

'Holy Man from the east,' she muttered absently.

Bregje looked around at the circle of expectant faces. Three out of five wasn't bad.

'Thanks guys,' she said. Then more earnestly, *'Dank-u-wel mijn studenten.'*

18

Burke or Hare

Against the odds, Munro arrived ten minutes early. He had given up on the A4 and skirted west of Leiden on the A44. It was a smaller road, but much quieter. It also had the advantage of delivering him to his destination without the hassle of a slow creep through the centre of Den Haag.

Wassenaar was quietly impressive. Plush suburban homes fronted by lawns larger than the average Amsterdam apartment block lined the smoothly modern, claret-coloured cobbled streets. Nearing the grandly named Kasteel de Wittenburg, Munro passed several unmanned police kiosks with attached steel barriers pointing like long fingers into the sky. More stately home turned conference centre than castle and located only a few kilometres from one of Europe's main centres of diplomacy, security was often an issue here.

After a turn around the overflowing car park, Munro decided to leave his car with the valet at the steps of the overstated sandstone entrance. When in Rome, he reflected, spotting a small group of chauffeurs smoking and chatting next to a gleaming row of sleek-looking

Mercedes and BMWs, it's better to be a Roman.

Exposing the burnt-orange dots of man-made illumination emanating from the ornate chandeliers as merely pale imitation, hard shafts of winter sunlight streamed through the four sets of French-doors lining the right wall of the long, wide, and spectacularly high ceilinged corridor. Only the first set of dark wooden doors on the left were open, and Munro could hear Sir James' amplified voice emanating from within. The tone was heavy with bass and strangely muted. The sound engineer's battle to counter the acoustical effects of Seventeenth Century architecture ending in muffled compromise.

'You're brave.' Sir James' secretary caused him to turn around quickly.

'Hello Nadine. Shouldn't creep around like that, made me jump there.'

Nadine Rahman was by heritage Bangladeshi, but by upbringing and nature: pure Dublin, and North Side at that. Exceptionally beautiful, her smooth dark complexion and large hazel-brown eyes always made an impression. The hour-glass figure didn't hurt either.

Throwing her wide, dark eyes up to heaven, she tutted, 'If I frighten you, wait 'til the big guy gets his hands on you.'

Munro clasped his hands together in mock supplication.

'Why don't you take me away from all this?' he begged.

'Why don't you go in there and start sucking up to the boss while you still can,' she fired back with a smirk. The smile abruptly faded as she stepped closer. 'Seriously Iain, he's really pissed off. What were you thinking?'

He shrugged sheepishly.

'Let me get a coffee, then I'll go in and try to look

interested. Might even clap a bit.'

A table had been laid out at the end of the hallway. Munro poured himself a small, black, tar-like espresso. Throwing it back in one swallow, he grimaced at the familiar burnt-metallic taste.

'Carbon coffee,' he murmured to himself, screwing up his face and peering into the tiny stained cup.

Suddenly, surprised by the sharp sound of a raised voice, he looked back along the corridor. Nadine had quickly lowered her tone to a hiss, but was still gesticulating angrily at a big, smartly dressed and well-built young man. Without meeting her angry glare, the man gave a nod of acknowledgement before turning away and walking casually into the conference room. Munro recognised the breed immediately. This particular pedigree was used to taking orders, and by the looks of things, used to taking a bollocking as well. Discarding his coffee cup, Munro followed him into the conference room.

Sidling up to his target he enquired, in what he hoped was a friendly tone. 'So which one are you, Burke or Hare?'

A square, thick head of closely cropped hair turned toward him. Puffy flesh around deep-set eyes and a nose someone had tried to re-straighten. I'd ask for my money back, thought Munro.

The dark eyes locked on him. 'What?'

The two men stood at the very back of the room, whilst, in a speech as impassioned as it was content-free, McFarlane was giving his all for the latest counter-terrorism initiative. A large crowd of journalists sat in front of the low stage. But while the photographers fiddled with their equipment, Munro could see the reporters lounging in their seats. Some were smoking, none were taking notes. Not good.

The shadow of a tattoo appeared from under his

companion's starched white cuff as he raised a bulky arm to take a short sharp draw of his cigarette.

Munro tried again. 'Famous body-snatchers from Scotland. Edinburgh in fact: Burke and Hare?'

'Oh, you're one of them are you? I saw you talking to Ms Rahman.'

The name and title were delivered with a sardonic twist and slight shake of the large skull. Munro nodded, trying his best to look sympathetic he let silence draw the man out. As it often did, the old copper's trick worked a treat.

'Shame that, he was a nice bloke.' London accent, not cockney, just sink-estate South-East.

Munro smiled. 'Gerrard?'

'Complete bastard getting the body back though. Weather was bloody awful. Seven and a half hours we were on that fucking ferry.'

When Sir James' speech ended with the usual appeal for questions, the room erupted in a furious flurry of shouted queries and camera flashes as reporters rushed into the space in front of the stage. Some held small pocket recorders in the air, and several photographers were clambering up onto the chairs to get a better angle. Munro could only hope the hurried shots of a red-faced McFarlane striding out of the room under a barrage of questions over the Amsterdam killings and the involvement of a totally unauthorised British Police Officer wouldn't be of a high enough standard for tomorrow's papers.

'Ten minutes Chief Inspector.' All business now, Nadine Rahman's smooth forehead dimpled into a frown when she recognised his partner. 'The Breda Suite, it's on the top floor.' She may have been addressing Munro, but her eyes were boring holes into the big man next to him.

His face began to colour. 'I thought you were-'

'Don't worry,' Munro winked. 'We're all on the same side. Aren't we?'

He followed McFarlane's secretary into the bright, sunlit corridor. Then, turning back and gesturing down the hallway, he added. 'You should try the coffee, it's delicious.'

'Have you *had* any calls?'

Much to his surprise, Sir James' reaction to his retelling of events had been unexpectedly calm.

'One crazy and a couple of journos who should have known better,' replied Munro.

The decision to place his number in the papers had been a calculated risk. He wouldn't have dreamt of it in the UK, the line would have been jammed with hoaxers and low-end reporters. He often felt, whatever the outside world may think, that The Netherlands had an altogether more mature culture. Even if these were the people who gave the world *Big Brother.*

McFarlane's tone bordered on the phlegmatic. 'Enlighten me Munro, when did the press ever know better?'

'Fair point, Sir,' he conceded.

The room suited McFarlane perfectly. Munro didn't like to think how much tax-payers money went towards the hiring of a walnut panelled luxury business suite in the Kasteel de Wittenburg. Maybe crime did pay after all.

As if reading his mind, his boss' expression grew colder as he leaned forward.

'Understand this,' the voice was quiet, yet unambiguously firm. 'I am a pragmatic man. From what you tell me, you've got a head start on the official investigation. *If* that's true. *If* your killer contacts you, and *if* you stop him committing another murder, then fine. We all did what we had to. But that's a lot of "*ifs*"

Munro, a fucking lot.'

For an instant, Munro saw something feral in the old man's sneer. Pragmatic my arse, he thought, remaining stony faced.

'When they *foisted* you on me,' McFarlane ground on. 'They told me you were clever. On the road to the top until, and please correct me if I'm wrong, you fucked it all up by trying to be too clever. The Branch wanted you out. The Met wanted you out. And if I'm not mistaken, the fucking Secretary of State for Northern Ireland wanted you out.'

Unfazed, Munro couldn't resist a wry smile at the incongruous sound of expletives from such an unexpected source.

'And yet Sir, here I am,' he said simply.

Surprising him again, the wily and consummate politician refused the bait. McFarlane appeared to relax. Treating Munro to a glimpse of the expensive looking red silk lining of his suit jacket, he leaned back in his chair and clasped his hands behind his head. As if on cue, his secretary appeared at the door.

'Ah, Nadine,' he smiled ingratiatingly over Munro's shoulder. 'Could you get me the dossier I received from the East Gelderland Bureau this morning.'

'I have it here Sir,' she replied.

Making a show of leafing through the thick sheaf of folders she held under her arm, Nadine Rahman placed a sheet of paper in front of MacFarlane. And a large, slim envelope on the desk in front of Munro.

'Thank you.' MacFarlane, all civility and good manners again. 'She is wonderful you know, I don't know where I'd be without her.'

Probably right here still shitting on me, reflected Munro silently.

Sir James waited until his secretary had closed the door.

'Take a look,' he nodded towards the envelope.

Munro pulled out an A4 glossy photograph. The grainy texture of the image did nothing to mask his own features, the twisted features of Jitske Bolthof's husband as he was pinned to the interview table, and the unmistakable grin splitting Remco's face.

'We received this, along with a formal complaint from a...' MacFarlane pulled a small pair of half-moon reading glasses from his jacket pocket. Taking his time, he peered down at the sheet, '...Commissaris Hesselink. Apparently you made quite an impression.'

Saying nothing, Munro slid the photograph back into the envelope before tossing it casually into the middle of the table. Under his full white head of hair, McFarlane's jowly features began to darken again.

'You better find your serial killer Munro, or I'll take considerable pleasure in being the one that buries you once and for all. Now, if you don't mind, piss off.'

19

a romantic spot

'I think I may have something,' Bregje had to speak up, hoping Remco would be able to hear her against the sound of his engine, and was that a siren she could hear too?

'Me too, I'm on my way back. Have you called him?'

'No, I didn't want to use his mobile number in case...you know.'

'It's alright, I'll call him. Can you meet us in De Kijkuit. It's a café on the Oudekerksplein in…say forty minutes?'

'Why there?' Bregje had enjoyed the mental legwork, but the Oudekerksplein would bring her physically closer than she would like to the actual event. Apart from that, any café in that part of town was bound to be a dive.

'I got an interesting call this morning, Munro has an appointment.'

'Who with?'

'I'll tell you when I get there. *Doei.*'

It was a long-standing joke between them. *Doei,* pronounced 'dooee' was, in Bregje's opinion, a dumb and girlish way of saying goodbye. As Remco well knew.

'Tot ziens Brigadier,' she replied formally.

It was the same Café they'd interviewed the Eastern European girls in on Friday night and Munro wondered if the floor had been swept since. Remco pulled a handful of napkins from a steel dispenser on the table and wiped down the plastic coated surface of the table.

'Doesn't look like the cleaners work weekends,' he said indifferently.

'What do you think he wants from me?' asked Munro.

Remco shrugged. 'Maybe he's read the paper and thinks you're in charge? Speaking of which, how did you get on with the boss?'

Munro talked him through the meeting. When he got to the part about the still photo from the interview room, Remco erupted. 'That piece of shit!"

'Look,' Munro sighed. He'd had more time than he wanted on the drive back from Wassenaar to consider events. 'Hesselink and McFarlane, they're both just covering their arses. Hesselink probably read the papers this morning, knows he fucked up with the interviews, and just in case I cause a stink he's got his retaliation in first. As for McFarlane?' Munro imitated his superior's effete Edinburgh accent. 'Politics Remco, it's a filthy business.'

As ever, his Sergeant was direct and to the point. 'Lullen.'

Munro didn't feel the need to protest.

Bregje only just managed to push the door open before being jostled to one side by Whisky's exuberant bid to gain entry.

'After you,' she commented sarcastically. Looking around briefly, she maintained the same tone. 'Nice place.'

The dog, after spending only a few excitable seconds greeting his master, began to snuffle around, vacuuming the floor of the cafe.

Remco laughed. 'What do you think he's found?'

Munro's mouth turned down. 'A veritable smorgasbord I should think.'

Suddenly flushed with excitement, Bregje called over for a coffee and sat down. 'Jitske Bolthof, Maartje Weidman and Anna Leys all had a connection with the Church in Winterswijk.' She emphasised the point by bouncing the flat of her hand off the table enthusiastically.

The response was disappointing.

'They're from Winterswijk,' Munro shrugged. 'It's the Bible-Belt. It would be hard to find someone not connected to the church.'

'No, not just ordinary parishioners-'

Remco cut her short. 'There's more, I did a bit of digging on our Predikant, or more particularly, on his van.' He pulled out his notebook. 'According to Mevrouw Steenmeijer, she's on the church Finance Committee, Predikant Kotmans has been in hot water with them for a while over his use, or as she put it, misuse of the church-van. Mileage unaccounted for…' he glanced down at his notes, '…and claims for petrol exceeding normal requirements.'

'Is this the same vehicle he was in when he was observed doing the horizontal rumba with Jitske Bolthof?'

'The same.'

'If only she knew,' smiled Munro. 'Mevrouw Steenmeijer might have checked out the suspension for wear-and-tear too.'

The coffees arrived, accompanied by the usual tiny ginger cookies, called speculaas, perched on the saucers. Whisky immediately ceased all activity and sat stock-still at the end of the table. The apparently obedient pose only slightly tarnished by a long string of drool sliding slowly from the corner of his mouth. The owner of the cafe watched impassively from behind the counter as Bregje tossed the dog a biscuit.

Munro inspected the oily dark liquid in his cup.

'How far back does this church-van abuse go?'

'All the way,' replied Remco. 'The yearly inspection of the vehicle highlighted the increase in mileage and our ever vigilant committee member followed up with the petrol receipts. She's a lot more thorough than some cops I know.'

'I bet she is,' nodded Munro thoughtfully. 'Listen, I know what you're both saying, and to a certain extent I agree. There is something not quite right about Kotmans, but the problem with him as a suspect is his profile. It doesn't fit. We're looking for a loner. Someone with the privacy and time to both plan *and* carry out these attacks. Remco, you know what it's like for a Predikant in a town like Winterswijk. I mean, take Mevrouw Steenmeijer for example. His congregation is all over him.'

Remco looked sheepishly out of the window.

'Remco?'

'Boss?'

'What have you done?'

'You do agree there's something fishy about him?'

Munro nodded.

'Well,' Remco continued hesitantly. 'While I was in Winterswijk, I popped into the Bureau van Politie and had a chat with our Desk-Sergeant friend.'

'Verboven.'

'That's him. I…I guess I kind of hired him.'

Munro raised an eyebrow. 'Go on?'

'Well, he had some leave coming, so I asked him to keep his eye on Holy Man for us.'

'Holy Man?'

'That's what we're calling him. It was Bregje came up

with it first. In the Doelen, remember?'

By scrutinizing the outside of her coffee cup, Bregje managed to keep it down to a low smirk. Munro could feel a headache coming on.

'You say you *hired* him?' he asked, exasperated.

Remco remained unaffected, 'I told him he could put it in as overtime. He was quite excited. He's never been in plain-clothes before.'

'And how exactly do you think an arch bean counter like Hesselink is going to react when that particular overtime sheet hits his desk?'

'The way I see it,' Remco stated confidently. 'Commissaris Hesselink doesn't get the overtime figures until the end of the month, and by then we'll have our man.'

Munro, somewhat speechless, stared at his Sergeant.

Remco returning the look, casually hunched his shoulders. 'Or not.'

'You know I hadn't finished.' Bregje piped up sulkily.

Surprised by her outburst, both men turned their faces toward her. Munro raised his palms in surrender and wondered if these two weren't intent on making him redundant, or in Remco's case, getting him fired.

'Excuse me. By all means, please *Rechercheur* Van Til, go on.'

Bregje smiled, undaunted by the lead-weighted irony in Munro's voice, she began.

'Bolthof, Weidman, and Leys: three of the victims we know about so far. They weren't just ordinary members of the church.' She went on to explain Weidman and Leys' connection. Noting, with some satisfaction, Munro's increasing interest. Finally, she posed the question. 'Surely the least we can do is see how much contact they had with Kotmans?'

Munro rubbed his chin thoughtfully. 'We?'

Looking him straight in the eye, Bregje beamed. 'You

just called me a detective.'

'Alright,' he conceded with a rueful half-smile. 'Let's look into it. But just look, understand?"

Remco, making one of his determined faces gave Bregje a, not so discreet, thumbs-up.

'I'll make sure our man in Winterswijk stays on the job,' he chirped, before fishing for his cell-phone in his jacket pocket and heading for the door.

'So,' Bregje pushed her untouched coffee into the middle of the table. 'Who's this mysterious appointment with?'

'Derk Merel,' replied Munro.

'Shit!' Bregje instinctively placed her hand on his. 'You should be careful. If half the things they say about him are true-'

'Oh, I think they probably are,' he interrupted, trying to mask his surprise at the small charge of electricity he suddenly felt deep in his chest. Slowly, without looking up, he turned his hand over. Her palm was soft and cool. Her fingers slender. Delicate. She made no attempt to pull away. Eventually, he worked up enough courage raise his head. She met his gaze with a slightly puzzled expression. As if she were making her mind up about something. Then, surprising them both, she burst out laughing, holding his hand for a few seconds before rapping his knuckles gently on the surface of the table and letting him go.

'What fucking age are we?' she giggled.

Hiding her embarrassment in a flurry of activity, she picked up her handbag and called the dog. As Munro couldn't think of anything to say, he paid the bill and followed her meekly out onto the Oudekerksplein. The cold air felt good. Looking around, Bregje spotted Remco leaning against the wall of the church. Still on the phone, he gave her a wave. A little way off to her left, and obviously negotiating a price, a tall man, his shoulder blades visible through his thin beige raincoat, hunched in one of the doorways. A thick African accent barked at him to make up his mind as it was *'too fucking cold'* to keep the door open. What a romantic spot.

'Bregje.'

She turned to face Munro.

'Erm…I'm meeting Merel on the Oudezijds, so maybe you should head back along the Warmoesstraat. Not worth the risk of him thinking you're involved in this.'

'He doesn't know me.'

'And I'd be happier if we kept it that way.'

His expression was one of concern. She kind of liked that.

'The thing is,' she hesitated, looking at her feet for a moment. 'I am involved.' Standing on her toes, she reached up and kissed Munro on the lips. He looked stunned. She kind-of liked that too.

On her way out of the square, Bregje noticed the tall man looking her up and down.

'Creep,' she called out, twisting her lips and raising her middle finger as she passed.

20

colourful curses

'It's a good plan. He'll be confused.'

Remco was lighting a pre-rolled cigarette with the one he'd just finished. Munro leaned against the corner where the Oudezijds Voorburgwal met the Oudekerksplein. Both men were watching Joop Huisman obsequiously cower at the driver's window of Derk Merel's garishly overstated cherry-red Range Rover Sport.

Munro gave Remco a sideways look. 'What plan?'

'Meeting the most dangerous criminal in Amsterdam with a fucking great goofy grin on your face.'

Munro let his head fall forward.

'I mean,' his tone deadpan, Remco continued, 'you two keep this up and you should be sleeping together by…' he made a show of looking at his wristwatch, '…next September at least.'

Huisman began to back away from the car, his head bobbing up and down all the way. Munro felt relief at the distraction.

'Grovelling bastard,' spat Remco in disgust.

'I'll say,' Munro let out a half-laugh. 'He's got more than a touch of the Uriah Heeps about him.'

'Who?' Remco looked up at him.

'Uriah Heep: Dickens character from,' he thought for a moment. 'David Copperfield.'

'Who?'

Munro let out a sigh and slapped Remco on the back. 'Looks like I'm on. You waiting here?'

'Fuck that. I'm coming with you.'

'Fair enough.'

As they approached, the passenger door of the Range Rover opened and a ludicrously large, six-and-a-half foot slab of muscle emerged.

'The bigger they are,' murmured Remco from the corner of his mouth.

'the harder they hit you,' completed Munro.

Merel's bodyguard held up a meaty palm toward Remco.

'Not you,' he barked sternly.

'Then not him.' Remco jabbed a thumb at Munro.

'Let it go,' Munro playfully grabbed his Sergeant's shoulder. 'He's not worth it.'

Remco chortled. 'You're lucky he's here.'

The slab just looked confused. He pointed a thick finger in Munro's direction.

'Please to take off your jacket.' he barked.

The accent was not Dutch.

'How polite,' noted Remco affably.

Munro did as he was told. He removed his tie too, handing them both to Remco.

'If he starts to take his jacket off, shoot him.'

Remco made a face. 'I'm not sure that would help.'

When the slab started to frisk him, he'd had enough. Knocking the hands away, Munro called over to the car. 'You wanted to meet me. Remember?'

'Alright, alright. Enough Victor.' Merel, one arm hanging lazily out of the car, waved him over.

In the flesh his thinning blond hair was sparser, his

deep set eyes seemed farther apart, and his thick pink lips looked wetter. A tall man too. Six-four, if Munro remembered the file correctly. His shoulders, though broad, had become rounded and thick. Muscle turning to fat under what could only be described as a truly hideous, canary-yellow golf sweater.

Colour coordination was obviously not Merel's forte.

'Seriously, his name's Victor?' Munro nodded towards the giant clambering back into the passenger seat.

'No.' Merel's reply was good-humoured. 'It's something unpronounceable in Russian. Get in.'

Reflected in the car's mirrored glass as he opened the rear door, Munro caught a glimpse of Huisman's leering rat-like visage peering furtively out of the shadowy lane opposite. Relieved to be out of the cold, Munro slid into the plush leather interior.

'Is he waiting for someone to lift up a rock so he can get home?' he jibed casually, interested in Merel's response.

Glancing over at Huisman, Merel seemed to think about that for a moment. Then he laughed. It was an unpleasant throaty cackle and it departed as quickly as it had arrived.

'We need to talk,' he said flatly.

The surrounding thunk of the central-locking system was unmistakable.

'I read in the newspapers some psycho killed Kwaaie Ali.'

'Actually,' Munro began cautiously. 'We think the psycho only wanted to kill the girl and Ali Absullah just got in the way.'

Merel shrugged. 'I don't give a shit.'

In the distance and drawing closer, Munro could hear the thin rasp of a scooter. Impatiently, Merel closed his window. The inside of the Range Rover fell silent.

This was what luxury was about. Not soft leather and walnut veneer. Those things were nice, aesthetically pleasing, but ultimately this kind of opulence was about seclusion. Exclusion.

Merel spoke slowly and deliberately. 'Kwaaie Ali worked for Huisman, and Huisman works for me.'

Munro tutted. 'Please don't tell me you got me here to talk about your injured pride.'

The scooter dawdled as it passed, eventually parking directly in front of them.

'No, I want to talk about being arrested for owning a silver Porsche.' Derk Merel squinted round to look at him, but Munro was distracted. Looking past Merel's decidedly undistinguished profile, he watched the rider dismount. Face obscured by the visor on his helmet and slightly built, he wore faded jeans and a black leather jacket. As he carefully untied, then removed a bright orange plastic bag from the pillion, Munro felt there was something familiar about the figure; and something ominously familiar about the shape of the bag. His mind beginning to race, he searched around for Remco. Eventually, he spotted his Sergeant on the other side of the canal. Still carrying Munro's jacket over his arm, he had started to run, his mouth opening into an 'o'. Munro turned back.

Time slowed.

Watching the dark barrels of the sawn-off shotgun emerge from the carrier, he automatically shouted a warning. Taken by surprise, now both men in the front of the car had turned to face him. He pulled at the nearest door-latch. Locked.

'Get out! Open the fucking car!' He began kicking at the rear door frantically.

'Hey,' Merel called out angrily.

At the moment the windscreen snapped to grey-white and his view was obscured by a million tiny fissures, two thoughts passed through Munro's mind. A frozen image of Jitske Bolthof's naked body blinking behind grey glass, and from somewhere else in his head, a small voice whispered: *maybe Remco was right about the scooter thing.*

A thin cloud of red mist hung in the air. Jumping forward, Munro began to thump at the buttons on the centre console. Glancing up in desperation, he saw a jagged, fist-sized hole in the windscreen. Against the grey it looked strangely solid. Colourful.

He turned to the bodyguard. 'For fuck's sake, the doors, open the fucking doors!'

Slab/Victor didn't even acknowledge his presence. He wasn't just shaking; he was positively vibrating. Wild staring eyes looked straight through Munro toward the driver's seat.

Instinctively, he followed the gaze.

The top third of Merel's face was gone. Hollowed out. A flap of skin, sparse blond hair attached, had fallen into the dark void. Lower, blood and air mixed to bubble obscenely through exposed gums and teeth. Oddly calmed, Munro looked down slowly and selected the button to unlock the car. A second blast, this time totally shattering the windscreen, threw him back into the rear seat. He reached up and pulled something gelatinous out of his hair. Sitting in silence, he could feel a numbing sensation begin to creep slowly across the left side of his face.

The noise of the scooter, painfully loud this time, snapped him back. Quickly scrambling out of the car, Munro felt his gorge rise. Almost gagging, he was pulled from the edge by a sudden surge of adrenalin as the cold wind cut through his thin, bloodsoaked shirt.

'Are you alright?' Remco puffed, holding his gun loosely at his side, he pulled out his cell-phone.

Munro's face now began to sting. 'I think-'

A screech of metal squealing against stone cut him off. Both men, turning toward the sound, watched in amazement as the scooter slid noisily into a shop doorway forty metres away. The rider leapt to his feet and, still clutching the plastic bag, started to run.

Munro turned to the nearest bystander. Obviously stunned by what he had just witnessed, the man stood stock-still, frozen with fear.

What he meant to say was: 'I need your bike.' What he actually did, was to scream hoarsely and unintelligibly in the man's face. In testament to his horrific and outlandish appearance, the stunned witness practically threw his bicycle at him.

That'll be the shock talking, the small voice chipped in helpfully.

Munro pumped his legs. Which way? His head was spinning. Which way would you run from here? If the shooter headed west he would enter Dam Square. It was crowded, but a minimum of two police units were stationed there at all times. Straight on down the Oudezijds was an option. No, it was always very quiet south of The Dam and he would be easily spotted.

East. He would go east.

Turning left, sliding the rear wheel of the bicycle on the icy, flat-brick roadway, Munro pulled up on the handlebars and bumped up the three low steps of the pedestrian bridge across the canal. Halfway over, and much to his satisfaction, he saw a black helmet and a flash of orange moving across the parallel road bridge to his right. Still pedalling the heavy bike furiously, he rattled down the steps on the other side and powered into the Stoofsteeg.

As potential customers threw themselves against the glazed doors lining the narrow lane in an panicked effort to get out of his way, a volley of surprised shrieks and colourful curses emanated from the working girls within. Miraculously unhindered, he emerged at the other end. Another pedestrian bridge. Unfortunately, as he already knew, there was no alley leading east on the other side. He almost had to stop to make the sharp turn, but as he did so, a sprinting figure emerged on to the busy, tourist laden bridge to his right. Then, slowed by the crowd as he crossed the Achterburgwal, his quarry disappeared into the street opposite. Gritting his teeth and almost out of breath, his rear wheel still slewing on the uneven and slippery surface, Munro attempted, once more, to accelerate.

Once they were both on the same street, the chase was essentially over. Ignoring the shocked stares of natives and tourists alike, he slowed down. It occurred to him there was one slight problem with his clever shortcut. For a few crucial seconds, the killer had been out of sight and may have taken the opportunity to reload. Biding his time and cursing the fact he'd left his mobile in his jacket pocket, he decided to follow at a distance. Almost immediately the cold started to bite. His fingers and wrists were starting to ache and the left side of his face now felt tight, as though coated in some kind of sticky web. In these temperatures, riding a bicycle in a cold, bloody, and now sweat soaked shirt, was not to be recommended.

After crossing the Zwanenburgwal, the shooter darted right. Dropping down the stone steps, he quickly made his way towards the Waterlooplein. This was Amsterdam's most popular and largest flea-market. At any other time of the year, the traders would have packed up by this time, but now, in the middle of December, it was mobbed. Munro made up his mind. He wasn't going to risk losing his man in the packed square. Finally getting some traction from the recently salted pavement, he put on a burst of speed. Leaping off the bicycle at the last moment as it careened down the short flight of stairs, he aimed the point of his shoulder into his target's right kidney. Distracted by the clatter of the bike against the metal railings, the black helmet spun left. As planned, the blow from behind arrived as a complete shock. Munro heard the air rush out of his victim, accompanied by the relieving rattle of metal on concrete as the plastic bag fell to the ground. Spinning the surprisingly light body around. He knelt across the man's chest and ripped at the Velcro chinstrap. Fixing his frozen fingers underneath the helmet, he began to pull upwards.

It was then, having witnessed an alarmingly bloodied and crazed lunatic attack a seemingly innocent man, the market traders chose to step in. As he was about to reveal the shooter's face, Munro was hauled backwards and up onto his feet by two strong sets of arms. Seizing the opportunity, Dirk Merel's assassin rolled onto his front before clambering on to his knees. Ripping off his helmet as he reached down to retrieve the sawn-off from the orange carrier, the youth winced as his bruised kidney sent his back into spasm, and Munro immediately recognised the tear stained and pain twisted face of Youssef Absullah. He felt the grip on his arms loosen as his captors backed away from the gun.

'Why?' Hardly an original question, but he didn't really feel on his best form.

Absullah slowly climbed to his feet.

'He killed Ali,' he said quietly.

Saying nothing and feeling suddenly exhausted, Munro took a slow step forward. The gun came up quickly and he realised both barrels were only inches from his chest. Youssef's hands were trembling, causing the twin dark barrels to glisten like wet stone in the artificial floodlights of the marketplace.

This time the words were delivered more forcefully.

'He *killed* Ali.'

A professional would have used tape on the gun to mask any fingerprints, discarding the weapon immediately after the deed was done. Plenty of canals around here for that. A professional would also have had planned more than one escape route. And more importantly, Munro told himself, it would take a professional to have the presence of mind to reload a double barrelled shotgun on the move. Youssef Absullah was no professional. Munro gripped the barrels of the gun with his right hand and slowly pulled the weapon from the young doctor's grasp.

In the minute or so it took for the sirens and flashing blue lights to arrive, the two men crouched in silence and waited patiently. Holding the shotgun vertically in two hands with the stock on the ground to help him balance, Munro stared blindly into the crowd, and tried in vain to banish the image of Derk Merel's ravaged face from his mind.

21

up the hill

The hot water felt good. Better than good. Munro pressed a shaky hand against the smooth tile of the shower wall. Under his palm, the cool flat surface soothed him. He'd been here before. The adrenalin-rush slow to leave. Nerves jangling, ready at a moment's notice to send blood coursing to an urgently required muscle group. Fight or flight. Live or die. As he bowed his head under the pounding spray, the left side of his face began to nip. Reaching up, he rolled a tiny fragment of glass from a small cut above his eye. *That hurt.* Best leave the rest to someone else.

With a single look, Remco had stilled any protest from the uniforms on the scene, and the pair had walked the short distance from the Waterlooplein to Munro's apartment in silence. Munro could tell he was angry. It was the only time his friend appeared totally calm and in control of his emotions. The notion made him smile, causing his face to sting a little more. Underneath Remco's gruff and aggressive exterior lay a cool and aggressive interior. And under that? Heart of gold. Probably.

Through the wall he heard his apartment door open

and close. The sound was accompanied by muffled voices. Stepping out of the bathroom wrapped in a towel, he passed the heavily stained shirt to Remco.

'Have you something to put this in?'

'In here.' Esther Van Joeren held out a clear evidence bag. Pulling the airtight seal closed with her fingers, she squinted at him. 'Sit down in the kitchen, it's lighter in there.'

'Haven't you got a murder scene to investigate?' Munro felt slightly disconcerted by the Professor's interested gaze. Esther and he were exactly the same height. It felt odd.

'That one looks to be pretty open-and-shut don't you think?'

She unclipped the large metallic case she'd placed on the table as he sat down.

'You got stuff for living people in there too?' he asked, trying to lighten his own mood more than anything else.

'It's all flesh and blood,' she answered with a surprisingly gentle smile. 'Besides, according to Remco, you're pretty much brain dead anyway.'

'He told you?'

'You,' Esther's smile became positively beatific, 'are a fucking idiot.'

'Fucking right,' added Remco. Taking a step forward, he waived the two unspent cartridges extracted from Youssef's shotgun in his face.

'Isn't that evidence?' asked Munro.

'Here.' Remco tossed the cartridges into the pathologist's case.

Esther laughed. 'Touching. But if you two don't mind, I'd like to get on with removing the glass and…' she leaned over, peering through a rectangular magnifying glass, '…if I'm not seeing things, fragments of leadshot out of this head?'

The tiny pieces of black metal and slightly larger chips of glass gave a dull *chink* as they dropped into the small stainless steel bowl.

'Oh,' Esther stopped to examine one fragment held in her tweezers more closely. 'Remco, could you open one of those plastic tubs?' She motioned her head toward the table.

'What is it?' enquired Munro, understandably curious.

I think that's probably a teensy little bit of Derk Merel's skull.'

Her smile never faltered.

'That's some job you have,' sighed Munro.

'Came out of your face.'

'Fair enough,' he conceded gracefully.

Satisfied she'd removed all of the debris. Esther once more sprayed the affected area with an antiseptic.

'Now for the good part, this stuff is magic.' She held up a small white plastic bottle.

'What is it?'

He seemed to have lost the ability to frame questions longer than three single syllable words; could cause a problem in the day-job, he thought to himself.

'A new type of liquid-skin. We've been testing it for a pharmaceutical company. It's really a glue of sorts, but it also has enough genetic material in it to dissolve naturally over time. Ideal for your kind of superficial injuries.'

'When you say *you've* been testing it?'

'We've had some great results. Obviously with my subjects we've had to pump blood into the veins and fire electric pulses into the muscles to keep a flow into the affected areas.'

'You mean dead people,' Remco's mouth turned down in mock distaste, Munro suspected he was beginning to enjoy life again. Esther nodded in a matter-of-fact way.

'You do understand why,' Munro began in a serious tone. 'The townsfolk will come up the hill to your place with the flaming torches.'

'No problem,' she chuckled. 'We're in Holland, there aren't any hills. Now,' leaning over him again, she pulled a tiny brush from the top of the bottle. 'When a doctor says this might sting a little, you know what that means?'

He gritted his teeth.

22

lack of evidence

'Did we get any info on the charity in the end?'

They were back in the office. Munro, consciously trying not to pick at the already blackening scabs on his face, was keeping his hands busy on the laptop's keyboard.

Sitting on a filing cabinet with his feet dangling inches from the floor, Remco pulled out his faithful notebook.

'Only what Youssef told you. Once a month the lorries are loaded up with medical supplies in Amsterdam before making the trip to Morocco. The charity is registered, and the paperwork all seems above board.'

'What about the brothers themselves?'

'Nothing unusual, when I ran their names through immigration Youssef turned up with his parents in Rotterdam about eleven years ago. There was a notation that his father had been here longer, but of course he would have been working black.'

'Black' was how the Dutch described all mildly illicit activities. Everything from sneaking a free ride on the tram to working unlawfully as an illegal immigrant. The origin of the phrase was almost certainly racist, though now common usage looked to have stripped it of its more unpleasant connotations and the most liberal country in the world didn't seem to mind.

'What about Ali?' asked Munro.

'Standard practice. He would have been old enough to work by then. Probably a good idea to keep at least one earner in the family tax free. If he'd been caught the legitimacy of the rest of the family's residency would have prevented any deportation procedures.'

Munro let his chin fall onto his chest. 'I know Baart arrested Derk Merel, but then he let him go, *and* we had our big story out there.'

'Maybe Youssef doesn't read the papers?'

'About his brother's murder? No, he must have at least have heard the news. But he still went for Merel.'

'I've got to admit,' conceded Remco. 'I never had him down as the *blow-your-head-off-with-a-shotgun* type.'

Munro could only nod in agreement. Both men, deep in thought, jumped at the chirping sound of Munro's cell-phone.

'Chief Inspector Munro speaking.'

Unconsciously, his left hand gripped the table's edge as he listened.

'Hello matey, how they hanging?'

Munro let out a sigh. 'Chief Superintendant Doherty, they're suspended slightly higher than usual at the moment actually, but thanks for asking.'

'Well, with what I'm about to tell you, they won't be dropping for a while yet.'

'Sorry Mickey, can you make it quick. I'm hoping for another call on this line.'

'Suits me. Gerrard's not Gerrard. His name's John Patrick Doyle. Low grade Belfast drug-dealer. In '94 he got himself in a jam and turned grass. By '96 he was relocated to Manchester by Special Branch after several successful court cases featuring our boy as star witness. Little scrote couldn't go straight though. One arrest since then; selling Class B drugs in a pub in Salford. Reading between the lines, word came down from on-high and charges were dropped due to a 'lack of evidence', if you get my drift.'

'Intriguing. Not helpful, but intriguing.' Munro finished scribbling in his notebook.

'One more thing.'

'Yes?'

'I'm making this call on my daughters mobile.'

'That much heat?'

'They dropped on me from a great height. Whatever this bloke was up to, the big boys don't want anyone poking into it. Of course, I swore I'd keep any information I'd gathered 'top secret'.'

'Well, you never told me anything.'

'Precisely.'

'Thanks Mickey. There is just one more favour you could do for me.'

He heard a resigned sigh from the other end of the line.

'Speak.'

'Just one more name for you to check on. And with this one, you really should be careful...'

'We've got about fifteen minutes.' Remco opened the door of the observation room. 'Baart's upstairs with Uylenburg and we've orders to join them in twenty.'

To be expected, thought Munro. Baart would want some alone-time with the Hoofdcommissaris to set out his stall and explain the many and varied ways Munro had found to fuck-up his investigation.

On the other side of the one-way mirror, Dr. Youssef Absullah sat quietly. Staring absently at the blank wall and dressed in a white one-piece evidence suit, he looked strangely at peace. Entering the room and taking the seat opposite, Munro thought he saw a shadow of a smile flicker across the young man's smooth features.

'I'm not meant to be here,' he began candidly.

'I am. Haven't you heard? I'm the guy who killed Derk Merel.'

Munro smiled, nodding his head as if in appreciation of Youssef's bravado, but as he spoke his face quickly straightened. 'There's no point Doc.'

'Point?'

'In acting the tough guy. You said it yourself: *you killed Merel.* The right people and, unfortunately for you, all the wrong people already know that. Your reputation's assured.'

'And my fate sealed.' Youssef seemed to relish the thought. 'I am not afraid.'

'Of course you are, we *all* are,' Munro tried hard to keep the exasperation out of his voice. 'You're a medical man. Do you know what we find when we examine suicide victims? The ones who jump: fingers bloody, nails torn from a last-second change of heart. The ones who drown are worse. It only takes a thimble full of water in the lungs to do the job, but every single time *their* lungs are full. A final heaving gasp for air to fuel the body's frantic last-ditch effort to claw a way to the surface. Don't tell me you won't be crying for your mother when you're lying in your own piss and blood on a prison-shower floor with a broken blade in your back.'

He waited for a reaction. He needed some answers. Answers a calm and reasoning Youssef Absullah wasn't likely to give. Hence the tirade.

'Why are you here?' There was a slight edge to young man's voice now. Good.

'I want to know why?'

'I told you.'

'You told me Merel killed Ali. But why? Why would notorious gangster and criminal mastermind Derk Merel take the time out of his busy schedule to murder mop-boy Ali Absullah? You can see my problem.'

The clear olive skin began to colour. Munro watched impassively as Absullah's eyes filled with tears. He was missing something here. He pictured Youssef carefully placing the flowers in the vase in the Absullah's kitchen. The hand gently pulling on Ali's arm as he held on to Munro's collar.

'I killed him, and you caught me. That's all.' Rubbing his face with his hands, Youssef Absullah regained some composure. 'The why doesn't matter.'

Bollocks, thought Munro as he left the room. *The why is all that matters.*

'Is that what you think?' Hoofdcommissaris Hendrik Uylenburg eyed Munro suspiciously.

'No,' he answered simply, ignoring the angry snort from Baart in the seat next to him. He had been patient, hiding his frustration at Baart's explanation of events. The Inspecteur's convenient contention that the whole business had blown over. A short and bloody gang war between rival factions. Merel killed Boos Ali, Ali's brother killed Merel, and thanks to Munro's brave, if completely reckless work in apprehending Youssef, the case could now be closed.

'Please elaborate Chief Inspector.' The flat-tone of the request from Uylenburg lead Munro to believe the Hoofdcommissaris was more inclined toward his own view. And, like the experienced copper he was, prepared to dislike what he heard.

'You've read my report?' asked Munro.

'I have.'

At this, Baart shifted uncomfortably in his seat.

Munro had guessed correctly that his findings would hit the buffers on the Inspecteur's desk. Controlling the stream of information upwards was the best and most overused tool in any over ambitious policeman's armoury. Side-stepping the problem, Munro had asked Remco to deliver his neatly typed and well thought-out report, along with Esther Van Joeren's medical files, directly to Uylenburg's secretary as she entered the building at nine this morning.

'Well, it's all there,' he shrugged. 'The medical evidence is overwhelming.'

'What about this whole *dates* thing? It sounds...' the Hoofdcommissaris searched for the right word, '*ongelooflijk*.'

'Incredible? I would agree,' Munro conceded calmly, lining Uylenburg up for the big hit. 'If Professor Van Joeren hadn't picked a body out of the harbour today. Female, pretty messed up, but with at least one of our identifying marks clearly visible on the right side of her body. She reckons the girl was killed and dumped in the water on the 11th of December. And that fits our man's calendar.'

The room fell silent as Uylenburg thought for a moment. Still looking down at his desk, he began to speak. 'This Predikant. You don't rate him as a suspect?'

'Can't say. His profile doesn't really fit,' shrugged Munro.

'Rule him in, or rule him out. I assume you haven't had any calls from the newspaper stunt, so he's all you've got at the moment. Get it done.'

'Might have a problem there, Sir,' chipped in Remco.

Munro hadn't known of Remco's overtime deal with Hesselink's desk sergeant when he'd written up the report in the wee hours of this morning. And as for the supposedly incriminating picture from the Winterswijk interview room...

'I'm afraid Commissaris Hesselink isn't exactly on-board,' he said quietly, then added. 'In fact, I'd say without your intervention it's unlikely we'll get much done in East Gelderland.'

Uylenburg took the news in his stride. 'I called that *potlood-lul* this morning. Told him the picture he sent me was obviously a still from a surveillance camera and if he wanted *me* to do anything about it he should send the whole film.'

'He's thorough that Hesselink,' observed Munro dryly.

'He's an idiot,' retorted Uylenburg. 'Met him on a course a couple of years ago.' A sorry shake of the head told the rest of the story.

Brightening, he turned to Baart. 'Inspecteur, you're running interference on this. Get me a magistrate to sign off on all the searches and surveillance we might need for this Holy Man character. You're also now in charge of our relationship with Commissaris Hesselink. Keep him off our backs. I can't help thinking you two should get along famously.' Uylenburg's sneer was more good humoured than cruel. At least Munro thought so.

Back in his office, Munro noted his surprise at Uylenburg's change of direction.

'He's good,' he acknowledged simply.

'The best,' agreed Remco.

'Mind you, he had a little help on the inside.'

'What?'

'Holy Man? I don't remember calling Kotmans that in my report.'

'Don't you?' smirked Remco. 'He must have heard it somewhere else then.'

Munro's reply was lead weighted. 'Aye, right.'

Then, cheering up at the thought of a beer, he slapped Remco's shoulder. 'We might as well pack up for tonight. It'll be tomorrow morning before Baart gets us a search warrant for Kotmans' place. I do have one more question though.'

Remco pulled on his overcoat.

'Ask away,' he said.

'What's a *potlood?'*

'It's a pencil.' The diminutive detective guffawed loudly.

'Figures,' Munro nodded appreciatively.

23

Christmas card

The Cafe de Doelen was an oasis of calm. Safely closeted in the snug atmosphere, Munro took his first sip. Felt good. Two swallows later, and Remco was signalling Martijn for two more glasses. Betty herself brought the beers over and took a seat opposite the two detectives.

'You've had a busy day.' she commented blithely.

It was no surprise. Each little section within the Centrum district of the city functioned as a self-contained village. Each had its own shops, its own delicatessens…and its own cafés. In this environment news travelled fast.

'Busy enough,' Munro replied casually, toasting Betty with his glass.

'So tell me,' she enquired with a tilt of her head. 'Which one are you: brave or stupid?'

Munro tried on his best Sean Connery face. Unfortunately, as he raised his left eyebrow it made the skin on his forehead wrinkle, causing him a not inconsiderable amount of pain. He ended up grimacing and sucking air in sharply through his teeth.

'I think that answers my question,' she sighed.

Standing again, she leant over the table and gave him a peck on his good cheek.

'*You should be more careful,*' she whispered in his ear. '*Idiot.*'

Once Betty had returned to her place at the bar, Munro turned to Remco.

'I'm getting that a lot today,' he stated reflectively.

'What?'

'Being called an idiot.'

'It's a Dutch thing,' chortled Remco. 'The harder we are on you, the more we love you.'

Munro knew exactly what he meant. It was a Scottish thing too.

Bregje was furious. She had actually heard the shots as she crossed Dam Square with Whisky. Naturally, assuming the sharp sounds to be fireworks, she'd paid them no mind.

Traditionally at midnight each New Year, millions of euros worth of privately purchased pyrotechnics exploded in the city. And during December, students, kids and adults who should know better, could never resist letting a few off early.

Betty's daughter, Daphne, had called her with the exciting news. *Exciting?* She'd wring his bloody neck.

The walk to the Doelen calmed her a little. You couldn't stay angry watching Whisky dart from bakery to deli. It was the same hackneyed routine each time: sit at the door and raise a paw, wait patiently, and eventually a piece of pastry or slice of sausage would be thrown over the counter. He managed to catch three out of the five offerings first time - which was about average. After all, she thought, it would be difficult to underestimate this dog's athletic abilities. Annoyingly however, her determination to maintain her composure as she entered the cafe was sorely tested.

The top left quarter of Munro's face was a mass of small cuts and abrasions. Although some had become nothing more than small, angry looking red blotches, a few of the wounds sported thin black crusts of dried blood.

'You are such a fucking *idiot!'* she hissed.

Bregje couldn't quite believe it, but she had a sneaking suspicion she may have stamped her foot too. Munro looked up from Whisky's enthusiastic greeting.

'I beg your pardon?' he replied calmly, with more than a measure of polite sarcasm.

'I said,' she was almost shaking. 'That *you* are a *fucking idiot.'*

The second time she spoke Bregje could feel herself calming down...well, a little. A fleeting look passed between the two men; leaving Munro with a pleased smile and Remco's face split by a huge grin.

'Dumb and dumber.' Bregje pointed to each in turn. Then, sighing resignedly, and if she was honest, blinking back a few tears of relief, she said simply. 'I'll get the beers in.'

When Esther arrived it felt as if the group had been completed. The vivid and shocking discoveries made the previous evening had connected them in a strange way. Only exposure to death could create such a bond so quickly, surmised Munro; giving in for once to what he considered to be his darker, Nordic side.

'So,' she began brightly. 'Where are we?'

'No calls yet,' stated Remco. 'But Uylenburg's on-board, so you should get all the resources you need from now on.'

'And Baart?' she enquired, brows furrowed.

'Pencil-pushing and paperwork. Strictly admin from now on.'

A smile of approval lit up the Pathologists face.

'How about your end?' Munro asked.

'The latest find is definitely one of our man's victims. We're having some trouble identifying her though.'

'No dental records?'

'No head.' Esther Van Joeren took a long draught from her glass, showing some things could still slip through her professional chainmail. 'Oh, we don't think he decapitated her,' she explained quickly to the table of shocked faces. 'The lacerations on her neck and shoulder suggest the corpse was caught by a ships propeller after it was dumped in the harbour.'

'You confirmed his calling card?' enquired Remco.

'Clearly visible on the right leg and a partial on the ribs.'

'Can I ask a question?' Bregje looked around the table for approval.

'Of course,' Esther smiled back at her warmly. 'They told me about the church connections you found. It was good work. Let's face it, you've added more to this enquiry than the dashing Inspecteur Baart.'

Bregje felt she had passed some kind of test, and as always, began to blush.

'It's just that,' she ploughed on, 'we've got all this evidence, but no one's mentioned DNA. Just tell me if I've been watching too much television, but from all of these murders; don't we have anything?'

Esther shook her head. 'There's nothing wrong with the question.'

'And it tells us something else about our killer,' added Munro leaning forward in his chair. 'This guy's not just educated, he's informed. He knows how to hide evidence. He meticulously cleans up after himself, and that takes a particular type of personality.'

'Holy Man looked to be the tidy sort,' interjected Remco.

'He did,' conceded Munro. 'That he did.' For a moment he was lost in thought. There was something in the back of his mind; an itch he couldn't scratch.

'What about the Peepshow?' Bregje wasn't going to be put off so easily. 'He changed his pattern. You said it yourself, he wants us to know what he's doing. Was there no DNA left there?'

A shadow of a smile crossed Esther's face.

'Quite the opposite actually,' she smirked.

'How do you mean?'

Bregje watched another knowing look pass between Munro and Remco, and it was starting to piss her off.

Munro spoke first. 'I'm sorry, we should have told you. Esther gave us a little light show yesterday morning.'

'Light show?'

The Pathologist took over. 'We call it a black-light. Set to a certain frequency it lights up any…' she paused briefly, picking her words carefully, '…organic material present.'

'And?'

Munro tried to put it as delicately as he could.

'Let's just say the guy on mop duty that night hadn't bothered with the bleach.'

Remco couldn't resist. 'The whole place looked like a fucking Christmas card!' Laughing hard, he slapped the table.

Obviously surprising herself, Esther joined in.

'It really did,' she giggled, dabbing at her eye with the back of her hand. 'God! Men are disgusting.'

Munro wondered briefly why he felt so good. Maybe it was the happy, childish sound of snow scrunching underfoot. Or was it, he reasoned, a feeling of heightened sensitivity - not uncommon after a near-death experience such as today's. Of course, it could simply be down to the fact he was walking Bregje home from the Doelen. The adolescent thrill of her hand once more in his. Bregje, speaking softly, broke the comfortable silence.

'Did you know?' she asked.

Fucking Remco, he cursed inwardly. 'Know what?'

She raised an eyebrow to show him she wasn't buying his clumsy attempt at obfuscation. 'Did you know Youssef Absullah had reloaded the gun?'

'No.'

'Did you think he hadn't?"

'Of course I did. I might be daft, but I'm not crazy.'

He thought of elaborating, but she huddled closer, his reply appearing to have satisfied her curiosity.

At the front door of her apartment building, Munro hesitated. Feeling totally out of his depth, he made a show of watching Whisky dance around in the snow. They both laughed as he misjudged the kerb and rolled into the street. Finally, he forced himself to raise his face to hers.

'Come on,' she met his gaze evenly. 'I'll make you a coffee.' Widening her eyes as she spoke, Bregje thought she'd made her intentions plain.

'And?' He'd meant it to sound funny, *Jesus* he was crap at this.

Sensing his awkwardness, Bregje abandoned subtlety. 'Appropriately enough,' she pulled him closer. '*And* is a copulative conjunction, not a question. Now get your mutt and come in out of the cold.'

Tuesday

18th December

24

cold comfort

Munro stared absently up at the cold shafts of pale blue light stretched across the smooth plaster of Bregje Van Til's bedroom ceiling.

'What time is it?' she whispered croakily.

'About three...I thought you were asleep.'

'I was,' Bregje rolled into him and kissed him gently on the shoulder. He felt a warm hand open against his ribs. 'But your feet are dancing a polka.'

He tensed for a moment. 'Sorry. I was thinking.'

'About today?"

'Amongst other things.'

'I want to tell you something.' She sat up.

With a supreme effort, Munro managed to keep his eyes focused on her face.

'Feel free,' he smiled, more than grateful for the distraction.

'It's about Martijn. I want you to know that I was feeling a little...well, old I suppose. It was just one night, and the next day I felt so-'

'dirty?' he interrupted.

'No,' she giggled.

'tired?'

'Shut-up.' She put a hand over his mouth. 'I don't know, sex is sex, there's nothing wrong with that. But maybe now I want something more. There, I've said it.'

'So you're not going to take me on the long walk to the Vondelpark with Whisky and dump me there?'

'Don't. I feel terrible about that.'

'So you should,' he sighed loudly. 'Poor kid must have suffered.'

The hand on his ribs closed and gently punched him.

'So what do you think?' she asked in a whisper.

'About us?'

'About us.'

'Well,' he said, his Scottish genes kicking in. 'Whisky seems to like you.'

Her laughter warmed him. 'That'll do for now.'

Bregje lay down again, facing him. After a few moments of silence she could feel his body tense again.

'If it does happen,' she whispered softly. 'It won't be your fault.'

'I know.'

Cold comfort for the next victim, he thought. Shuddering unconsciously, he tried to shake off an overwhelming sensation of helplessness.

'Are you cold?' She pulled the covers up on his chest.

'A wee bit.'

'A wee bit,' she imitated his accent.

'You lookin' fur trouble darlin'.' He reached under the sheets and tickled her.

'Might be.' This time, she rolled onto him, the smooth sensation of skin on skin making him gasp. She raised an eyebrow suggestively. 'What are you going to do about it?

'Still nothing on the mobile?'

'Not a peep.'

'Looks like we're off to Winterswijk then. Where am

I picking you up from?' Unusually for the crack of dawn, Remco seemed to be in an exceptionally good mood. Munro heard the shower start to run in the bathroom across the hall.

'I'm at Bregje's,' he said.

'I know.' A rasping laugh reverberated down the line. 'I'm right outside.'

Munro pictured the grin. 'I'll just have a quick shower. Why don't you find me a coffee for the journey and I'll see you in a minute.'

'Don't rush on my account,' the laughter died down to a wheeze. 'Oh, and check your work voicemail, Esther says she left you a message.' Remco hung up.

Outside, Munro heard the rumble of the old Citroën's engine as his friend pulled away to find a coffee bar. Saving the battery life left on his mobile, he used the phone beside the bed to call the office. An robotically impassive female voice told him he had two messages.

'Hey lover-boy, it's Esther.'

Munro was beginning to realise he had no secrets.

'Unlike you, *I've* been working all night, and I might have something interesting. We think we've found another two victims. Both were from across the border in Germany. One fits in with our missing date in September, but the other was earlier. Thirty-seven days earlier than our previous first body to be precise. In case you're wondering, that fits with his schedule perfectly. Had a bit of a panic too. Our search of the Winterswijk medical files came up with a dead woman with head, rib, and leg injuries almost a year ago. Luckily for us, if not for her, the wounds were sustained in a road-traffic accident. Witnesses and everything, thank God. Anyway, Remco's got me looking into Holy Man's wife's records too. I'll call you if I get anything.' There was a moment's hesitation followed closely by a short fit of the giggles. 'And tell Bregje I want to hear all about it, bye.'

'Second message.' The voicemail's lifeless voice droned on. 'Message received today at six-thirty a.m.'

'Chief Inspector.'

An icy hand clutched at his heart. The voice was unnaturally low. The words were slowed. Artificially deformed. And although the language was Dutch, the message was simple, deliberately ensuring Munro understood every word.

'I must admit, it was a good try. For a moment I was genuinely angry.' Through the distortion, he could just make out a note of surprise in the voice. 'Don't feel too bad. In a way I suppose you *have* succeeded. Here I am after all, speaking to you.' There followed a slow laugh. Each peal grotesquely amplified. 'Actually, I'm considering a change of plan.' The intonation suddenly turned vicious. 'Perhaps that whore you just fucked should be next.' There was a short high pitched tone. 'End of messages. To listen to your messages again press...' Munro stared down at the phone.

'What is it?' Bregje came into the room towelling her hair.

'It's...it's a message.'

When he looked up at her, she watched his expression turn from a mask of concern to one of stony determination. He pressed a button and handed her the receiver. As she listened, she unconsciously pulled her dressing gown tighter.

'Fucking creep.'

'Correct.'

He moved closer and pulled her in toward him.

'We're going to have this bastard.' he hissed.

His arms around her felt right. He wasn't coddling her, but he wasn't letting her go either.

'Give me your voicemail number and passcode.' she

commanded.

'What?' he pulled away slightly.

'I'll download and isolate the voice with the studio program I use for my students. Then I'll tell you where this *lul* grew up, went to school, *and* learned where to be such a shithead.'

He played dumb. 'I have no idea what you're talking about, but it sounds good.' They kissed. 'I'll call a squad car to take you to work - and before you even think of arguing, it'll be waiting outside your office until we get this bastard.'

He gave her his sternest look.

Pointedly ignoring it, she smiled up at him. 'So we still have time for a shower?' she enquired coyly.

'Thought you just had one?'

She turned, looking at him over her shoulder.

'I may have missed a bit,' she giggled.

25

a viable candidate

They met up in the car park behind the Winterswijk Bureau, the police station's outward appearance as beautiful as ever. Esther winced as she looked up at the building from the passenger seat of the unmarked forensics van.

'What a shithole,' she said.

'It's not much better inside,' added Munro. 'How long have you been here?'

He was leaning on the side of the forensic van, glad to be standing in the fresh air after the stuffy drive.

'Ten minutes.' she replied. 'I grabbed Michael and headed out as soon as we heard about the body. Anything from Baart?'

'He's on his way with the paperwork, should be here soon.'

Since leaving the message for Munro, Esther had discovered the final resting place of Maartje Weidman. With the exception of Jitske Bolthof and the incomplete floater from the harbour, all of the other victims had already been cremated.

Munro frowned.

'Do you think you'll find anything useful? I mean,

she's been down there a while.'

'Probably nothing that'll help the investigation. But if you're going to prosecute this guy, she's going to have to be re-examined anyway. At least it should be interesting, I've never taken a body out of a church-vault before.'

'So what you're saying is: you're bored looking at pictures.'

Esther broke into a tired smile. 'What can I say? I'm a hands-on kind of a girl.'

A sleek new convertible Saab pulled up beside Remco's car. Inspecteur Baart climbed out. Dressed in dark jeans and a kind of trendy woollen crewneck sweater, he looked as if he'd just stepped out of an advert.

'If vanity does not overthrow all our virtues, at least she makes them totter,' murmured Munro.

'What?' Esther turned to face him.

'Don't worry,' interjected Remco. 'He's always doing that.'

Flicking a cigarette butt into the gutter, he joined them at the van.

'Rochefoucauld,' Munro gave Esther a sly wink. 'I feel it's my duty to educate the Sergeant whenever possible.'

'I'm not really a big fan of French cheese,' stated Remco amicably.

'Chief Inspector,' Baart waved a brown envelope in the air. 'I have the disinterment papers and permission to search the church's properties.'

'What about Kotmans' farmhouse?' asked Remco.

'No chance. We've no workable proof of his involvement. I only managed to get the search warrant for the church on the grounds that evidence may have become detached from Maartje Weidman's body. On the plus side, his house in town is technically owned by the church and as such…'

Munro nodded his approval. 'May legitimately be searched by us. There may be hope for you yet Inspecteur.'

Baart began to smile, then quickly remembered himself.

'Thank you...eh, Sir.'

'Call me Iain. I assume Remco's reputation precedes him, and this is-'

'I know. Hello Esther.'

As Esther stepped out of the van, Munro noticed a look pass between them.

'Franck,' she replied.

'Such a small town, Amsterdam,' commented Remco sagaciously.

Obviously discomfited, Esther turned toward the Bureau.

'Shall we go in?' she enquired brusquely.

'Let's not.' Munro started walking back to Remco's car. 'There's a cafe up the street, we can work things out there.'

Munro, Remco, and Esther took a table at the back of the Cafe Oostboom. Baart had gone into the Bureau to calm Commissaris Hesselink's troubled waters, and Michael had taken his camera to scout out the church; under strict instructions to maintain a low profile.

Esther warmed her hands on a large cappuccino.

'So how do you want to do this?'

Munro thought for a moment before speaking. 'At this stage we need Holy Man out of the way. If he is our guy we don't want to tip our hand. The last thing I need is him getting jumpy and losing his tail.'

Remco drummed the table with his fingers.

'Poor old Sergeant Verboven's been trailing him since yesterday afternoon. Your friend Baart will relieve him when he's finished with the idiot-Commissaris.'

'Franck Baart's not exactly a friend.' Esther took a sip of coffee. 'We had a thing a few years back. Didn't work out. Let's just say you should never shack up with a guy who has a larger wardrobe than you, or uses more hair-product.'

Remco laughed uproariously. 'Seriously?'

'Don't get me started.' She was smiling now. 'It only lasted a week. His hair-dryer used to wake me up in the morning.' Artfully, the professor then changed the subject. Arching her eyebrows in Munro's direction, she asked, 'So, how was your night's sleep?'

'Blissfully sporadic,' he replied smugly. 'Shine got taken off a bit this morning though.'

In answer to her puzzled expression, he keyed in his voicemail number and handed her the phone.

'Fucking creep.' Esther sneered after listening to the message.

Munro sighed. 'That seems to be the general consensus.'

'This was left on your office line. Not the mobile number you gave the papers?'

Munro nodded.

'So who has that number?'

'Anyone with reasonable computer ability and access to the Internet. My name's listed on the Europol and Joint Police Operations websites.'

'You're sure it's him?'

'Most hoaxers don't get up at six-thirty in the morning. He knew where I was, where I'd been, and he took the time to find the office number. It's him alright. They're running a check at the phone company to find out where the call came from.'

'How's Bregje?'

'Working on cleaning up the recording and giving us a voice profile.'

Esther nodded approvingly. 'Good for her.'

Forty minutes later, the call came in from Baart. Within fifty they were pulling up on the Grotekerkplein. Munro briefed Esther on the way in.

'Holy Man's visiting an retirement community on the outskirts of town, so we think we should have at least an hour. Long enough for you?'

'Easy,' she replied. Then she stopped. 'Did he mention the name of this community?'

He looked up for a second. 'Jasmine, or Jasmijn as you would say.'

'Interesting.' Esther started to walk again. 'That's where Maartje Weidman died.'

In the vestry they met the only representative of the church committee Remco reckoned they could trust to keep quiet. Mevrouw Steenmeijer looked exactly as Munro had pictured her. Nineteen-fifties twinset just visible under a patterned scarf and thick grey woollen coat. She even wore a hat similar to the one his granny kept for Sundays. Remco introduced him.

'You are not Dutch.' she stated bluntly, unashamedly squinting her pinched face up at his blood speckled forehead. 'Are you even a policeman?'

'Well Mevrouw, it is true I have no powers of arrest in The Netherlands. I am also not permitted to carry a weapon,' he opened his coat to emphasise the point. 'But I assure you - I am a policeman.'

He fired up his best smile. Obviously unimpressed, she turned to Remco.

'Let me see the documentation.'

'Certainly Mevrouw Steenmeijer.'

Remco handed over the brown envelope, and after scanning the contents for what seemed like an age, she finally ordered them to follow her to the office to get the key for the vaults.

'This one opens the iron gate in the knave. Follow the steps down and I believe the Weidman vault is at the end of the corridor on the left.'

She handed the large set of keys to Esther.

'I'll get suited up. See you outside in about forty minutes.' As she made for the door, Esther turned to Munro. 'Good luck with her,' she murmured quietly.

'There is another thing you could help us with Mevrouw.' Munro had never heard Remco sound so deferential. 'It's about Predikant Kotmans.'

'Yes?' The old lady's eyes seemed to light up. 'Have you found out where he's been going with the van?'

'Not exactly, no. But to that end, we were wondering if you were in possession of a key to the Predikant's house? Perhaps we could just have a look around while we're here.'

Munro waited for an explosion of righteous indignation, but instead there was a moment of silence as Mevrouw Steenmeijer mulled the idea over.

'I would have to come with you,' she said. 'To make sure nothing is disturbed.'

With some effort, Remco's smile remained frozen on his face.

'Of course,' he agreed.

Bregje was losing patience. The recording was so short she'd put it on a loop as she fiddled with the sound. At first, being called a whore over and over again gave her a chill, but it wasn't long before she had zeroed in on the tone. If the recording had used the same software as hers it would have been easy. As it was, whenever she modulated one section of the message, another part would slip out of synch. The pitch would sound wrong. Not fit the pattern. In frustration she snapped off the program and glared balefully at the blank screen. Unbidden, a thought came into her head. She wondered what this Holy Man character looked like. Munro wasn't so sure about him, but Remco certainly thought him a viable candidate. Bregje opened her browser and keyed in the name: 'Kotmans'. Lists of sites from all over the world came up. Dumb. She had to be more specific. Selecting a search engine, she first clicked on the sub-group 'images', then typed in 'Hersteld Hervormde Kerk Predikant Kotmans'.

In a mild state of shock, she stared at the screen. Just like the other sixteen images the search had thrown up, the thumbnail was small. She tapped on it once, and then again, bringing the image up to its original size. Her hand shook as she fumbled for her phone.

'Iain?'

'Bregje? Are you alright?' A note of panic in his voice.

'Yes,' she assured him. 'I'm fine.'

He sighed. 'Sorry. We're just tiptoeing through Holy Man's house. I'm in his front room, and I have to agree with Remco on one thing, this guy's tidy. Gives me the creeps.'

'I've seen him,' she said.

'What? Where...I mean, when?'

'Calm down.' She couldn't believe she was telling *him* that. 'Yesterday. On the Oudekerksplein before you met with Merel. He looked straight at me as I left.'

'How do you-'

'Looked him up on the web: Predikant Kotmans.'

Silence.

'Is the squad car still there?'

Bregje peered out of the window.

'Yes,' she replied, surprised by her relief.

'Alright,' snapped Munro. 'Stay there. I'll find out where he is.'

26

a heavy burden

Guaranteed by Baart that Holy Man was still inside the Jasmijn Community Centre, Munro pulled Remco aside. Away from the prying ears of Mevrouw Steenmeijer, he told him about Bregje's call.

'Arrest Kotmans.' Remco's expression had darkened. 'We can keep him for a while, grill him.'

Munro could see that part was already appealing to his Sergeant.

'At least it'll fuck up his timetable.' Remco added.

Munro considered the option. It was the classic policing dilemma. By preventing the crime, no evidence is gathered and no charges could be brought. Or take the risk: use surveillance, catch the criminal in the act. His instincts had always directed him toward the latter course. But now, when *the act* might involve someone close to him?

'We still can't be sure its him.'

He felt dirty.

Remco sensed the cop out.

'This could be Bregje we're talking about?' he grumbled.

Munro gave him a look. 'If it is him, he's killed at

least seven times, probably more, and he's left no evidence. Nothing. Trust me, if we get something solid on this guy I'll be all over him. Until then get looking. In case you've forgotten, we're on the clock here.'

'In more ways than one,' muttered Remco, defiantly meeting Munro's angry glare before turning on his heel and striding into the hallway.

Munro took a deep breath. Sufficiently calmed, he surveyed his surroundings. In keeping with the rest of the house, this room had retained its historical integrity. He imagined the other townhouses lining the Grotekerkplein would have been updated and modernised long ago, losing the low ceilings and dark burnished wooden beams. Shame. Although the room was freakishly tidy, not a speck of dust or a cushion out of place, it was comfortably furnished. A single sofa and large armchair filled the slightly cramped space in front of the large stone hearth. A small pyramid of neatly chopped logs sat to one side, whilst on the other, a gleaming set of brass tongs, poker, and a toasting fork hung from a row of hooks designed for the purpose. They looked unused, as did the fireplace itself. Not only had the grate been swept clean, it also had the burnished tint of fresh polish.

He called out, 'Mevrouw Steenmeijer?'

He had insisted, much to her displeasure, that she wait at the front door.

'Yes?' she replied, appearing at the doorway of the lounge just a little too quickly.

Munro let it slide.

'The Predikant hasn't stayed here for a while?'

'I'm really not sure of his comings and goings,' she protested. 'But I must say, the clock in the hall doesn't look to have been rewound for at least a week.' In answer to Munro's mystified expression, she went on. 'It was a gift from the parish for the last Predikant, I picked it out myself. It has an eight day mechanism and as well as keeping excellent time, it also displays the day of the week.' She took a step back into the hallway and pointed to a wooden-cased, antique wall-clock. 'Woensdag, you see?'

'Yes Mevrouw Steenmeijer. Wednesday, I see.' He scrutinised the old lady a little closer. 'I was under the impression Predikant Kotmans only visited his farmhouse at the weekends.'

He waited for the reply, letting silence draw her out. It didn't take long.

'Oh, you know about that do you?'

Munro nodded silently, and Mevrouw Steenmeijer couldn't resist.

'Well, it has been brought to the Finance Committee's attention that such a valuable asset belonging to the Church should not be squandered. For this beautiful house to be left unused...' Her sentence trailed off with no small amount of tutting and shaking of the head.

Yes, and I think I know who brought it to the Committee's attention as well, mused Munro. The Steenmeijers of this world formed the tightly knit and often stubbornly inflexible backbone of quite a lot of the churches back home too.

'Absolutely,' he nodded, his ingratiating smile making his peppered forehead nip. 'I couldn't agree more Mevrouw, such a *fine* building.' His commiserations were munificent. 'I don't suppose...?' he began, then looked abashedly at his feet. 'No, it doesn't matter. You've been so helpful already.' He broke away and called upstairs to Remco.

'What?' she asked, suddenly interested. 'If I can assist the police it would surely be my duty to do so.'

'No,' he shook his head dismissively. 'You might unwittingly hear or see something, and then I would have to insist you kept it secret. That can be a heavy burden Mevrouw. One which I would not wish to place on you.'

Remco's voice could be heard from the top of the stairs.

'Nothing here sir, I don't know what to suggest next,' he called down, adding a despondent sigh.

Nice touch, thought Munro, assuming his Sergeant had been listening in.

'Please Chief Inspector, Munro isn't it?'

He nodded politely.

'Yes, Mevrouw?'

'Please ask. What is it you want?'

Her tiny, dark, bird-like eyes were positively gleaming.

'Well, I wondered if the Predikant kept a set of keys to the farmhouse in the Church?'

If she did hesitate, Munro didn't notice it.

'I think so,' she nodded enthusiastically. 'On the spare set for the van. Let me get back to the office and I'll meet you outside.'

Instantly, and with an urgency of movement one would find surprising in a woman half her age, Mevrouw Steenmeijer hurried out of the door.

More than a little unsettled, Bregje moved away from the computer and made her way over to the kitchen. Whisky, recognising a move to the cookie area, padded over to join her. She had to smile when, his lowered face a mask of supplication, he tried on the paw routine. The trick worked so well it was only after she had relented that she wondered which of them was in charge.

She had kept on at the recording; more from curiosity than anything else. The cold look on Holy Man's face, both on the screen and in the flesh, had left her in no doubt as to the killer's identity.

'Maybe I'm going about this the wrong way?' she murmured, assuring herself that, as Whisky was present, she wasn't talking to herself. Coffee in hand, she peered down at the large black identifying letters on the roof of the Police car parked three floors below: 'GH' - in English the combination could either be silent, or make the phonetic sound '*f*'.

That was it.

Bregje was furious for wasting so much time. She *had* been approaching the recording from the wrong angle. By concentrating solely on the key consonants, she could at least make a start. The most obvious place to begin was the letter *G*. In the south of the country, near the border with Belgium, it was pronounced *Je*. To the north, Amsterdam included, it was more rasping, grinding, rolling sound produced in the back of the throat, and finally to the east: the sound emanated still from the back of the mouth, but it was more solid, guttural, sharp, and if the truth be told, Germanic. The vowels would have to come later as they were the most affected by the distortion. Munro had told her there was a unit working on the recording at Police Headquarters. Somewhat optimistically, she hoped they'd had more success than she'd managed.

Bregje listened carefully to the recording again.

Interesting.

When she reached the more emotionally charged last sentence, she snatched up her pen.

Very interesting.

27

back a long way

'I'll take the body back to the lab. Give you a call if I find anything.' Standing by the forensics van, Esther began to peel off her evidence suit. Then, observing the Steenmeijer woman climb into the back of Remco's car, she gave Munro a sideways look. 'What are you guys doing now?'

'Nothing,' he replied.

The flat tone of his reply told her all she needed to know.

'We'll follow you,' she said.

'I can't ask you to do that. At best this'll be an illegal search.'

'And at worst?'

'Housebreaking.'

She seemed to chew on that for a second. 'If you do find something, you won't be able to remove it or it'll immediately become inadmissible. We, on the other hand, have a mobile lab here. We can test stuff. Take away samples so small they won't be missed. And if we come up with something you'll know what you're looking for when you come back with a search warrant.'

Munro still looked unconvinced, so she took a step

closer.

'You know this is a whole different kind of enquiry. We need to know right now if Holy Man is the guy. Someone may already be scheduled to die tomorrow.'

He knew who she meant.

'Okay,' he conceded. Secretly delighted by the offer, he smiled across at her. 'But if it all goes pear-shaped,' he motioned with his head toward Mevrouw Steenmeijer perched on the back seat of Remco's car. 'One of us is going to have to take care of Miss Marple here.'

As their little convoy bumped down the hardened dirt track making up the last half-kilometre of the journey to Holy Man's farmhouse, Remco's mobile started to chirp. Fishing it out of his inside coat pocket, he handed the phone to his boss. This road was playing havoc with his beloved old car's suspension and he needed two hands on the wheel. Munro answered with a flourish.

'Meneer Elmers' manservant speaking. How may I assist you?'

'Who?'

'Sorry sir,' Munro pulled a face. 'Hoofdcommissaris Uylenburg?'

'Is he with you?'

'I'm afraid the Brigadier is driving at the moment.'

'Doesn't matter, you'll do. I have the location of this morning's call from the phone company. Thought you might like to know.'

'Don't tell me: a disposable mobile or public phone box.' It stood to reason, this was a very careful killer.

'The latter. But not just any public phone box. This phone box is located on the north-eastern corner of Winterwijk's Grotekerkplein.'

Munro's mind raced.

'Chief Inspector?'

'Yes sir...still here, sorry.'

'How are you getting on?'

'Still looking into Hol-' Munro quickly remembered their passenger, 'things in Winterswijk.' he finished clumsily.

'I bet you are. Never had much time for coincidences myself.' The Hoofdcommissaris hung up.

After the ageless grace of the townhouse, Predikant Kotmans' rural retreat was not quite as Munro had expected. The modern cement coated building was all large double glazed windows and broad angular tiled roofing. A stone path protected by a small wooden garden gate led up to the front door. Off to the side, and more in keeping with the rustic setting, stood a scruffy courtyard with several brick outbuildings dominated by what looked to have once been a stable block.

Munro held Remco back, waiting as Mevrouw Steenmeijer led Esther to the front door, then he told him about the call from Uylenburg.

'You still don't want to pull him in?' hissed Remco.

'First we call Sergeant Verboven. See if he was keeping tabs on Holy Man at that time.'

'What about this place?'

'Esther knows what she's looking for.'

They climbed back into the welcoming warmth of the car. Remco keyed in Verboven's number and switched his mobile on to speaker so they could both listen in. Frustratingly, the call went straight to voicemail.

Remco's message was curt. 'Call me.' He hung up.

'Fucking yokels,' he cursed, using a word Bregje had taught him in the Doelen after his first visit out here. Reminded of her, Munro couldn't hide his smile.

'We'll try again in a few minutes.' he suggested, before pushing the car door open again. 'Let's have a look round the yard.'

The first shed didn't offer much in the way of encouragement. A flimsy unvarnished door hung loosely on even looser hinges. As Remco pushed it in with his shoulder, the ugly scraping squeal of damp wood on stone echoed around the courtyard and set Munro's teeth on edge. The inside was musty, empty but for a few rusting farm implements left dangling from a row of vicious looking wire hooks cemented into the far wall. Although used for the purpose they were intended, the hooks gave him a chill. Trying to shake off the feeling, he turned to Remco.

'How come you've got the Chief of the Amsterdam Police Department running your chores?'

The little man shrugged. 'We go back a long way.'

He didn't ask Remco to elaborate. If he'd wanted to say more, he would have.

'This looks like our best bet.' Munro led the way across the slippery courtyard to the stables. Feeling the cold wet cloth of his trousers flap against his ankles, he noticed the snow underfoot was slowly turning to slush. In town he'd felt the wind change direction. And now clouds, rolling in from the west, had turned the previously crisp blue sky to a gloomy, and distinctly ominous, grey.

Obviously more cared for than the other buildings, the windowless block was well built. Four large rectangular indentations in the wall faced on to the courtyard. Munro assumed they were the individual stable-gates, long since bricked in. The centre of the low structure was dominated by an impressive set of double doors. Recently painted a glossy black, the block's only entrance was secured by an equally impressive padlock.

This time Munro's phone rang out, echoing eerily against the empty buildings.

'He's on the move.' Baart sounded anxious.

'Where's he headed?'

'Back into town. I'm trying to avoid being spotted, but it's not easy. This place isn't exactly busy and I'm doing this alone.'

'Have you heard from Sergeant Verboven?'

'No, he looked pretty tired when I relieved him. I imagine he's tucked up in bed at the moment. I don't think he's done this sort of thing before. He's left me a log-book of sorts, but it's a shambles.'

'He recorded Holy Man's movements?'

'After a fashion.'

Munro could hear the scorn in Baart's voice.

'Open the book.' he commanded.

The young Inspecteur's demeanour quickly flipped from disdain to distraught. 'What do you want me to do? Follow Holy Man, talk to you on the phone, or read Verboven's notes?'

'Alright, call me back when he stops or if he changes direction.' Munro conceded with a sigh.

More anxiety crackled down the line from Baart.

'Were getting close to the church now, are you guys clear of the townhouse?'

'We're at the farm.'

'What are you doing there?' Distraught gave way to distress, and Munro found himself wondering just how exhausting being Franck Baart was. Involvement in illegal searches doesn't go down well with the Promotion Board, and black-marks like that tend to hang around.

'Do you really want to know?' he asked unkindly.

'No sir. I'll call you in a few minutes.'

'Thank you. That would be greatly appreciated Inspecteur.'

Recognising the sarcasm in Munro's tone, Remco gave a short grunt of derision.

'Another one with a broomstick problem?'

'This one might need surgery,' chortled Munro.

'So how do we get in?' Remco rapped his knuckles on the solid sounding door.

Munro eyed the stainless steel latches.

'Maybe Esther's got a screwdriver in her big box of tricks?'

Sloshing their way back around to the front of the house, they saw Michael storing his camera gear in the back of the van. Esther and Mevrouw Steenmeijer met them at the front gate.

Looking put out, Esther folded her arms.

'Apart from clear evidence of compulsive cleaning? Nothing.'

Even the indomitable Mevrouw Steenmeijer looked a little crestfallen. Munro took her elbow gently and pointed over to the courtyard.

'I don't suppose you know if this is Predikant Kotmans' property as well?' he enquired gently.

'Yes of course. He bought this place about two years ago, after old Dr. Roemer died. He was the vet, used the stables over there as a surgery. A lot of the local farmers weren't too pleased when the Predikant moved in, they were hoping another veterinarian would take the practice on. And quite naturally, we wondered why he would waste so much money when he had the use of a perfectly good house in town. Rent free too.' She added indignantly.

Esther seemed to be thinking out loud. 'That's around the time his wife was first diagnosed with cancer.' Pointedly, she turned to the old girl. 'They may have wanted a little more privacy.'

If the implication resonated in any way, Mevrouw Steenmeijer showed no sign of it.

'How did she die in the end?' asked Munro.

The old lady tutted. 'Brain tumour. Treatment held it at bay for a short while, and they did once try to operate, but it was unsuccessful.'

'Do you happen to know which side of the head the tumour was on?'

'The right I think, yes, I remember her wearing a beret to cover a scar from the operation.'

Unnoticed by Mevrouw Steenmeijer, a knowing look passed between the Detective and the Forensic Pathologist.

28

for the blood

The first part of the recording was, in origin, almost pure East Gelderland. Almost. By pulling up the research on the web, she could even pinpoint certain sounds exclusive to Winterswijk itself. So far so good. But without a true rendition and reliable measurement of the length of the vowel sounds, it was proving to be heavy going. And as for the final outburst? Careful study was beginning to reveal it to be nothing of the sort. The clearly pronounced consonants alone showed the expressive content to be strictly controlled. This was no emotional outpouring. In fact, to her laboriously trained ear it was a carefully rehearsed statement, calculated to shock the listener, jog him into action.

It had worked.

A cold chill tightened the skin at the nape of her neck. There was something else. However well practised, the urgency of the delivery had opened cracks in the accent. Minuscule lesions that, from her unique point of view, allowed slivers of light in. And it would be these slivers that, in time, would illuminate the tiny clues she needed to build an understanding of the speaker's history. Unfortunately, concentrating for so long on the fluctuating and warped sound was giving her a pounding headache.

Lack of sleep could have something to do with it too, she reflected with a wry grin as a warm trickle of physical memory buoyed her spirits.

Whisky, watching Bregje lean back in her chair and stretch, joined in with a stretch of his own. Slowly climbing to his feet, he gave her one of those high-pitched sinuous yawns utilised exclusively by bored dogs in need of exercise. He followed that with a short full-body-shake for good measure.

'Alright,' Bregje ruffled his ears. 'A walk might do us both some good.'

The light was growing dim by the time she made it to the bottom of the steps outside her office. A depressingly young-looking uniformed policeman jumped out of the patrol car.

'Pardon, Mevrouw?'

'Just call me Bregje.' She gave him a pained smile. 'Mevrouw' was mostly reserved for older, married women.

'Sorry, I-'

Bregje stopped him before he dug himself any deeper.

'I'm just going to walk the dog and get a bite to eat. Why don't you take a break, we'll be back in...'

He was shaking his head. 'Sorry Mevr...erm, my orders were very explicit.'

Bregje straightened up in surprise. 'How explicit?'

'Have you met Sergeant Elmers?'

She could see concern, or was it fear in his eyes. She imagined Remco often had that effect on junior officers.

'Can I help?'

The familiarity of the voice made her turn quickly. Martijn stood by the steps. Shoulders hunched against the cold, he had his hands stuffed deeply into his jacket pockets. Suddenly assertive, and almost brushing her aside the young Policemen moved between them.

'Do you know this man?' he asked bluntly.

What exactly were Remco's orders she wondered. Bregje let the dog go. Watching him bounce around Martijn in a fit of excitement, she smiled at the policeman.

'I think that answers your question.' He looked as if he was about to apologise again, so she went on. 'Now you can have a break. I have a friend *and* a ferocious dog to protect me.'

All three of them looked down at the dog. Right on cue, Whisky responded by sitting down and raising a paw.

'Well,' she laughed. 'A friend anyway.'

The young officer relented. 'You know if the Brigadier finds out he'll have my-'

Bregje cut him short again. 'Shall we say an hour?'

Esther had gone one better than a screwdriver. Her heavy-duty electric drill's wide range of parts included a bit which fitted the screws on the stable door latch perfectly. When asked why she travelled with an array of tools that would make a joiner happy, she shrugged off the question by reciting a list.

'Coffins, artificial hips, iron railings-'

'Alright, we get it.' Munro had interrupted hurriedly, one eye on Mevrouw Steenmeijer.

'Here you go,' she handed him the power tool. 'We'll wait in the van, call us when you get it open.'

Remco had noisily removed two of the screws when Munro's phone rang again. Moving away, he checked the display: Baart.

'I have Sergeant Verboven's notes now sir.'

'Good. Does he describe any of Holy Man's movements at around six-thirty this morning?'

'Let me see...' Munro could hear pages being flicked back and forwards. 'No sir. Not that I can...hold on. It's at the end, on the last page. Jesus this is a mess, it isn't even in any kind of chronological order.'

'Inspecteur!' He hadn't meant to shout.

Remco turned off the drill and turned to face him.

Baart sounded flustered. 'Sorry. Six-thirty a.m.: subject observed making a call from public phone box on Grotekerkplein.'

With some difficulty, Munro retained his composure.

'Right. Here's what you do next,' he ordered. 'You call Hoofdinspecteur Uylenburg and tell him what you've just told me. After that, you call the Magistrate and get a Search Order for the farmhouse. Don't worry, Uylenburg will back you up.'

'What about Kotmans?' asked Baart, clearly put out by Munro's commanding tone.

'Where are you?'

'Far end of the Grotekerkplein. He's in the church.'

'Alright, if he starts to move let us know, and tell whoever's coming with the search warrant to pin a copy on the stable door and clear off.'

'Why?'

'Because we'll be finished by then.'

He hung up, took the drill from Remco's hand and jamming the business end between the loosened latch and the wood, ripped out the rest of the screws. With barely a sound, the doors swung open. Casually, Remco scratched the back of his head.

'I assume this operation is no longer covert.' he said quietly.

The dimming light from the courtyard gave out after venturing only a half-meter into the black interior.

Munro fumbled along the wall until he found a switch. The fluorescent bulb flickered a few times before coming on, the glimmering light once more involuntarily resurrecting the image of Jitske Bolthof's pale corpse in his mind.

'Get Esther.' Munro issued the order quietly, and with an authority in his voice he wasn't sure he still possessed. A huge stainless steel table almost filled the centre of the room, and like the rest of the large space, it was spotless. Attached to the walls, the smooth progress of the expensive looking granite work-surfaces were only interrupted up by a twin-set of deep porcelain sinks. The taps were the medical type you could turn on and off with your elbows. To his right the far wall remained in darkness, and as he started to walk towards it he felt himself stumble on the uneven floor. He regained his balance as Esther appeared in the doorway. She was not alone.

'Well, who would have thought that would still be here.' Mevrouw Steenmeijer bustled in. 'It was Doctor Roemer's.'

'What was?' Munro moved forward, trying to usher her back toward the door.

'The operating table of course,' she tapped the steel surface with her fingers. 'Do you see the pulley?' She pointed up into the rafters. 'That was so you could get the horses on. Took a couple of men though. He operated on my daughter's pony,' she offered, by way of an explanation. 'Saved its life.' Then, just in case Munro thought she may have been getting sentimental, she added darkly. 'For a price.'

'And what about the rest of the place?'

'It's a lot tidier than I remember. Animals, especially sick ones, do make a terrible mess.' She looked around. 'The sinks are new, and the walls have obviously been painted. Other than that...' The old lady seemed to be thinking for a moment. 'Do you think he means to sell the place to another vet?'

The unexpected innocence of the question made

Munro pause for a moment.

'Maybe,' he answered quietly.

Looking down at his feet he could see now what had nearly upended him. A narrow channel with a gently sloping curved bottom had been carved into the tiled floor. It led from the foot of the table to the guttering at the door. Steenmeijer saw him looking at it.

'For the blood,' she explained helpfully.

Esther instructed Michael to return Mevrouw Steenmeijer to the van. She also gave him a list of things to bring back.

'Wait for the gloves,' she admonished Remco as, turning back, she caught him reaching to open one of the three drawers set into the table. He picked a pen out of his pocket and used it to pull on the handle. Seeing her scowl, Munro raised his hands in surrender.

'What can I say? He's not known for his patience.'

The drawer opened easily. Neatly lined-up on soft black velvet, and looking like some kind of twisted cutlery collection, a set of pristine silver medical instruments slid into view.

'Could they have belonged to the Vet?' Munro asked Esther.

'Only if he was into antiques,' she replied in a whisper, obviously fascinated by the assortment.

Michael returned with the same aluminium case Munro remembered from Esther's application of his own running repairs. Unconsciously, he reached up and rolled a thin crust of dried blood from one of the tiny wounds on his forehead.

'Don't you dare drop that,' she hissed.

He put it in his pocket. With a brief look to the heavens, Esther handed out the latex gloves.

The middle drawer was larger and deeper than the others. Inside, fitting snugly, sat a squat green metal box. It was the type used by small businesses for petty cash with a handle on the lid and a small lock on the front. Esther lifted it out and placed it on the steel surface of the table.

'Feels light,' she said, pulling open the third drawer. It held a set of handcuffs, a roll of gaffer tape, and several white plastic pill bottles. She lifted the handcuffs with one finger, waiving them in front of Munro. 'Maybe you think these were the vets too?'

'Can you open the box?' he asked.

'Only if you don't mind me popping out the lock.'

Remco grinned. 'Have you seen the door?'

Two taps with a delicate looking hammer and chisel, and the mechanism was loosened enough for her to prise open the lid. Apart from a moulded foam insert and a label glued to the inside, it was empty. One part of the vacant mould was almost the shape of a gun, the difference being the barrel, which appeared to jut out too far behind the handle. Above that, there was a space for something pipe-shaped and slightly wider.

Munro squinted at the label.

'What does it say?'

'*Gevangen Boutkanon.* This is a safe-box for a captive bolt gun.' She read on from the short description outlined below the title. *'For the humane euthanizing of livestock.'* Looking up at Munro she started to explain. 'This type uses a compressed air cartridge to drive a steel bolt into, well...into whatever you like really. The fitted barrel would do for sheep and perhaps younger pigs, but you'd need the top attachment with the bigger bolt for horses and cattle. Now those probably did belong to the vet.'

'Will they do?'

She pulled a small plastic ruler from her breast pocket and measured the two ends of the foam outline.

'They'll do,' she replied softly.

29

write a book

As she sat in the cafe on the corner, where the Prinsengracht met the Elandsgracht, Bregje washed down a mouthful of her filled roll with a swig of beer and looked across the table at Martijn. His face was ruddy with cold, and a study in youthful melancholy.

'Are you telling me you've been waiting outside my office all day?' she asked in amazement.

He nodded sheepishly. As they had walked through the Negen Straatjes - Nine Little Streets that criss-crossed the canals in the Jordaan - she had noticed his waterlogged shoes and the damp darkness creeping up the legs of his jeans. Grabbing a couple of broodjes from the deli down the street, she'd ordered him into the warmth of the bar. His roll, however, sat untouched.

'Why?' she asked incredulously.

'I wanted to talk to you, but I was too...' He left it hanging there.

'Listen,' she began, trying to pick the right words. 'What happened the other night was my fault. I was feeling a bit down and...' There was nothing else for it, '...you were available. I'm sorry if you thought it would lead to more, but for me it was just a physical thing.'

As she spoke, Bregje had a horrible feeling she was repeating, almost verbatim, something said to her in her own student days. She was also pretty sure it had taken a her a while to get over *that* guy. Martijn slowly got to his feet.

'I'm going to go,' he mumbled sullenly.

She looked up at him. 'Martijn. Go home, have a hot bath, put on some dry clothes and go out for a drink.'

She choked back the urge to tell him there were plenty more 'younger and prettier fish in the sea' on the grounds that, having turned into her mother, she would have to kill him and everyone else in the café, and that wouldn't be fair.

Martijn left quietly. She felt sure Whisky had wanted to accompany his friend to offer some kind of consolation, but there was now an untouched ham roll on the table, and this was a dog with strictly adhered to priorities.

The young policeman was pacing nervously outside her office building when she got back.

'I thought that guy was going to stay with you?' he complained.

'He has to meet someone.' Not a complete lie, she thought. 'Anyway, we've not been gone an hour.'

'This came for you.' He held up a CD case. 'From Headquarters. It was lucky I was here to take it or Sergeant Elmers would have-'

'I know,' Bregje snapped, thinking: policemen don't only look younger, they're more immature too.

'I'm sorry,' she held up her hands and smiled cordially. 'What is it?'

'Some recording they've cleaned up. They had orders to get a copy to you as soon as it was done.'

'That was quick,' she marvelled. 'Thank you.'

Taking the disc from him, she quickly ushered Whisky up the stone steps to the front door.

The same rough workmanship. The same wire hooks. Different appendages. Violating an almost sacred silence, Remco nudged Esther's assistant with his elbow.

'Shouldn't you be getting a few snaps of that?' he chirped.

With a start, Michael ran out of the stable block and could be heard splashing through the yard in his hurry to retrieve his camera equipment from the van.

Fumbling around on his search, Remco had accidently found the light switch that lit the far end of the stables. Inexplicably, it was located on the underside of the work-surface at the opposite end of the room. He found it, and being Remco, he pressed it. Two high powered halogen spotlights suspended from the rafters illuminated the wall with a sheet of almost blinding white light.

As in the other outbuildings the hooks had been primitively cemented in. On each but the last two, standing out in dramatic relief against the rough surface of the exposed brick, there hung a small item of clothing. A scarf, a blouse, a shoe, a bra, white panties... Munro counted eleven pieces.

Eleven.

'Trophies?' he asked, already knowing the answer.

'Trophies.' replied Esther flatly. 'And a Kill Room.' Clasping her hands on the top of her head she heaved a sigh. 'This is the one I write a book about and retire.'

Leaving Esther and Michael behind to wait for both the local forensic team and the belated Search Order, they dropped Mevrouw Steenmeijer at her house in town before heading for the church. The quiet stillness they had fallen into while the old lady had been in the car lingered on.

It was Munro who spoke first. 'How should we play this?' It was an admission. He'd been wrong about Holy

Man and it was only fair Remco should be allowed to plan and execute the arrest. As he knew he would be, and unlikely as it would seem to someone who did not know him well, Remco's reply was gracious.

'I wouldn't leave it to me. If I was left in charge I'd drive the bastard back up to that farmhouse and hang the fucker up on one of those hooks.' Well, as gracious as Remco got. 'And not by his neck either,' he added contemptuously.

Inspecteur Baart was leaning on his car when they arrived. A large cardboard cup of coffee in one hand, he was, with some difficulty, trying to remove the foil wrapping from a cheeseburger with the other. Remco took the burger from him.

'Allow me, Sir,' he said with a friendly smile.

Munro took the coffee. 'Thanks, just what I needed.'

Baart watched helplessly as Remco took a huge bite out of the cheeseburger, but before he could start to object, Munro tapped his chest with his forefinger.

'Officially, you're still the most senior Dutch officer on this enquiry.' he stated.

The Inspecteur eyed him suspiciously. 'Yes?'

Munro told him what they'd uncovered at Kotmans' place, but the initial reaction was predictably disappointing.

'What about the Search Order?' Baart enquired.

'Did you call Uylenburg and get one?'

'Yes, straight away.'

Munro glanced at his watch. 'Then it should be there by now.'

'But you didn't have it when you broke into the place.'

Remco piped up through a mouthful of food. 'I beg your pardon Inspecteur, that door had been forced before we arrived. And just in case you doubt my word, we have two forensic experts and one locally respected pillar of the community as witnesses.'

'We merely investigated the break in until the Search Order arrived,' added Munro. 'So, I guess the arrest is yours to make.'

Munro could see Baart begin to salivate at the prospect. But then, prematurely lining his handsome features, a shadow of doubt crept across his face.

I bet you don't see that very often, thought Munro.

'You wondering what to wear for the press conference?' he enquired dryly.

Baart ignored the jibe. 'I've already made one mistake on this enquiry.'

Munro could see Hoofdcommissaris Uylenburg's words had stung him, leaving the ambitious young man's carefully planned career path in serious jeopardy.

'I'm not making another.'

Remco, having wolfed down the burger, noisily scrunched up the wrapper.

'Let me get this straight,' he began. For once abandoning his usual confrontational style, he sounded quite calm. 'We're handing you the arrest of the year - no wait - decade, on a plate. And you're too chickenshit to take it?' At least he'd managed a reasonable tone.

Baart examined his shoes.

'Was there *any* physical evidence in the stable-block?' he asked without looking up.

'Hard to say,' replied Remco. 'Apart from eleven items of clothing belonging to each of the victims, a cutlery drawer from a horror movie, and a case that was built to keep a bolt gun set exactly matching the unique wounds found on the corpses...nothing really.'

'No,' Baart persevered. 'I mean DNA, fingerprints. Anything that ties Kotmans to the murders.'

Remco's frustration bubbled over. 'It's *his* fucking building.'

'Inspecteur Baart might have a point.' Munro

conceded quietly. He hated himself for having to admit it. The evidence may well be damning, but it *was* circumstantial. Even if Hans identified Holy Man as the guy leaving the peepshow in a hurry. What about the Porsche? And what would a defending lawyer make of the Kapitein's well documented alcohol intake on the night in question?

No, they had no reliable witnesses. And more importantly, no real physical link.

'He's going to be tried here,' he went on, thinking aloud. 'Before a jury of his peers. How keen are they going to be to see a Predikant, a representative of *their* church go down for murder?'

'And if he says he rented out the space?' Baart added. 'What do we have? An old lady unhappy about the amount of fuel he uses. An affair with Jitske Bolthof; noticed by the police, but undocumented at the time. Any half decent lawyer would have *that* thrown out before a jury even got to hear it.' He looked to Munro for support. 'No, I'm telling you, to make this watertight we need more.'

Baart had made a huge error in judgement when he arrested Derk Merel, and Munro wondered if a small part of the usually self-assured career cop felt responsible, however indirectly, for Merel's death. It was the price you paid for wanting in on the big cases. Mistakes, missed opportunities, and moments of just plain bad luck had a way of chipping away at an eager detective's glossy veneer. Meanwhile, the musty smell of past horrors, witnessed, packed away and left to fester in the memory would get to work from below. In the end something always had to give. Maybe in five or ten years, assuming they both survived in the job, he would be able to talk about all that with Franck Baart.

But not now.

'Then we follow him,' Munro stated calmly, taking a

sip of Baart's coffee.

He made a face and handed it back.

'Let me guess, decaf skinny latte. That, my dear Inspecteur, is nothing more than a dirty cup of lukewarm water.'

30

Mokum born

Startled, Bregje looked up from her computer screen as, caught by a sudden gust of wind, an almost solid sheet of rain noisily rattled the elderly window frame. She then waited a few seconds before, true to form, Whisky acknowledged the event with a semi-interested half-bark.

'My brave boy,' she murmured, giving him an exhausted smile.

It was slow work. The cleaned up version was a great help of course, but there was still something wrong. Warmth, emotion, sentiment: the essential oils that normally served to smooth a person's personality and character into timbre and tone, were all missing. The absence wouldn't stop her from completing her task, but she found it disconcerting, the deficiency made the job harder. She could cheat of course, judging by the ease with which she had been able to find Holy Man's picture, she assumed there would also be quite a few articles about him on the web. Bregje considered the idea, then rejected it. Iain and Remco wouldn't be back in town for ages, and she had to have something to occupy her mind in the meantime. At least she had one more sliver to work on. This guy was born and brought up in one of the poorer neighbourhoods of Amsterdam and had most likely left the city to go east in his mid to late teens. It was all in the 'A's. Slightly nasal with a tiny hint of flatness. He'd tried to disguise it and probably thought he had succeeded over the years, but that sound. Indisputably Mokum born, and almost without doubt, Mokum bred.

'Here he comes,' grunted Remco.

They both slid down in their seats as the white Volkswagen van passed. The motion was automatic, but unnecessary. An almost impenetrable darkness had descended, the lighting around the square in front of the Grote Kerk barely coping with the black sky and now driving rain. They waited a few seconds for Baart's Saab to slip by before Remco pulled out into the light evening traffic.

As the tiny convoy crossed the bridge at Arnhem, Munro and Remco exchanged a fleeting look. This was where one of the victims had supposedly committed suicide. Remco's foot pressed on the accelerator.

'Easy,' ordered Munro quietly. 'Baart's on him.'

'If he gets within a half-kilometre of Bregje-'

'I'll take him down myself,' assured Munro.

The acknowledgement seemed to satisfy Remco and his hands relaxed their grip on the wheel. Forty uneventful minutes later, as they passed the turn-off for Ouderkerk-aan-de-Amstel, Remco's mobile rang. He put it on speakerphone.

'I've arranged for two units to take over surveillance when we enter the city,' announced Baart.

It was Munro who replied. 'Tell them to hang back, you've got the lead on this and he hasn't made you yet.' Just because you had resources, didn't mean you had to use them.

Surveillance rule one, don't overcomplicate.

'But I've been on him all day, the risk-'

'Inspecteur Baart. The risk of losing him on a hand-over is far greater. Stick with the van and keep back-up informed and out of sight.'

Munro sighed as Remco hung up.

'And maybe try growing some balls,' he murmured.

The rain was beginning to ease as they reached the outskirts of the city. Turning right on to President Kennedylaan, they then followed the meandering line of the ever broadening Amstel before taking another right over the bridge and on to the Weesperstraat. The traffic now heavier as they neared the centre, Munro had time to think of Gerrard as they passed the hospital, or as they now knew, Doyle. Of his altercation with Boos Ali, his fake passport and driving licence, and the subsequent removal of his body before a full autopsy could be undertaken. In his mind he filed away a question for Esther.

Watching the van disappear into the underground car park of the Albert Hein supermarket on the Jodenbreestraat, Remco bumped the car onto the pavement on the other side of the Meester Visserplein. Following at a discreet two car distance, Baart's Saab slid out of sight into the darkness beneath the store. Remco leaned back in his seat, clenching and unclenching his hands, he stretched his fingers.

'Now what?' he asked simply.

Munro thought for a moment, before making his mind up and tapping the dashboard.

'Now we head for the Police Bureau on the Nieuwmarkt and wait for him to pass us on his way to the Walletjes.'

It was where Bregje had seen him on a day he wasn't scheduled to kill. Selecting the next victim. Doing his homework.

Tracking Kotmans on foot, Baart passed the steps leading to the Waterlooplein where Munro had thrown himself and his bicycle down in pursuit of Youssef Absullah. Then, as if meeting an old friend, he briefly shook hands with a member of the surveillance team. Waving a warm farewell, he discretely slipped in the earpiece and attached the microphone behind his jacket collar.

Moving to the small couch in the kitchen area of the office, Bregje lifted her feet and curled up. The lack of sleep and intense effort involved in deciphering each and every sound on the recording had made her suddenly very tired. Pulling her phone from her pocket she laid it beside her. She had gleaned everything she could, and they would call her when they got back to town. As she drifted off, the darkness of the week's events caused her a pang of anxiety. Luckily though, she was instantly comforted by the sound of Whisky's padding feet, the slump of his body against the sofa, and a long and relaxed doggy sigh.

'We're getting closer to you now.' Baart's voice came through, carrying with it the background patter and hiss of the rain. The drive around to the Nieuwmarkt hadn't been simple, but his sergeant's knowledge of the streets and total disregard for the traffic laws meant they had arrived in good time.

'There,' Remco grunted, ducking his head and pointing at Kotmans' figure as it emerged through the crowd. The windows on the ground floor of the Police Bureau on the Nieuwmarkt were both mirrored and made of strengthened glass, a decision taken after the riots that proceeded the erection of the new Town Hall and Opera House. The protest at the demolition of a large swathe of the old town lending the government building its everyday nickname: the Stopera.

To their surprise, Holy Man seemed to be coming straight toward them, suddenly stopping at their window and separated by only a few feet, the Predikant's face formed itself into a grey mask of cold hatred. Startled and chilled in the same measure, Munro and Remco could only stare back in silence. Then, as if suddenly shocked back into animation, Kotmans moved off.

'What the Hell just happened?' Baart's voice sizzled into Remco's hand-held radio.

'Nothing, just stay on him.' snapped Munro. Thinking out loud, he then laid a shaky hand on Remco's shoulder. 'He hates himself. He hates what he is about to do. What he has to do.'

The pair followed at a safe distance as Baart guided them across the Nieuwmarkt Plein and into the alleys of the Red Light District.

'Fuck me!' exclaimed Remco, as Baart described how Kotmans had made a bee-line for the Sexycastle Peepshow, entered, and climbed on to the escalator.

'How can that place be open again so soon?' asked Munro, amazed.

'I'm guessing forensics was finished,' sighed Remco. 'And you should never underestimate the connections these people have with the authorities,' he added, with a knowing tap on the side of his nose.

Baart posted men at the entrance and at the private rear door of the peepshow before seeking out Munro and Remco.

'What do you think he's doing in there?' he enquired anxiously.

Watching the lascivious grin spreading across Remco's face, Munro answered before his sergeant could get himself into any more trouble with a senior officer.

'If he follows his schedule he can't kill until

midnight. So, I'm assuming he was selecting a victim when Bregje spotted him, and he's just biding his time.'

'Are you sure it wasn't Bregje he was following?' asked Remco grumpily.

'No…I'm not. But he's here now and there are no other ways out of that place. If, when he does leave, he starts heading across town, we'll pull him in and take our chances in spite of Inspecteur Baart's reservations.'

Somewhat placated, Remco still treated Baart to a withering scowl.

31

why not

By the time Holy Man left the peepshow, Munro was heartily sick of the weak coffee and greasy smell from De Kijkuit Café on Oudekerksplein, and would have happily burnt the place to the ground.

'He's on schedule,' Remco placed his elbow on the table and tapped his wristwatch. 'Eleven-fifty.'

It took all of Munro's willpower to stay put as one of Baart's team reported in.

'He's leaving the club by the main entrance and turning left.'

Then another, 'I have him, he's on Oudekerksplein and walking anti-clockwise around the church.'

There was silence for a few moments, suddenly Baart's voice broke in. 'Well come on, update?'

'He's stopped by the billboard for the Sex Cinema, I've had to keep moving to avoid him spotting me.'

Baart again, 'Fuck! No, it's okay, I have him, he's on the move again and…wait…he's just gone into an alley, I'm following…'

Remco jumped to his feet. 'Come on!'

Munro followed instinctively. As they passed the Cinema, Remco puffed an explanation.

'That alley leads to a small courtyard lined with windows, if he goes into a room without Baart spotting which one, we may not get to him before he finds a way out the back.'

They all but ran into Baart as he exited the alleyway.

'Did you see the door he went in?' quizzed Munro.

'Yes, I have the number, but what do you want to do now?

'Time?'

'Five-to-twelve.'

'We need to go in,' he pushed passed Baart, and three steps later found himself in a tiny space with eight, no, ten glass doorways. Around half were occupied by girls, the rest empty or in use, their signature red curtains drawn.

'Which one?'

'Here.' Baart pointed out a doorway directly opposite the entrance to the square.

'Have we got something to open this door?' His heart had started pounding. This felt bad.

'Don't need it,' replied Remco knowledgeably. 'The two doors on either side are connected through a corridor at the back. The girls leave them unlocked in case a punter gets out of hand so they can escape or call for help.'

'And if they can escape…' Munro rushed toward the first door on the right, then had to stop, nonplussed, as it swung open and a black woman of startling proportions cupped her breasts, squeezed them upwards at him and exclaimed in a husky African accent.

'Fifty euros; suck and fuck baby?'

Thinking on his feet, Munro smiled.

'Why the Hell not,' he replied.

She stepped aside to let him in, and then began to protest as Remco and Baart followed.

'Hey, that's gonna cost…'

Remco silenced her with his Police ID and a finger to his lips.

The corridor was empty, and Munro moved as quietly as he could toward the next room. The handle turned easily in his hand, but the door refused to budge. Suddenly a shriek sounded from inside, and it was all he could do to get out of the way as Remco came barrelling in, pretty much reducing the cheap hollow door to splinters. Unsurprisingly, more shrieks ensued.

Bregje jumped when heard the Police car's engine start up. I am so stressed, she thought, then wondered if the sound had only been a part of her dream. Stretching as she climbed on to her feet, she made her way to the window. The young policeman's car had gone, replaced by a police van. A change of shift. A low growl emanated from Whisky's prone figure.

'What's up with you?' she groaned, rubbing her eyes.

Boredom had won, as long she was stuck here she might as well get on with it, she would look up Predikant Jan Kotmans history on the Internet, check it matched what she had already gleaned from the recording. It only took a few seconds to get his name up on the search engine and click on the first history offered, but something wasn't right. Bregje backed out to the search engine again and clicked the second link.

Fingers trembling, she frantically dialled Munro's number. Fucking automated answer. She left a message and marked it urgent before throwing the phone down in frustration. A few moments later, Bregje couldn't be sure if the dog had started barking before the doorbell sounded, or just after.

If Munro had thought the prostitute who had allowed them access next door was big-boned, he was in for a shock. The enormous shifting bulk of 'Princess', as she insisted on being known, was pulling on a skimpy one-piece, her huge frame all but filling the doorway to the courtyard at the other end of the room. Her voice was as husky and African, but her tone was up a few octaves, and right now, close to deafening. In front of him, Predikant Kotmans was on his knees, half-dressed, handcuffed, and pinned to the bed by Remco. Pinching the bridge of his nose, Munro leaned back against the wall. Wrong. This was all wrong. When he spoke, it was calmly.

'Remco, let him sit up. Baart, call Verboven now, and Princess..?'

The mention of her name created a momentary pause in her raucous monologue.

'Have you seen this guy before?'

Her reply caused his heart to sink to his boots.

'Of course, he is my best regular. Pays good too, here he is in my diary.'

She turned abruptly, and bending low at the waist, reached into a holdall stashed in a small cupboard beneath a tiny sink. Munro averted his gaze and caught Kotmans looking at her bent form.

'The Lord God made them all,' he said. Then, in reply to Kotmans puzzled frown, he added. 'All things wide and wonderful.'

Princess, one hand on the sink to help her back up, turned back around and thrust a battered school notebook into Munro's hand.

'There, you see? We have legitimate business here. No'ting illegal. No'ting!'

Munro examined the contents and found Princess had painstakingly ruled the lines into each page of the book, with the days and dates in her 'diary' handwritten in neat rows. Munro checked the days off against the dates he could remember from the 'murder list', and as he now knew they would, several dates clashed.

'Boss?' It was Remco. 'He's on the line now.'

Munro grabbed the phone, 'Verboven?'

'Ja…I mean, yes sir.'

'The telephone call, the one Predikant Kotmans made this morning, did you actually see him make it?'

'No sir, but I can assure you he did…'

'Bastard door,' cursed Bregje on the way downstairs. It was always sticking. 'Bastard wimpy policemen too.' By simply opening the window and peering down, the blue circle of the cop's hat confirmed her suspicions. That'll be why he won't just barge it open like everyone else, she thought. Whisky's frenzied barking wasn't helping her mood either. The dog had scrabbled to get out of the office door before her, and she'd only just managed to grab his collar and haul him back inside before slipping out herself. The doorbell sounded again.

'Alright, alright,' she called down, refusing to rush on the steep staircase. Finally, in the tiny vestibule at the bottom of the stairs, she grabbed the lock and yanked the door open.

'Commissaris Hesselink told me, he was out on his morning run and he observed the Predikant using the phone box on the Grotekerkplein. Told me I was doing a great job, thinks I might be in line for a promo-'

Munro hit the hang up button. Throwing the cell phone on to the bed, he grabbed Kotmans by the front of his shirt and hauled him to his feet.

'The surgery?' He shouted.

A blank look.

'Workshop, whatever…at your farmhouse, who…who uses it?'

'Oh, I see,' Kotmans frowned, confused.

'It came with the house, but I had no real use for it…so I rented it out.'

Eyes bulging, Munro tightened his grip, causing the fabric to protest.

'Johan…I rented it out to Johan Hesselink.'

The blow that sent Bregje flying back into the wall scattered her wits. Her brain, flickering into survival mode, suddenly raced, sending partially-formed thoughts fluttering through her mind. He had more…stuff, on his uniform, decorations, and his hat had a line of white on the brim, and he had punched her in the chest. Why would a policeman punch her? But when she looked down, she saw it was not a punch. The policeman's hand was still there, and it was red.

Wet and red.

It took more effort than it should to lift her head again, and she became aware of a tightness. As if an iron band had been placed over her shoulders and pulled down over her arms, squeezing, crushing, until her breath could only just fit into the rapidly diminishing space in short panting gasps.

'You know we have a lot in common, Johan and I,' Kotmans burbled on. 'Both of us losing our wives like that. Of course, his loss was much more sudden than mine. A little time after the accident he said he needed some extra space to store his wife's possessions, to help himself to move on…'

Munro's exhausted brain somehow dredged up the memory. Esther's call.

'It was a road accident; a lorry knocked her off her bike?' He asked quietly, already knowing the answer.

Kotmans looked up, surprised.

'Yes, how did you…?'

'He didn't move on Predikant, he didn't move on at all.'

It seemed an age before the hand released her, and though she felt herself sliding down the wall, in a strange way she had become detached from all physical sensation. Dark shadows now appeared in the periphery of her vision, and when her head fell to the side as her body crumpled, the view tilted too, the way it does when someone drops a camera. He moved closer then, crouching. A tram rumbled by, the overhead line sparking in the rain, causing something metal to glint in his hand. Bregje, her sight growing dimmer still, watched helplessly as the policeman's fingers worked on the long barrelled silver object.

Munro slumped on to the bed next to Kotmans and rubbed his face with his hands.

'The connections, coincidences, it wasn't the church. It was us, the police. We were just too close to see it…' He was so tired. He had been on the go for eighteen hours straight, and hadn't had much sleep before that. The thought jolted him on to his feet.

Bregje.

He fumbled in his coat pocket for his mobile, realising he had switched the ringer off as they pursued the Predikant through town. One message.

'Iain? Pick up the fucking phone. It's not Holy Man. I looked through his history and he's never even lived in Amsterdam, the man who left that message did though, grew up here. Call me.'

Munro winced at the breathless urgency in Bregje's voice, and immediately pressed the button to return the call.

I must move, she told herself. I must make myself move. Bregje felt him come closer, his hot breath on her face, his burning spittle on her cheek as he rambled, his words blending together into a fluctuating hiss.

Pleading, begging his God for forgiveness.

Amsterdam, she thought randomly, definitely Amsterdam.

There was a loud 'click' and a black circle at the end of a steel tube drifted across her line of vision. With a supreme effort, she gritted her teeth and tried to pull her head away.

A blast of colour exploded behind her tightly closed eyes. Then…nothing.

Wednesday

19th December

32

Elsje Christiaens

Blue lights danced on the walls and bounced off the slick watery pavement of the Nieuwezijds Voorburgwal in an epilepsy inducing display of intermittently indiscriminate flashes. In turn, each burst of illumination revealing a dramatic tableau of individual moments frozen in time.

A tall woman in a blue coverall shouts from the top of a flight of stone steps. Beneath her, a young man crouches in the back of a large van, looking up from his task of wrapping expensive looking camera equipment in plastic sheeting.

Two paramedics, one speaking into his radio-set, the other shrugging as he closes the doors of an empty ambulance.

A baby-faced policeman is pinned to the wall by a short, overweight man. The man's thick white knuckles distinct against the black leather of the uniform jacket.

A figure stands alone on the edge of the scene, only occasionally picked out by the swirling lights. His head to one side, the rain runs down his face and falls from his hair. His hands hang limply at his sides, tiny droplets of water trickling from his fingertips. As his shoulders slump and his knees bend a little, he looks as if he could be dissolving in the pounding rain.

The sound of frantic barking snapped Munro back into life, and he made himself move toward the entrance of Bregje's office building.

'Esther?' he called up to the pathologist on the top step.

'Okay,' she replied. 'The rain has washed away anything we might get from the outside, but make sure you step directly onto the bottom step inside…and carry him out, please.'

Esther's tone was as professional as ever, but Munro could see the deep lines of tension in her face. Try as he might, he couldn't help looking down as he jumped on to the stairs. Esther's giant flashlight pointing into the stairwell blinding him at first, but then revealing the amount of blood on the floor.

So much blood. He paused, turning.

'Could she have survived this? Wherever she is…I mean, is there any…?

Esther's expression hardened. 'You don't have time for these questions.' she scolded, pointing him upstairs. And in that moment, he knew she was right. Protocol meant someone else would take over this enquiry, but what had happened here occurred only minutes ago, perhaps even as he and Remco had been running through the streets of Amsterdam, breathlessly calling for assistance on their mobile phones.

Whisky did not greet him with the wild abandon the high pitched yelping, which had increased in urgency as he climbed the stairs, had suggested. Instead, the dog backed away, then cowered toward him, ears pinned back and tail between his legs. Munro lowered himself onto his knees.

'No my boy, no. There's nothing you could have done.' As he spoke the words choked him, his body shaking as Whisky gently pushed his large white head into his chest.

The sudden sharp screech of a police siren sliced through his already frayed nerves. Feeling his knees creak as he straightened up and moved to the window, he watched in confusion as Esther's forensic van's doors were noisily slammed shut, and the vehicle driven off at speed. Another shrieking burst, and his eyes were drawn to Remco, one hand still inside one of the patrol cars working the siren, his sergeant's other hand was waving frantically up at him.

They were running again. The icy rain pounded down, obscuring dips and ankle-breaking upturned kerbs in deep puddles of inky rainwater and melted snow. Munro had handed Whisky over to the care of the still shocked young uniform, and told him to deliver the dog to The Doelen. Pausing only briefly as he turned to flee, he had called back.

'Don't worry. This wasn't your fault.'

'Elsje Christiaens,' Munro's legs were giving way. 'Elsje Christiaens.' he repeated, this time slurring the words. Remco's firm grip held him upright, and Munro tilted his head to the smaller man. 'You know who…?' Remco grunted his affirmation.

They had splashed their way from Bregje's office, along the Spui, across the Kalverstraat and on to the Rokin; Munro's routine journey transformed into the blackest of nightmares.

In the distance, across the broad street and on the far side of the wide canal, they could just make out a white figure strapped to a black mooring post. Two motorcycle cops and a patrol car were closing off both ends of the Oude Turfmarkt, the narrow street hemmed in on either side by the canal and the impressive frontage of the University's Allard Pierson Museum. Esther's white van and the ambulance, having just been let through, were coming to a halt by the occupied stanchion. Blindly, Munro stepped out into the Rokin, and by some miracle made it to the other side unscathed. Closer now, across the broken rain-spattered surface of the water, he could make out Bregje's short blonde hair.

She had been dressed in a long white smock that now sagged limply in the rain; the saturated cloth gathered untidily where ropes had been wound under her arms, binding her lifeless form to the post. At head height, sodden but still recognisable, several newspapers had been nailed into the wood.

Franck Baart had arrived, and was standing behind the two men.

'But I thought this was Bregje Van-' he began.

Remco interrupted, speaking quietly, and unusually calmly. 'Elsje Christiaens came from Jutland with nothing, and lasted exactly two weeks in Amsterdam. We don't know if her landlady on the Damrak tried to force her into prostitution, or just refused her credit. Either way, when the she started beating Elsje with a broom handle, Elsje turned on her, cracked her on the head with a hatchet causing her to fall downstairs. Whether it was the fall or the hatchet that did for the landlady? We don't know that either.'

Baart looked confused. 'When was this case? I have never-'

It was Munro's turn to interject. The sound of his own wavering voice disconnected, as if someone else were speaking. 'She was no older than eighteen years old in April 1664. The Aldermen's court ordered that she be garrotted on a pole, and then to be beaten upon the head several times by the hangman with the same hatchet she used on the woman. As was the custom, they left the body, with the weapon nailed on the post next to her as an example for others.'

Baart ran a hand over his wet hair, 'I still don't understand.'

Remco turned to him.

'The reason we know all this is because an old man by the name of Rembrandt Harmenszoon van Rijn was passing a couple of days after the execution and decided to make a sketch of the scene.'

'Two sketches,' corrected Munro, his voice breaking.

'And this,' Remco's arm reached out across the water. 'Is what he drew.'

Munro felt suddenly nauseous, bending over; he rested his head on the cold cast-iron railing lining the canal. Remco's hand came to rest on his back. With a voice like gravel, he rasped in Munro's ear.

'We should go, there is nothing for us to do here.'

As they stumbled past the end of the street and into the Grimburgwal, they watched Baart flash his ID and make his way towards Esther's van. Then, when they were almost out of earshot, Munro and Remco heard Esther's distinctive voice as it barked out his name, no doubt chastising the dashing Inspecteur for contaminating her crime scene with his expensive Italian footwear.

33

bollards

When they reached The Doelen, Martijn was stacking the chairs on the tables as Jean-Baptiste chased out the last of the evening's customers. One of the stragglers made to protest as the two detectives entered the bar unhindered, but was instantly cowed by the thunderous look on Munro's face.

'One for the ditch, gentlemen?' enquired Jean-Baptiste with a smile. 'You certainly look like you need it.' Remco placed a hand on the student's shoulder, his expression stopping him in his tracks. Not understanding why, Jean-Baptiste then helped Remco take four chairs back down and place them around a table by the window.

When Munro noticed another figure in the room, Martijn followed his gaze and waved dismissively toward the prone form stretched out along the bench on the back wall.

'Kapitein Hans,' he elucidated, with a weary shake of his curly locks. 'Pissed again, so we took his boat keys off him. Reckon he's rode his luck long enough for this week.' Martijn moving behind the bar, went on. 'Whisky is upstairs with Betty. It was weird; once he got here he wouldn't let her out of his sight. I'd imagine they're both asleep by now. So, as it looks like I'm in charge, what can I get you?'

'Four single malts,' ordered Munro, then more softly. 'Come and join us Martijn.'

Looking back at the single lit table in the darkened bar as he closed the door, Munro observed Martijn's hunched figure, a helplessly shocked looking Jean-Baptiste, arm around his friend's shoulders, and Remco. Whisky tumbler clutched tightly in his red fist, his sergeant's always animated face was now vacant as, glassy eyed, he gazed blindly at his own reflection in the rain streaked windowpane.

He had to leave. He had to think, to remember, to try and make some kind of sense of everything that had happened in the last twenty-four hours. Munro could also hear the whisky bottle calling to him, and he knew that wouldn't help. Not right now.

As he slowly climbed the stairs to his apartment, he tried to focus on the case, not Bregje, anything but Bregje. It had all been there, Hesselink's obsession with numbers, his interference in warning and preparing Predikant Kotmans' for their interview, and the skill in leaving absolutely no physical clues behind. As for the victims: all with criminal records, but with just the right number with links with the church to put them off the scent. Munro couldn't decide if that was a stroke of pure genius, or just dumb luck. He stopped, rubbing his fingers into his scalp in frustration. Even the fucking automatic bollards, and the van, the police van that Kapitein Hans had observed as he slipped past on the Oudezijds Voorbugwal.

Then, as he knew they would, the 'if only's began to surface. If only Esther had mentioned the name of the road traffic accident victim. If only Kotmans had told the truth at the interview. If only he hadn't decided to investigate the death of Gerrard/Doyle. Then maybe, who was he kidding, then *certainly* Bregje would still be alive. Perhaps it was the emotional turmoil, or maybe it was simply mental and physical exhaustion, but as he looked up at his front door, it took Munro a moment to register it was hanging open.

A moment too long.

The flash of a uniform, the swishing sound of a police baton. Munro, three steps lower than his assailant, had no time to raise a hand in defence.

Warm blood trickled down the back of his neck. He heaved, and in accompaniment to his own retching he heard the chair he was strapped to creak loudly in protest. Munro had nothing to throw up, which he quickly realised was a good thing, as the thick tape across his mouth would almost certainly have caused him to choke. He tried raising his head, the bedroom spun around before his eyes causing his stomach to lurch again. This time he felt his old wooden kitchen chair move beneath him.

'One hundred and forty-three seconds.' Johan Hesselink's calm tone filled his brain, his breath hot against his ear. Munro tried in vain to twist his head up and around to see the man standing behind him.

'You were wondering how long you had been unconscious, no?' The tall Commissaris, still in full uniform, moved slowly, coming to a halt directly in front of Munro. 'Now, when I remove the tape, there can be no shouting.' he warned. Bizarrely, his tone reminded Munro of a kindly schoolmaster. Two painfully solid taps of a police baton on the top of his head however, dispelled any illusions he may have had. The strip across his mouth was removed slowly and carefully; giving him a close look at Hesselink's pale, yet strangely calm face. The watery grey eyes focussed on the task, then, when the gag was removed, they moved on to his own.

Someone so close, staring into your eyes, should be very uncomfortable, and given the situation even more so now, thought Munro. But there was something separating the two men. It was as if a thin, yet unbreakable film had been placed between them. As Hesselink moved away, disappearing into the kitchen, it dawned on Munro that the disconnect had come from Hesselink himself. He was separated from reality, his consciousness was now in another place, and even his vision was altered. Johan Hesselink had his own actuality, and so disturbed was his mind Munro suspected that even the evidence of his own eyes backed it up.

For the few seconds Hesselink was out of sight, he tested the chair, feeling it move a little more. His arms pulled down at his sides, his wrists were attached to the back legs of the seat by what felt like the same kind of tape used for the gag. His ankles were strapped to the front legs, and it was there he could just about sense some give in the ancient joints.

His captor returned with the only other chair from the kitchen and placed it carefully opposite Munro. As he sat, Munro's eyes focussed on the door directly behind him, and noted that it remained slightly open, the lock having been damaged in the earlier forced entry. He tried to speak, but the sound came out as a rasping croak. Forcing a cough, he tried again, settling for a single word.

'Why?' he asked simply.

A scowl further creased Hesselink's already lined features.

'To save her. You of all people should understand that now.' he replied, fussing, pulling on his uniform tunic. Straightening the front before concentrating on the sleeves, then, satisfied, he settled into what sounded to Munro to be a long and rehearsed explanation.

'My wife did not die when that lorry collided with her bicycle. At first I believed her soul had risen, and as would have befitted her, she dwelt amongst the angels. This was the story Kotmans sold me, before I learned of the depravity of his sins, and more importantly, before I heard her voice. Imagine that. She spoke to me. At first I was elated; overjoyed she was still here, beside me.'

Hesselink leaned toward Munro, thin hands flattening themselves against his chest, his long tapered fingers spread wide and vibrating with emotion.

'Inside me!' he exclaimed breathlessly. There was a pause. The hands were lowered, the breathing brought under control, and Commissaris Johan Hesselink regained his composure.

Munro noted just how much effort it had taken.

Voice calm again, the madman's attempted rationalization continued. 'Over time though, I began to realise that just as Predikant Kotmans proved to be false, his church was also counterfeit.' Suddenly, Hesselink tilted back on his seat, smiled broadly, and waved a finger in the air. This abrupt alteration of mood appeared so startlingly unnatural to Munro, it caused him to involuntarily lean away from the man in his own chair.

'What do you know of the Great Schism, Inspector?' he asked abruptly.

Caught off-guard by the seemingly arbitrary nature of the question, Munro thought for a moment, trying to recall his childhood Sundays in the painfully protestant Outer Hebrides.

'The Reformation; ecclesiastical differences; theological disputes. The Pope's claim to universal jurisdiction, of course…' He was surprised just how much he could remember.

'Excellent!' Hesselink clasped his hands together. 'I

knew you were the one.'

The phrase sent a shockwave through Munro.

'What do you mean?'

'How can you doubt it? By God's divine hand you made yourself known to me.' Hesselink beamed, as he continued his questioning. 'And what else? What other major sticking point was there in the Great Schism between East and West?'

Munro hung his head. He was so tired; he just wanted to give up. Bregje was gone; let this crazy bastard do his worst. He was about to tell Hesselink to fuck off, when the notion jumped into his head. Without thinking he said it out loud.

'The existence of Purgatory?'

'Exactly.' Hesselink's reply was not triumphant this time, but delivered with a despondent shake of the head. Yet another monumental mood swing to discomfit Munro.

'Purgatory.' The voice had become a whisper. 'That is where my love is. It is the only explanation. The woman who saved me is being held back from entering heaven because of my sins.'

Munro wanted to ask just how killing other women helped her case, but bided his time, gently pushing his chair back and forth as subtly as he could.

'The living can help those whose purification from their sins is not yet completed, not only through prayer, but also by gaining indulgences for them as an act of intercession.'

Munro kept his voice low. 'You indulge in murder.'

This time a tired smile accompanied Hesselink's calm reply. 'I don't expect you to understand, that is not why you are here. It is your mission to explain why I have done these things to those who will follow.'

Munro raised his head, his face a mask of puzzled exasperation.

Hesselink met his gaze. 'I have removed sinners from this Earth, sent them straight to Hell. The specific number of sinners and the times of their sacrifice have been ordained by God himself.'

'Oh, does he speak to you too?' Munro jibed.

'Not at all,' replied Hesselink unfazed. 'His will is made clear to me in a myriad of ways. His plan, His mathematical glory shines as the most obvious constellation in a night sky.'

'And how many women does this plan require you to kill before your wife is set free?' sneered Munro, past caring about the consequences.

'The same number as the Lord's disciples,' answered Hesselink matter-of-factly. Then, as if indulging a simple child, he went on. 'That wasn't the important part; it was the dates that really mattered, the prime numbers, and the alignments that lead me to this day.'

Munro forced his mind to work, to sift through the dates and deaths they had established were the work of this Holy Man.

'You are finished.' he stated abruptly.

Hesselink raised an eyebrow.

'Twelve,' Munro went on. 'You have killed twelve women, the number of disciples, and now what? Your wife ascends to heaven, and you…where do you go Johan?' As Munro had suspected, the use of Hesselink's first name rattled him. Somewhere inside the twisted mind of this particular serial killer, there remained a small corner office, within which, there resided that part of him that continued as an officious pencil-pusher. Munro pressed on.

'The Holy Trinity,' he let out a short laugh. 'You've got it Johan. You have them all.'

Hesselink's expression darkened.

'Do not make jokes with God.' he warned.

'I'm not,' spat Munro. 'Let me count them off for

you. One: Bi-polar, that's where all the manic stuff comes from, like seeing all those crazy connections. Two: Schizophrenia, that'll be the voices. And three? You, Johan, are a nine carat, dyed-in-the-wool, one hundred-fucking-percent, psychopath.'

It worked. Munro needed him standing, and the moment Hesselink leapt up, the force of his sudden angry action tipping his chair to the side, Munro made his move. Straining every sinew he exploded upwards, and, as he'd hoped, the front legs of his own chair splintered and came away from the base. On his feet now, he had no time to curse the fact his hands had remained secure as, bent awkwardly, he charged.

34

hope

Smashing the heavy door against the railing, the two men sailed through the air and landed heavily on the stairs in an untidy rolling tangle of arms, legs and splintered wood. Quickly realising he now had one hand free, Munro raised his arm and brought it, and the partially broken piece of chair leg attached, down on to his assailant's face. Hesselink immediately brought his knees up and pushed. Head over heels, Munro tumbled the last three steps down to the half-landing. A stinging and instantly debilitating pain shot across his shoulders.

'Everyone forgets,' snorted Hesselink, as he lifted Munro off the floor by his shirtfront. The neat Commissaris was unrecognisable. Thin strands of hair in disarray, nose bloodied and broken, he paused to spit blood, and what appeared to be white shards of broken teeth aside, before hauling the still dazed Munro to the top of the next flight of stairs.

'Everyone!' he barked, kicking the barely conscious body off the top step. Munro was drowning, spinning down into a black whirlpool. A sharp slap brought him round. More spinning.

'Do you hear me?' Hesselink bellowed into his face.

'They all forget!'

Just at that moment a door on the first floor landing swung open, and a shrill female voice called out from inside. 'I am calling the Police!' The door slammed shut again.

Hesselink's shoulders slumped at first, and then after sucking in a whistling breath, he began to shake.

'Did you…did you hear tha…? Laughter wheezed out of him in an almost girlishly high tone. In spite of everything, or more likely because of it all, Munro could feel his own hysteria rising and felt his ribs ache in protest at the beginnings of a sob.

They sat together in silence for a few moments. Hesselink composing himself. Munro trying to pull the pieces of himself together. Suddenly, at the sound of a distant siren, Hesselink slapped him hard on the back.

'Thirteen, Chief Inspector Munro. Everyone forgets, there were thirteen.' With that, he got to his feet, clipped easily down the final stairwell and out of the door into the street.

'How many?' asked Remco.

'Three, I think,' replied Munro

'He threw you down three flights of those stairs and you don't think you might need a scan, or maybe even just an x-ray?' Esther Van Til protested, as she cleaned him up with her kit from the van and a basin of hot soapy water supplied by Martijn from The Doelen's kitchen.

Munro shook his head, which was a painful mistake. He had somehow dragged his battered body to the bar, just arriving as Esther's forensic van had pulled up outside. She had come with news.

Amazing news.

Bregje was alive.

Munro spurned all offers of assistance until he'd

heard the facts. Patiently, Esther tried to explain something she couldn't really believe herself.

'The first thrust with the knife missed her heart, punctured her lung, but missed her heart. Her leg and two ribs are broken, as per his MO, but the blow to the head? Maybe he was distracted, or Bregje managed to move at the last second, we may never know. She has a fractured skull and even if she recovers it's unlikely she will ever remember.'

Into the stunned silence that met her words, Esther Van Joeren poured more wonder.

'Here's the thing,' she held her hands up, eyes wide in amazement. 'The way he tied her up to that post meant her lungs didn't fill with blood the way they would've had she been left prone. Also, by keeping her upright he reduced the blood pressure on the brain from the fractured skull.'

Munro began to speak, but the Professor wasn't finished and cut him off.

'Add to that, the rapid cooling of the freezing rain slowing her metabolism, my arrival on the scene so quickly…so many factors, which…' she stopped then, and looked at Munro directly. 'May still mean nothing at all. The blood loss is beyond borderline, and they will keep her in an induced coma until the swelling on her brain recedes.'

He had no idea where it was coming from, but Munro felt a warm flow of energy feed back into his shattered system. Bregje was alive. There was hope. When he spoke, it was with purpose.

'He's not finished.' He went on to relay his conversation with Hesselink. This was turning out to be a night for stunned silences.

'Judas,' stated Esther flatly. 'The thirteenth disciple.'

'And the thirteenth victim,' added Remco.

'Has to be a woman,'

'With a criminal record?'

Munro chipped in. 'Not necessarily. He selected Bregje much later. It has become more personal. This feels more…important?'

Esther spoke quickly as she pulled out her phone. 'Then what do we know of his history? Stands to reason a psychopath like this would have exhibited some anti-social, aggressive or violent behaviour in the past.'

'Obviously nothing has come to light since he became a policeman,' observed Munro.

'And if criminal behaviour had been recorded while he was a minor it would have been expunged by now.' Remco's tone conveyed his personal view of such liberal procedures.

'Criminal records, yes,' grinned Esther. 'But medical and social records, that's another matter. Bregje said he was a Mokum boy too, didn't she?'

She dialled her assistant, and twenty minutes later Michael arrived with his laptop.

'I saved the whole medical and psychological file in here,' he said, looking exhausted. 'You're lucky, those years were all digitised and put on the system for research students last August.'

Remco tutted petulantly, 'Nice to know all my personal information's floating around out there as well.'

Michael replied with an easy smile. 'Not at all, it's quite secure. The names are kept in a separate file and can only be matched with a special code.'

Remco pointed a stubby finger.

'A code you have.' he said.

'A code the Pathology Department have,' stated Esther firmly. 'Don't worry Remco, I'll make sure you're really dead before we go looking to find out who you really were.'

35

sea legs

'This is textbook.' Esther tied her hair back as she read. 'Abusive father, extreme aggression, lack of empathy…'

'How the Hell did he become a cop?' quizzed Remco reasonably.

'The aberrant behaviour all ended when he was around fifteen. Incredible.' Esther looked genuinely nonplussed.

'That'll be around the time he met his future wife.' sighed Munro, biting his lip. Nothing about this whole thing could be tagged as typical. He drove on. 'Listen, if any of this information is to be of any use we need to find a likely ' Judas', otherwise it's all too late…again.'

'The father?' Martijn had been sitting a little way from the table, and the sound of his voice over Munro's shoulder gave him a start.

'Already deceased. Heart attack twenty years ago…but,' Esther jabbed at the keyboard. 'There is a red flag here from a psychologist who attended a panel meeting with young Johan. She claims a Predikant attending the meeting irresponsibly exacerbated the boys already strong sense of betrayal by his…his mother.'

Munro grasped the straws in front of him.

'His mother? She must be pretty old if she's still alive?'

'You would think so wouldn't you, but actually…?' Esther swung the laptop around to face Munro. He scanned down the page.

'Fuck.' he said finally.

'What?' barked Remco, reaching the end of his infamously short patience.

Esther looked up at him. 'Johan Hesselink's mother had just reached the age of fourteen when she gave birth.'

A hat trick of stunned silences, thought Munro. *Someone should get a prize.*

'So, is she still alive?' Martijn again, and silently Munro thanked him for keeping their overwrought and exhausted minds moving.

Esther smiled. 'I don't know, but I do have her full name and date of birth?'

'I'm on it.' snapped Remco, pulling his phone out of his pocket and hitting speed-dial for the information section at Police Headquarters.

Munro winced as he pulled on the jumper Jean-Baptiste had fetched for him from his apartment.

'That apartment is a mess,' the neat law student stated sympathetically when he arrived back. 'I'm afraid he really did a number on the place.'

'Actually, he only damaged the door,' replied Munro, deliberately ignoring Esther's smirk.

'Oh, okay,' came the flat reply. 'I'll just…eh, just go and get Hans a coffee.'

Esther's face straightened.

'You think we're too late.'

It was a statement, not a question.

'He's had access to the same information we have, if it was his mother he was looking for, there would be nothing to stop him going straight there after leaving me.'

'Actually, there might be.' Remco stood over the table, trusty notebook in hand.

Munro looked up, 'You have a current address?'

'I do, she has a houseboat on the Westerdok, but I also know she isn't at home right now.' Expertly, Remco single handedly flipped over a page. 'Sanne Pietersen is the night warden at a women's refuge by the Westerpark. The exact address of the refuge is protected by court order.'

Munro hauled himself to his feet.

'When does she get off work?' he asked.

'They usually change shifts at around six in those places.'

'And what time is it now?' He rubbed his wrist where his watch used to be, and wondered briefly if it was still in his apartment, or lying smashed beneath a stairwell.

'Just after four.'

'Let's go.'

Esther frowned. 'You think he's waiting at her home?'

'If she is his Judas, then I would bet on it.'

'Wait!' Remco barred the door. 'There's a ton of demolition work going on at the Westerdok at the moment, and only one road in and out. If he is there, he's going to see us coming a mile off.'

Esther laid her hand on Remco's shoulder. 'So, you don't think we should tell Franck Baart?'

'Absolutely not.'

'My van is unmarked, we could…'

Munro interrupted, 'I think what Remco's saying is that any traffic up there at this time of the morning would be pretty conspicuous.'

'So, what do you…?' Esther's voice trailed off as she followed Munro's, Remco's and Martijn's gaze toward a small figure in the corner nursing a warm coffee cup in both hands.

Kapitein Hans looked up.

'What do you lot want?' he enquired uneasily.

'So you're saying I can't get arrested?' Hans had his grubby grey-white cap on at its usual jaunty angle and was looking up at Munro with a mischievous grin.

'You can tell them I ordered you to take us,' Munro assured him, then quickly grabbed for a handrail as the small motorboat tilted alarmingly at Remco's clumsy attempt at boarding. The mooring rope was then thrown on to the deck, followed nimbly by Martijn.

'Where do you think you're going?' snapped Munro.

The boyish face looked determined. 'You're going to sneak up on this guy and creep ashore in silence are you? I've just witnessed Remco's athleticism, and your sea legs don't look too steady either. Don't worry, I'll just help you come alongside and tie up…I want to help.'

Munro could see no point in arguing.

'Alright, just be…'

At that moment, Kapitein Hans pulled the throttle back and it was all he could do to stay upright by gripping the forward rail with both hands. Remco and Martijn were less fortunate, collapsing on to the deck in a shadowy muddle of arms and legs.

'Take it easy,' Munro shouted above the engine noise. 'Just because you won't get nicked, doesn't mean we want to get stopped on the way.'

Hans winked his acknowledgement.

The rest of the short journey was uneventful, but strangely beautiful. The rain had all but stopped and a calm silence had descended. Above their heads, tall seventeenth century buildings loomed darkly, peering down at their own angular reflections. Another moment in the city he loved; time shifting like the constantly drifting sand under the brick red, herringbone streets.

The lowering tone of the engine signalled they were nearing their destination. Hans leaned his head toward him.

'The houseboats are around the next bend, what do you want me to do?'

Munro thought for a second.

'Can you cut the lights and the engine and drift through?'

'If I time it right, sure,' Hans replied with a shrug.

Just as you did that night on the Oudezijds Voorburgwal, and countless other nights when you've spotted the police, thought Munro.

They entered the Westerdok in complete silence, and Munro could see Remco's point. Even from their low angle, his eye-line only just above the height of the bank, Munro could see the area had been almost completely cleared. Good-sized piles of rubble stood sentry, interspersed by tall metal poles. The powerful lights attached three quarters of the way up were angled downwards, providing cold and clearly defined illumination on the unnaturally flat wilderness below. All too soon, their view of the former warehousing dock was obscured by the first of the houseboats.

'Do we know which one is Hesselink's mother's?' whispered Munro.

Remco raised his hands, 'No idea. They have names, not numbers.'

They coasted on, black hulls rolling by in the darkness. After a minute or so, they could see the end of the wharf and the widening expanse of the IJ estuary.

'I can come around here without the engine if you like?' volunteered Hans. 'The tides coming in and the current will push us toward the corner.'

Munro was already nodding his agreement, when a

tiny movement in the shadows ahead caught his eye. Remco's firm grip on his arm confirmed he had spotted it too. As they drifted closer to the bank, the shape began to take on definition. Finally, as they turned the bend the temporary lighting on the demolition site outlined an unmistakable form. The peaked policeman's hat pushed back on his head, Commissaris Johan Hesselink sat on one of three large concrete breezeblocks blocking the entrance road to the dock. The movement they had observed had been his left hand, impatiently tapping on his knee.

Using hand signals, Munro directed Hans to pull the boat in a further fifty metres around the wharf. A small mountain of uneven bricks provided the cover they needed to disembark as Martijn, true to his word, silently clambered on to the bank and tied up the boat. Munro envied him the balance and confidence he had obviously gained from a lifetime mucking around on the water. Keeping his voice as low as he could, Munro looked from Martijn to Hans.

'You two wait here. Hans, do you have a phone?' he asked.

The little man shook his head, and when Munro turned back to Martijn, the lad shrugged.

'I must have left it at the bar.' he admitted sheepishly.

Munro fished his own mobile out of his pocket and handed it to Hans.

'Take this, if we're not back in ten minutes, call the police and tell them Commissaris Hesselink is here. Then get out of Dodge.'

Hans looked puzzled.

Munro placed a hand on his shoulder and looked him in the eye to make sure he got the message.

'I mean, turn on the engine and get out of here as fast as you can. This guy is very dangerous.'

36

dark star

They picked their way around the edge of the rubble as quietly as they could, doing their best to stick to the shadows on the opposite side of the nearest light source. Unfortunately, as Munro had feared, there was going to be another thirty-five metres of open ground between them and their target. By his calculations Hesselink should be facing in the other direction, but it was still a long way. Peering into the darkness, he began to signal Remco he should take out his gun, when something made him stop. Not something; his mind raced; a lack of something. Hesselink.

It was hard to make out, the contrast between the white of the breezeblocks and the almost impenetrable black of open water, meant it took Munro a few seconds to realise Hesselink had gone.

'You are incredibly resourceful.'

The disembodied voice came from a ragged area of pitch-blackness around ten metres to their left. If he had been less tired, if his body didn't feel like it had been through a tumble drier, or if his head hadn't been splitting from the combination of extreme prolonged stress and repeated blows with a police baton, then perhaps Munro would have reacted differently. As it was, he let out a long sigh.

'For fuck's sake Johan. Give it up, it's over.' he said wearily. Noting as he did, Remco's fumbling hand flap against an empty holster on his hip.

He almost laughed.

'For you I'm afraid,' replied Hesselink with a sigh of his own. Stepping out of the darkness, his face bloodied and swollen, the skeletal figure raised his service weapon. His arm straight, the muzzle was pointed directly at Munro's sternum.

The shot was deafening, the sharp report bouncing off the buildings on the opposite side of the canal before echoing across the wasteland of the empty building site. Munro lurched back, his hands involuntarily clutching at his chest. Then he stopped. Peering down in the dim light, he gazed at his torso, and at his impossibly dry hands. Absently, he began rubbing his thumbs and fingertips together.

'Fucking Hell!'

Remco's outburst jump-started his brain. Looking ahead, Munro could see the light brown sole of a shoe, the foot held in the air by a small pile of broken bricks. The only other part of Johan Hesselink's body visible in the gloom behind a low, uneven wall of rubble, was his left forearm. Pointing up, wrist limp, and pale hand twisted inward. Munro then turned toward Remco, and watched in disbelief as the little man stepped aside to reveal another figure. Remco's regulation Glock, thick and black in his hand, the smoke from the muzzle merging with his shuddering breath in the cold air, Martijn stood stock-still.

'That was for Bregje,' he rasped.

Remco reacted immediately. Reaching over, he pulled the gun from the young man's hand. Then, facing Munro, he pointed the gun into the air and called out.

'Boss?

Understanding immediately, Munro agreed.

'Do it,' he replied.

Remco fired the shot into the air, and without missing a beat, grabbed Martijn's collar. Dragging the young man back toward the boat, he bellowed orders into his ear.

'You get back to Hans, and you both fuck off as fast as you can. When you're clear…' he bent down and picked up a half brick, shoving it into Martijn's pocket. 'You dump this coat into the canal. Then you go home and have a long hot shower, and make sure you scrub that arm with soap until it's raw.'

'But…' began Martijn.

'But nothing,' interrupted Remco. 'You sit tight until I call you tomorrow morning. Got that?'

Not moving, Martijn looked back at him blankly. Remco clouted him around the head twice with an open hand.

'I asked you a question,' he barked. 'Have you got that?'

The thumps seemed to do the trick, and Martijn staggered off in the direction of Hans' boat.

A guttering cough sounded from the darkness. Munro moved over to Hesselink's prone form and was shocked to see the pale grey eyes glitter in the half-light. He knelt quickly. The battering his body had taken almost causing him to topple over. Regaining his balance he looked for somewhere to place his hand, some way he could try and stem the bleeding, but Hesselink's life was pulsing from his chest at an inexorably lethal rate. Another wet cough. Then, with surprising strength, a tremulous hand grabbed Munro's sleeve.

'Was it…?' The voice was impossibly hoarse.

Munro leaned forward, bending his head to the side

to hear.

'Was it enough?' asked Johan Hesselink.

Munro's first impulse screamed at him to shout out, 'No, of course it wasn't, you lunatic. You killed all those women for nothing.' But something stopped him. No, not something. Someone.

Bregje.

The way his world had collapsed when he caught sight of her limp body across the rain-dimpled waters of the canal. As if his very soul had become the densest, blackest, heaviest dark star in the universe.

The way it had changed him.

'Yes,' he whispered into the dying man's ear. 'I think it was enough.'

'Then she is saved, and now I…' the pinpoints of light in Hesselink's eyes seemed to dull as a shadow of a smile shaped his thin lips. 'And you must understand this Chief Inspector…I go straight to Hell.'

Monday

24th December

37

smell a mouse

It was clear to Munro that Esther could, in Glasgow parlance, 'smell a mouse'.

She knew something didn't quite add up.

Their accounts of Hesselink's demise, of Remco's warning shot, of their valiant efforts in trying to dissuade a cold-blooded serial killer to drop his weapon before being forced into a final, regrettable, and fatal action. Witnesses had come forward to confirm they were disturbed in the night by two clearly distinct shots, and Remco's gunshot residue test had come through as expected. Not as much residue as you would expect for two shots, but by Remco's own admission, he had tripped on one of the many bricks lying around and may have used that arm on the wet ground to get up. Still, Munro could see a shadow of doubt in her eyes as she summarised her report for Hoofdcommissaris Uylenburg.

The old man sighed as he dropped the report on top of an alarmingly tall pile of identical manila folders situated perilously near the edge of his desk. The stack teetered, but remained upright.

'Here is what happens next,' he began in his usual direct manner. 'Hesselink is confirmed as the murderer of Jitske Bolthof and Ali Absullah, and the attempted murder of Bregje Van Til. We'll give the press everything on those cases, and those cases only.'

Munro had already figured as much when he'd noticed it was only himself and Esther invited to attend this morning's meeting.

'And the other victims?' asked Esther.

Munro saved Uylenburg the bother of replying, 'No physical evidence, you said so yourself.'

He could see Esther wasn't happy, but he could also see she had known where the meeting was headed before entering the room. The query had been made for the sake of her own professional integrity. She gave it one last try.

'What about the trophies from the farm building in Winterswijk?'

Uylenburg frowned sympathetically, 'Hesselink had access to almost all of the mortuaries the victims ended up in. Picking up items from there may have been both disturbing and illegal, but not proof of murder.'

At that, Esther gave up, as she had known she would.

Munro abruptly changed the subject, 'Actually Esther, We have a question for you. It concerns a fellow you had in your care by the name of John Patrick Gerrard…'

It was only four in the afternoon, and already Munro felt it had been a long day. If anything his body had stiffened up in the four days since his battering at the hands of Johan Hesselink. The bruises on his ribs, hips and legs had exploded into a myriad of colours, something noticed by Esther as she had checked on his progress immediately after the morning meeting.

'Looks like you've been run over by a paint truck,' she had quipped, utilising the bedside manner that ensured her a permanent place among the deceased.

He shouldn't complain though, he thought. He had been driven around all day by one of the most senior policeman in the country.

Their first port of call had taken just under an hour and a half to reach. The town of Vught in North Brabant was pretty enough, until you reached the high fences and concrete walls of Nieuw Vosseveld High Security Prison. Terrible things happened in Vught during the war, with the transit camp originally built to house Jews and dissidents on their way to concentration camps in Poland, itself becoming a final destination.

Bad things still happened in Vught, observed Munro, as he stood by Youssef Absullah's bed in the prison hospital. The young doctor's eyes had a yellowish tinge, and an ashen hue coloured his, once smooth, olive skin. Munro assumed the makeshift knife must have damaged his liver, or kidneys…or both. When Youssef spoke, it was with a voice as brittle as spring ice.

'They are transferring me to a better-equipped hospital in the prison at Scheveningen tomorrow. Be nice to visit the seaside.' The attempt at a smile quickly turned into a grimace, and Munro felt an almost overwhelming sadness wash over him. He had spent a lot of time in hospital over the last four days. He also knew the prison at Scheveningen wouldn't have the security levels Vosseveld had. Levels that had failed.

'We need to talk.' he said simply.

'Yes,' replied Youssef. 'Before it's too late.'

Munro nodded, deciding Youssef Absullah's courage deserved honesty.

'Tell me first about Ali, then fill me in on John Patrick Gerrard…'

'What's going to happen to Remco?' asked Munro.

Hoofdcommissaris Hendrik Uylenburg shifted in his

seat. It had taken another hour and a half to get from Vught to Wassenaar on the outskirts of Den Haag, and the traffic had done nothing to brighten his spirits. 'He has two months obligatory leave, during which he'll have several sessions with the psychiatrist. After that, provided he gets the all clear, he'll come back to work.'

'With me?'

'If the stunt we're about to pull comes off, I'll bump him up to Inspecteur for the second time in his career, and he'll join you, yes.' Uylenburg lifted his eyebrows. 'He does get under your skin, doesn't he, the little bastard?'

'You two go back,' stated Munro.

'We started together,' replied the older man, a smile creasing his weathered visage. 'Fearless he was, fucking fearless.' A shake of the head and a pursing of the lips told Munro he was getting no more than that.

They drove in silence for the rest of the journey, Munro reminding himself to ask Remco about his relationship with the boss, and also to tell him that under no circumstances was he to assault the psychiatrist.

The sun had set, and the car park of the Kasteel de Wittenburg was, in contrast to Munro's last visit, virtually empty. Nadine Rahman met them at the entrance.

'This way please, gentlemen,' she said, with a sub-zero smile that didn't come close to reaching her eyes. As they followed her through the internal doors and along the grandly vaulted corridor, Munro could have sworn he heard Uylenburg tutting.

McFarlane came around his desk as they entered the room and greeted them both so warmly, Munro wondered briefly if he'd had a little too much Christmas cheer for lunch. A notion instantly dispelled when, as Hoofdcommissaris Uylenburg turned to sit, Munro was skewered by a poisonous glare.

'I hope you don't mind if we make this brief,' began McFarlane with an ingratiating grimace. 'It's just that, you know, Christmas Eve and all that, I'm heading for home to see the grandchildren.'

Uylenburg raised his hands.

'Shouldn't take long,' he said, his own demeanour, in contrast to McFarlane's, becoming decidedly chillier. 'I would very much appreciate it if your secretary would join us.'

Sir James looked flustered.

'Nadine?' he enquired, obviously off-balance.

'Nadine Rahman, yes,' replied Uylenburg.

Frowning, McFarlane pressed a button on his telephone and requested his secretary's presence. Nadine came in, looking decidedly wary.

Taking control, it was Uylenburg who spoke first.

'Please, Ms Rahman, take a seat.'

Munro stood up.

'Here, have mine,' he offered.

A look passed between Nadine Rahman and Sir James McFarlane as she lowered herself into the chair. A look that warmed Munro to his toes.

'Sitting comfortably?' he enquired rhetorically. 'Then I'll begin.'

'Look here!' blurted McFarlane, but Uylenburg silenced him with a forefinger raised to his lips.

'I suggest you just listen for now,' he said somberly.

Munro gave him the briefest of smiles, then started.

'They weren't terrorists, John Patrick Gerrard wasn't John Patrick Gerrard, and you Ms Rahman, are not a secretary. Let's take these three statements in reverse order.' Munro briefly glanced over at McFarlane. 'Some time ago, I asked a very well informed friend about your secretary Sir James. Nadine Rahman: a Dubliner, originally from a pretty dodgy estate on the North Side, but escaped. Educated at Trinity, where she received a first in Languages. Then a move to the dreaming spires of Oxford and another first class degree in Economics. I mean really, she is a smart one. Doesn't mean she can't be a secretary of course. I'm all for education for education's sake, but I'm forgetting something, oh that's right, the jobs she had before this one. First a spell at the Government Communications Headquarters in Cheltenham followed by a move to London. Strange that she should give a promising career like that up to become a run-of-the-mill secretary…spooky even.'

Nadine Rahman had folded her arms and was staring fixedly at the edge of McFarlane's desk.

Oh dear,' Munro ground on, turning to her. 'Don't tell me this was your first field op? Messy, very messy. In theory I guess it kind of made sense. North Africans running ecstasy into The Netherlands and sending the profits home. I mean, to fund terrorism, why else right? But you needed to get in on the deal, someone inside. Which brings me to Gerrard, or should I say, to small time drug dealer and former informer for the security services: John Patrick Doyle. You sling him in there, he's already known on the scene in Manchester, so you arrange a meet with a middle man in Amsterdam. Throw in a shed-load of money to start making deliveries to the UK, and you're very much in business. Better still, I imagine after the first shipment the operation was paying for itself. You see, that Economics degree wasn't wasted after all. How am I doing?' Munro tilted his head and eyed Nadine Rahman. No reaction.

'Okay, I was kind of hoping you'd want to stop me there, you know, before it gets ugly,' he sighed. Noting, as he spoke, that Uylenburg had fixed McFarlane with a long, cold stare. So far, so good.

'This is where it all goes wrong. Youssef Absullah is a smart guy, and senses something is wrong. You made it all too easy, the price was too good, your operation was too smooth, and it unnerved him. He decides to end your agreement, but when Kwaaie Ali gives your boy Doyle his marching orders, Doyle goes nuts. This deal has been the best thing to happen to him in his miserable drug dealing life. He causes a scene right outside the Sexy Castle Peepshow, in front of countless witnesses. This is not good, it compromises the whole set-up. Luckily, one of your goons drags Doyle away before he can be arrested, and quite possibly, blow the whole thing wide open.'

Munro paused, arranging the facts in his mind before going on. McFarlane grasped the opportunity, and attempted to fill the silence.

'This is supposition, you have absolutely no evidence that any of this took place,' he bridled.

Surprising everyone in the room, it was Nadine Rahman who spoke next.

'He doesn't need it,' she said flatly. 'He has me.'

'Please,' interjected Uylenburg. 'Chief Inspector Munro has not yet finished.'

Accepting the wily Hoofdcommissaris' request for more ammunition, Munro bowed briefly,

'Thank you, Sir. As I said, things had taken a turn for the worse, and so you did what anyone would do. You pulled the plug. A tip off to the Water Police gets the last shipment picked up. Not to Customs, they would have asked way too many questions. That, I must say, is neatly done. You have compartmentalised the operation well. No one on the ship knows anything other than the name of the person receiving the delivery in the UK, and that person only knows the name of the dealer he's passing the goods on to. One John Patrick Gerrard, a character you created: passport, driving licence and all. A fellow who didn't exist. Except, of course, he did. Doyle was by now, not only a loose cannon; he's also a loose end. Worse still, he'd gone missing. I have to admit, the thought did cross my mind that you'd dealt with the situation in the old fashioned way, but I just couldn't square that with the rest of the op. Sure, Doyle had a minder, but the security services don't just up and kill someone on foreign soil. The potential blowback would far outweigh the reward. That, and I assume you Nadine were the girlfriend who reported his absence. Hoping they would contact you first if he turned up, giving you a head start on clearing up this mess. Then I wondered what you thought when he did surface, literally in this case. I can only imagine the rising sense of panic; this thing really had spun out of control. Next step? Damage limitation. Get the body out before it can be identified.'

Munro crouched down, so his face was level with Nadine Rahman's.

'In case you were wondering, or even care,' he said quietly. 'Professor Van Joeren managed a quick examination of Doyle before your guys whisked him away. There were no head injuries, the water in his lungs was consistent with drowning, and his knob was hanging out. Well, what was left of it after the fish had had a go. Basically, he fell in the canal whilst taking a piss. Drunk or stoned probably, she didn't get the chance to run his bloods.' He straightened up again and addressed the room. 'Don't know about you lot, but I fucking hate coincidences.'

'Actually,' said Uylenburg calmly. 'I fucking hate the fact that the head of Interpol and Europol has a completely unsanctioned British Security Officer at the heart of its operations.'

With frightening ease, Sir James McFarlane sloughed off his blustering exterior, transforming his demeanour into one of cold efficiency.

'What do you want?' he asked.

Uylenburg said nothing, silently turning his head toward Nadine Rahman. McFarlane nodded.

'You may leave us now, Ms Rahman.' he said.

The dismissal had an air of finality about it, and Munro caught a fleeting look of disgust on her face as Nadine left the room. Uylenburg waited patiently until the door was firmly closed before speaking.

'It will be called the Secondary Unit,' he began without ceremony. 'A hand-picked group of officers dedicated to investigating cases that have either floundered, or, for whatever reason, have hit a wall. They will start these investigations as if the crime has just occurred, except of course, they shall have immediate access to all of the forensic and intelligence information already gathered.'

McFarlane frowned. 'I can only imagine such a Unit would be extremely unpopular within your force,' he observed.

'Not your problem,' stated Uylenburg bluntly.

'So what is my problem?' asked McFarlane, taking the hint.

'Funding. I can't get it through the normal channels, so I was wondering if Europol would like to sponsor an open ended experiment?'

Sir James McFarlane closed his eyes for a moment.

'And who would head up this Secondary Unit?' he enquired wearily.

'I suggest we transfer Chief Inspector Munro here to a permanent place in the Amsterdam Force.'

McFarlane was skeptical. 'You can swing that?'

'I can if you're paying his wages,' beamed Uylenburg, scenting victory.

Pushing open the heavy wooden doors, Munro was surprised to see Nadine Rahman waiting at the bottom of the stone steps leading down to the car park. She looked up at Munro, and then turned to walk towards a black, cast-iron bench several metres away.

'I'll meet you at the car,' said Uylenburg.

Taking a seat next to her, Munro felt the chill of the cold metal seep through his clothes.

'You've got one thing wrong,' she began, without looking at him. 'This wasn't my operation. McFarlane and I knew nothing about this whole mess until they called us.'

'After it had all gone tits up?'

Rahman nodded. 'We were just the cleaners.'

'Who are 'they'?'

'That's the point. Someone in London set this up, and not just this. There's stuff going on all over Europe right now that doesn't make sense to me. Operations that must have been sanctioned from on high, yet…' her voice trailed off as she shook her head. Munro turned to face her.

'Why are you telling me this?' he asked.

'There is someone in Amsterdam, someone who doesn't just work for them, but matters very much. Let me ask you a question.' Nadine Rahman met his gaze, her startlingly beautiful eyes narrowing slightly. 'Do you think Johan Hesselink killed Ali Absullah?'

Munro looked away before speaking.

'We have a witness who claims they saw a different man leave the peepshow at around the time of the murders. I also think it was that same man who called Youssef Absullah and told him Derk Merel had murdered Ali.'

'I suggest you don't tell anyone else that.' Getting to her feet, Rahman then turned back to Munro. 'Not yet,' she added, with a hint of determination.

'No.' agreed Munro, standing slowly with the help of the arm of the bench.

Nadine Rahman tilted her head and gave him a

sympathetic look.

'One more thing before you go.' she said. 'The third thing. How do you know for certain the Absullahs weren't terrorists?'

'Well,' Munro smiled gently. 'They weren't brothers; that was just a cover.'

'For what?'

'They were lovers Nadine. More than that, they had been together for years. An unlikely arrangement for a couple of fundamentalist terrorists, I'm sure you agree.'

'And the money?'

'A little went into buying the chemicals and the production of the ecstasy, the rest all went into the medical centre.'

Surprising Munro, Nadine let out a short laugh.

'This fucking country!' she yelled with her head upturned.

'Tell me about it,' sighed Munro.

38

souls

Framed within the large window separating the nurse's station from the hospital room, the scene within appears frozen in time.

A bank of machinery. Bregje's still form, her shaven head marked by a clearly defined fresh scar with the smooth contours of a sine wave, eyelids taped closed with slivers of white tape. From the side of her mouth, one thin, and one thicker tube emerge and lead out of sight on the other side of the bed. Her arms lie above the sheets, a clear tube connects the left to a drip on the nearside of the room. Her figure, unnaturally aligned, lies at a horizontal attention.

By her side in this colour-washed scene, a young man sits hunched in a plastic chair. As he speaks, tears are running down his face. Munro cannot hear his words, the room is soundproof.

What he can hear is the regular high-pitched ping of the life support apparatus. A nurse, one he has seen many times in the last few days, bends to check on the display, and then looks up at him.

'We were worried about you,' she says with a smile.

It took a second for Munro to snap back into the moment.

'Sorry?' he asked, with a start.

'You didn't turn up this morning, we were worried something had happened to you,' the nurse explained.

Munro rubbed his eyes with the heels of his hands. He had spent most of the last four days camped out in Bregje's room, only returning home to shower, change, and catch a few hours of guilty, fitful sleep before returning, and was, he admitted to himself, felling pretty spaced-out.

'Work,' he said simply.

The nurse nodded, understanding.

When Martijn left the room, he met Munro's sympathetic look with a nervous smile.

'I'm moving away,' he said. 'Erasmus University in Rotterdam have offered me a place.'

Munro nodded. Taking the young man's arm he lead him gently away from the desk. Bowing his head to meet Martijn's eyes, he said softly, 'I wanted to say thank you for saving my life.'

The student raised a hand, rubbing the back of his neck. His expression was one of pain. He looks lost, thought Munro.

'I mean it,' he reiterated. 'You did the right thing.' But as he spoke, he knew he wasn't getting through.

'Jean-Baptiste has my number,' said Martijn, his voice hoarse. 'You will let me know if there is any…you know…with Bregje.'

Munro nodded, then watched the slouched, broken figure walk away.

'Chief Inspector Munro?'

The voice came from behind him, causing Munro to wince as he turned too quickly. His bruised ribs' objection to the sudden movement lingered, making him catch his breath in short gasps. A tall, heavily built, balding man in loose fitting surgical blues reached out a supporting hand.

'Are you alright?' he enquired.

'Ribs,' replied Munro economically.

The man pursed his lips in sympathy before speaking. 'My colleague, Esther Van Joeren, tells me I can speak plainly with you. I am Miss Van Til's neurosurgeon.'

'Iain Munro.'

They shook hands, Munro hiding his discomfort as the large man's hand enveloped his bruised knuckles.

'Rob de Brusse.'

'You're kidding me.'

'I know,' said the surgeon affably. 'It wasn't deliberate. I only discovered the significance when I visited Scotland on holiday as a young man. Beautiful country, very friendly people.'

'I'd imagine the name helped.'

'Yes, I think so,' de Brusse smiled.

They wandered back to the observation window. The nurse had gone inside, and the two men observed her impassively as she replaced the bag on the drip with practiced efficiency.

The surgeon's countenance darkened as he began to speak. 'I must tell you this. There is no such thing as a miracle. The damage is extremely serious and has occurred in a vital area. In a very, very few cases, the organ can find a way around such a catastrophe; redirecting the blood flow or, in rare instances, it can train another part of the brain, enable it to take over. When that happens, it is not a miracle; it's a survival mechanism. It can also take some time.'

'How long do we wait?' asked Munro quietly.

'Unfortunately, being kept in this condition also takes a huge toll on the rest of the body.' de Brusse lowered his head. 'She has suffered many other serious injuries, as well as a colossal loss of blood. If we get no response in a few weeks…' The accompanying shrug was slow, and sad. They shook hands again.

As de Brusse turned to leave, Munro asked. 'I take it you're not a religious man doctor?'

A smile creased the big man's face.

'Quite the opposite actually,' he replied. 'In this job I am often asked about the existence of the soul. I heard something once though, a phrase that rung true for me. I believe we are all souls Inspector, but what we have, are bodies.'

Munro waited until the bulky form had ambled out of sight before turning away, entering Bregje's room, and settling down in the plastic chair to regale her with his news. The day's events delivered in faltering, and mostly grammatically incorrect, Dutch.

COMING SOON

The Shadowmaker

Alexander TARBET

A blast wrecks the penthouse suite in one of Amsterdam's most exclusive hotels. The suite had not been reserved, and was supposed to be unoccupied. So who were the four men inside? The Secondary Unit's DCI Munro and his Sergeant, Remco Elmers, have a personal stake in the answer. Not only was the atrocity committed directly opposite their favourite drinking den, but the person under arrest for triggering the explosion is a friend.

Acknowledgements

First and foremost, I must thank my wife Maggie.

As her infinite patience and support continue to defy reason, I am honour bound, once again, to rejoice in her peculiar madness and dance a jig of joy in the blind spot that is her love.

I also thank all you folks, too numerous to mention, who have encouraged and helped me in the creation of this book - not least my Amsterdammer friends, without whom this novel would have no heart (or names).

My humble thanks also to Geert Mak for his wonderful and inspirational book: *Amsterdam: A Brief Life of the City*. If you have visited Amsterdam and not read it, then shame on you.

Finally, my undying gratitude goes to a fine dog. Thank you Whisky, rest in peace my lovely boy.

22162714R00172

Printed in Great Britain
by Amazon